TO CURE OR KILL

A Novel

Sept, 2023
To Ben —
Thank you for all of your help!
Enjoy...
Michael

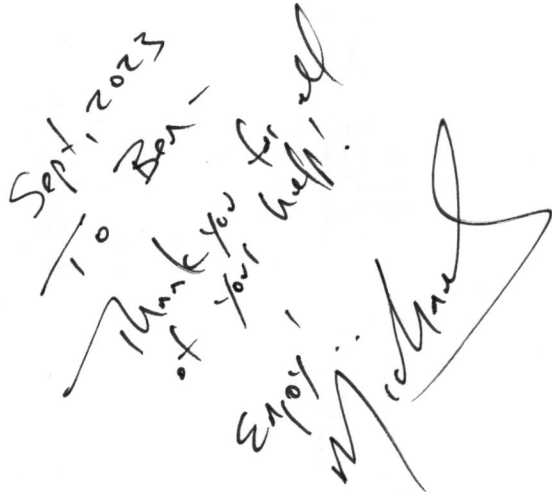

Michael J. Young, M.D.

Published in the United States by GM Books, Beverly Hills, California.
Library of Congress Cataloging-in-Publication Data

Michael J. Young, M.D. "To Cure Or Kill"

GM Books
269 S. Beverly Dr. #1054
Beverly Hills, CA 90212
(310) 923-2157
www.gmbooks.com

ISBN (Print): 978-0-9891627-4-6
ISBN (Hard Cover): 978-0-9891627-5-3

Publisher: William Dorich
Cover and Book Design: Randy Haragan, Senior Illustrator
Editor: Douglas May, M.B,A., Ed.D., Senior Editor

Printed in the USA

To the dedicated scientists and health professionals
who strive to do the right thing.

Also, by Michael J. Young, M.D.

The Illness of Medicine: Experiences of Clinical Practice (non-fiction)

Consequence of Murder

Net of Deception

Introduction

When you consider it, using a poison to commit a murder is somewhat of a passive undertaking. Generally speaking, it actually requires little more than appropriate planning and knowledge on the perpetrator's part. The victim takes on the active role in his or her own death as he or she actually does the inhaling, absorbing, or ingestion of the toxin. The victim's participation is performed without their knowledge–or consent. Yet, it is the victim who ultimately performs the final act.

In consideration of the variety of methods of poisonings (which drug or chemical to use) it is also understood that a main goal of the perpetrator, other than, of course, to cause the demise of the victim, is to be able to escape; that is, to be elsewhere at the moment of the last breath. Whether or not the intent is to also camouflage the cause of death is another matter that will dictate if the culprit chooses to hide the particular poison or route of administration.

Contents

CHAPTER 1 – *To Cure Or Kill*

CHAPTER 1

Chicago, IL

The man behind the horn-rimmed glasses turned off his laptop computer. As the monitor flickered and then turned black, he heard the machine's internal fan slowly spin down until there was absolute silence. The room was dark and the hour was quite late. He took off his glasses and wiped the lenses clean with a microfiber cloth. This activity of cleaning his spectacles was a habit the man did repeatedly as he considered his options. He was never in a hurry, and yet, he was never late—to anything. His compulsive nature was evident in everything he did. Whether considering his next job or getting dressed in the morning, all of his activities were performed methodically and with detailed planning. Jonathan Burksdale, III sat back in his grandfather's old burgundy leather chair and looked around the room that functioned as his small office. He could hear the worn and cracked leather in the seat cushion squeak as he changed positions. The walls were slightly yellowed from time. Faded photographs in wooden frames were spaced evenly throughout the small room. The desktop was immaculate. His compulsiveness was evident everywhere; everything in its place. Burksdale spun around in his chair and admired the many diplomas on the walls behind him. In the center of the wall was his most cherished certificate of achievement: *Doctor of Medicine*. As he pushed himself away from his desk, the oak floors creaked under the movement of the chair's wheels. Jonathan Burksdale understood what he needed to do, and now he had a clear idea of the means to do it. He understood the *why* and *how* of his next job. However, the question he had the most difficulty with was the *when*.

Doctor Burksdale's background was somewhat atypical of most physicians. Perhaps it was his unusual upbringing, or possibly it was both nature and nurture which was responsible for his peculiar personality and behavior. Burksdale was raised in a privileged New England home. The family's lavish turn-of-the-century house sat alone, hidden by a dense cluster of trees with its own quarter-mile private entranceway. As an only child, and the third in-line to have the name of Jonathan, he was overwhelmed by domineering parents who demanded his success. Burksdale found their tyrannical pressure for him to become part of their financial success story to be overbearing. The family made its money in business: he would not participate. More out of anger at the expectations put upon him, Burksdale pursued an education in biology—it was primarily a means to get away, rather than an effort to earn his parents' approval. What parent could argue when someone expressed an interest in medicine? But his disdain for his parents continued to fester throughout his life. He gladly took their trust-fund money, but always held contempt for them.

Burksdale was both bright and clever. Perhaps a consequence of the private tutoring he had when young, he sailed through his undergraduate program and then matriculated to medical school. There, his idiosyncrasies were evolving, but not completely mature. After receiving his medical degree, he entered a residency program in Emergency Medicine. Given the variety of problems he would encounter and the need to understand a variety of anatomical and physiological systems, he thought he would be a good fit. But after two years of training, he simply couldn't do the job. Oddly, Burksdale (as well as his fellow residents and teaching physicians) realized he couldn't deal with *people.* The good doctor enjoyed understanding the science of medicine, but he wasn't suited for dealing with the emotions or issues surrounding illness and injury. Burksdale repeatedly demonstrated his inability to show empathy for those he was supposedly treating. He was cited multiple times for his apathy in tending to those in pain or distress—some even thought he enjoyed watching patients suffer.

Eventually, Burksdale was asked to resign from the training program. Perhaps, many thought, he was better suited to pursue a career in Pathology, the scientific study of the causes and effects of diseases. Despite his medical training to learn how to heal, his only interest was to understand death.

Burksdale was drawn to the field of Toxicology. This is the branch of science detailing the nature, effects, and detection of poisons. It combines an understanding of biology, chemistry, pharmacology, and physiology. He applied for and was accepted to a Postdoctoral Fellowship Program in a forensic toxicology laboratory. One could surmise his emergency medicine program director had a hand in his landing the position—anything to get him away from (living) patients.

And, once again, after two years of tolerance, the toxicology program had had enough of this peculiar man. Recognized to be brilliant, Burksdale's inability to work with others and productively apply his knowledge was obvious to everyone in his program. More importantly, he simply could not get along with anyone. As a student spending the majority of his time alone, he could get away with his antisocial personality disorder. But in the *real* work environment, nobody could tolerate his rudeness and boorish behavior. Burksdale was out of a job for the second time during his short medical career. No one would hire him given his previous multiple employment failures, and he could no longer continue in an academic environment.

As his antisocial personality evolved, Burksdale became increasingly more withdrawn and separated from others. But this really didn't bother him as much as it did the others around him. At the rare family events he was invited to, Burksdale would often bring up inappropriate morbid discussions, and go into detailed descriptions of the pathophysiology of death in various circumstances. Nobody asked, nor cared to hear these grotesque descriptions of his obsessive interest. His invitations to such gatherings were stopped, and Burksdale's family and friends drifted away as he became consumed with the topic of death.

As Burksdale spent more time alone, considerable amounts of his day focused on reading voraciously about forensic toxicology. It was apparent he was fascinated with understanding how poisons affected a human body. Burksdale would study and review minute details of how poisons were acquired, transported, and reacted with the body's own natural defense mechanisms. How poisons worked became an obsession for him. Over time, Burksdale became a true expert of understanding poisons—their use, application, and more concerning, means of camouflaging their presence.

Despite his academic failures and inability to complete any training program, Burksdale had learned many of the principles and methods of the science of toxicology. What he didn't know from his training or previous experiences in laboratory work, he sought out, researched, and studied. He was an expert of poison laboratory protocols. Perhaps just as important, he understood the limits and capabilities of these specialized laboratory methods.

Given his medical background, toxicology expertise, and just the right amount of a progressive socialization disorder, Burksdale was becoming a very dangerous individual.

CHAPTER 2

Glenview, IL

Y*onie Pharmaceuticals Inc.* is based on an enormous campus just outside of Chicago in the suburb of Glenview, Illinois. However, the main entrance off Interstate 294 is actually quite ordinary. A small sign indicating the direction to turn onto the company's access road minimizes the grandiosity about to be seen. That simple sign would be the last ordinary thing seen as one entered the complex. Past this entry point the visitor would turn onto a half-mile, manicured private roadway. Magnificent foliage, flowers, and trees line the winding road up to the main gatehouse. Conspicuous speed sensors and cameras line the road which always appears to have a fresh coat of blacktop. At the end of the beautiful drive, a visitor on this private road would then encounter an innocuous appearing gatehouse. The gatehouse resembled a small, friendly home. In an effort to appear non-threatening, the red-brick exterior walls and white shutters were simply a veneer for this highly-fortified command post. Darkened bulletproof windows made it difficult to peer inside. When the front door of the gatehouse was opened, one could catch a glimpse of a wall of flickering monitors and a table lined with advanced surveillance computer equipment. The armed security officers stationed here would request visitor identification and prior approval for visitation before granting entrance. During this encounter, carefully concealed cameras will take digital photographs of the vehicle—its license plate and images of the driver and occupants.

Upon entering, all visitors were assigned an escort to accompany them during their *entire* visit. No visitor was ever allowed to roam the property without someone at their side. To walk from end-to-end on the vast property would take approximately thirty minutes. Given the average person walks approximately 2.5 miles per hour, the massive *Yonie* campus extends for slightly more than a mile in diameter. Observing the compound, one would appreciate a definite structural difference between the administrative and research buildings.

The administrative buildings are located inside the main campus entrance and are architecturally stunning. Their shimmering chrome and glass structures have opulent marble entranceways and foyers. Through huge panes of glass, one could see large trees adorning their atriums. Bright LED and growth lamps for the many plants and trees hang from the ceiling on fifty-foot cords. If the design objective is to impress visitors, then the architect's goal was accomplished.

The research buildings are industrial; both in their appearance and function. They are comparatively shorter than the administrative buildings, and standing only three stories in height, these mud-gray, massive buildings were the size of large warehouses. Many of these buildings were interconnected by a series of enclosed walkways allowing employees to move from one building to the other without stepping outside. These passageways improved work efficiency between the buildings, and eliminated the need to don coats and boots during the harsh Midwest winters. Attached to the research buildings themselves, another revelation can be made: cameras. Cameras are located *everywhere.* Cameras can be seen every ten feet along the roof lines of each building, as their presence was meant to be seen. Similarly, cameras could be seen at multiple locations at all entranceways. Oddly, no windows existed in the research buildings. It was doubtful any lovely trees would be growing in atriums in these facilities.

Other notable findings on the *Yonie* campus can also be seen. Perhaps the most obvious is the size of the surrounding wall. This was no ordinary wall demarcating a property line as it appeared to be nearly twenty feet high. Limited effort to camouflage the structure with shrubbery or trees is evident—probably by intent, as barbed wire and spikes could be seen atop the dark gray, steel wall. On close inspection, one could make out a series of horizontal wires near the top of the barbed wire. It's unclear from a distance to assess if the wires were electrified or acted as sensors. Given the size and location of the twelve-inch spikes, the barbs, and the wall height, it was clear that an attempt to climb or scale the structure would not be an easy task. Additionally, there appeared to be steel rods coming up from the ground adjacent to the seemingly impenetrable wall. Perhaps these steel rods were a deterrent to an intruder considering tunneling underneath. Without question, it was clearly obvious that security is a priority at *Yonie Pharmaceuticals*.

Yonie was considered to be among the top five of the largest pharmaceutical companies in the world. The company had divisions to cover most areas of pharmacologic need. *Yonie's* production capabilities in opioids was previously its largest division, but ever since issues surrounding illegal marketing strategies was identified years ago, the Pain Division of *Yonie* has been quietly reduced. The details of the company's shady *participation* in a Florida-based opioid distribution scheme had been carefully scrubbed from public scrutiny. In response to these events, as well as due to a change in global pharmaceutical demand, *Yonie* shifted its priorities. Over the past decade, *Yonie* has put increased resources into its Oncologic Pharmaceutical Division. At this time, the production of anti-neoplastic (cancer) drugs was taking on the dominant role at the pharmaceutical giant. Given the expanding anti-neoplastic drug market demands, revenue from oncologic pharmacologic therapies is forecasted to reach nearly $250 billion by 2028. This staggering estimation reveals not only the need for increased drug development, but also reflects the financial incentive for well-positioned companies to be part of this aspect of medical care. *Yonie* has every expectation to take the global lead.

Healthcare in the United States is big business, and Big Pharma is in the middle of the playing field. As one of the largest utilizers of lobbyists in Washington, Big Pharma plays hardball, and uses its financial and political strength to advance its financial objectives. Most individuals involved in the development of new drugs and therapies do so because of their interest in science, and the desire to apply that knowledge to the betterment of society. But the altruistic goals of scientists and healthcare workers in many instances is overshadowed by the greed of the medical-industrial-complex. This vast interwoven association of companies is pulled together by corporate structures that own and operate our medical centers, pharmacies, medical supply chains, and other health-related industries. This massive compilation of companies and products are collectively the largest industry in the country. Healthcare makes up nearly one-fifth of the U.S. Gross Domestic Product. Consequently, the pharmaceutical and associated healthcare industries dictate how health care is delivered. Ultimately, they have a stranglehold on how medicine is evolving and applied.

Neil Goodall is the CFO at *Yonie Pharmaceuticals*. As the director of an army of industry analysts, Goodall understands not only current medical needs, but he has the pulse of where medical dollars will be spent in the upcoming future. Having a clear understanding of past, current, and potential evolving trends in drug development and use, puts Goodall squarely in the middle of *Yonie's* efforts to secure a foothold in helping to shape how the country's healthcare dollars are spent.

Goodall enjoyed his status at *Yonie* and had been financially rewarded for his previous efforts at the company by being granted a cushy seven-figure salary. Important to Goodall, he also was given a large corner office. His focus at *Yonie* was legendary among his peers: he did not like to be disturbed at work, and if interrupted, you better have a damn good reason. Goodall, like many other high-achievers, was obsessive compulsive. With a Master's Degree in Computer Sciences along with his CPA, and having over a decade of experience working in the pharmaceutical world, he knew his job well.

Goodall and his team collated data from the World Health Organization, the CDC, and other health-related governmental agencies. They would collect prescription-use data gleaned from *Yonie's* contractual relationship with hundreds of pharmacies and other data mining resources. Using his own self-developed algorithms, Goodall would plug all the massive amount of collected data into proprietary computer programs to analyze and then project practically every aspect of healthcare-related issues and pharmaceutical trends. He would extrapolate these findings to predict pharmacologic needs in one-, five-, and ten-year estimations.

However, one of the most cryptic methods Goodall used to predict the direction *Yonie Pharmaceuticals* should proceed in drug development was not obvious—it didn't show up on any data spreadsheets or calculations. This part of his analysis wasn't formally written down, nor did it comply with any known economic or financial methodology used to forecast industry trends. Goodall had a means to *tap* into any number of competing pharmaceutical companies to learn what they were doing and projecting: Goodall had an inside source—someone knowledgeable of computer security programs and the skills to intercept and bypass them. Goodall sat nearly motionless at his desk chair in his large, opulent, corner office. He peered intently at his quad-setup of computer monitors. The game was hardball, indeed.

CHAPTER 3

Glenview, IL

Cancer is a disease in which abnormal cells grow uncontrollably and can potentially spread to other parts of the body. It is caused by changes to the genes that control the way our cells function—particularly how they grow and divide. These genetic changes can present themselves because of errors in cell division, damage to the DNA from carcinogens (substances in the environment that lead to the instructional misinformation from the DNA), or the inherited genes themselves were defective. Our immune system is a complex network of organs, cells, and proteins that defends the body against infection or disease. When the immune system is working properly, it can assess which cells are normal and which are foreign. It can detect and eliminate those cells abnormally dividing or appearing abnormal. In a healthy situation, the body's immune system will eliminate cells with abnormal DNA before they actually turn cancerous. However, as the immune system ages or has inherent deficiencies of its own, the abnormal cells can propagate.

The concept of immunotherapy is essentially a type of treatment that uses a person's own immune system to fight cancer. One of the principal ways the immune system finds and destroys abnormal cells or invaders is with antibodies. An antibody attaches to a specific molecule (antigen) on the surface of a target cell, such as a cancer cell. Once bound, the antibody serves to attract additional disease-fighting molecules or immune-responsive cells and may act as a trigger that promotes cell destruction by other immune system processes. Monoclonal antibodies are laboratory-produced molecules engineered to act as substitute antibodies that can enhance or mimic the immune system's attack on abnormal cells, such as cancer cells.

A vaccine introduces a small amount of weakened or mutated disease cells into the body. Although it is not intended to make a patient sick, the vaccine has enough cells or antigen to help the body build antibodies to recognize and fight off the disease. One of the most exciting new areas of immunotherapy is the development of cancer-directed vaccines. The premise behind therapeutic cancer vaccines is that the injection of tumor antigen can be used to stimulate an immune system response against the associated cancer cells. In essence, cancer vaccines can teach the body to protect itself against its own abnormal cells.

However, aside from the scientific aspect of cancer treatment, revenues generated from the sale of oncology drugs have increased by 70% over the past decade and now account for nearly one-quarter of the net revenues of these companies. More than 700 drugs are now available or in development for oncologic purposes.

Yonie Pharmaceuticals was aggressively promoting its research in therapeutic cancer vaccines. The company felt the future of cancer *management* was in cancer prevention—not just treatment. *Yonie* made a business decision to direct its large Oncologic Pharmaceutical Division towards research in this arena, and to limit current chemotherapeutic drug production. *Yonie* wanted to be the world leader in cancer vaccine innovation and development. This decision was not reached without internal resistance. Considerable in-fighting among upper-level executives resulted in a massive realignment of the oncology division leadership. One of those affected by the directional change of the division was its director, Dr. Jason Kogan.

Jason Kogan, Ph.D., had been with *Yonie Pharmaceuticals* for over 25 years and had a major role in navigating *Yonie* though some truly difficult times in the past. During his tenure, Kogan oversaw the expansion of oncology to become the most profitable of the company's five pharmaceutical divisions. He was a dedicated *Yonie* employee, and devoted a significant portion of himself, his family, and his career for the company. During his 25-year stint, Kogan went through two divorces, a mild heart attack, and as he would tell others, the loss of most of his hair.

Jason Kogan was a molecular biologist by training. After completing his doctorate at Stanford in the evolving field of gene mapping, he was hired as an entry-level research scientist at *Yonie.* His work focused on gene manipulation on chromosomes of specific bacterial pathogens. Later, he added to his research portfolio by successfully advancing concepts of new chemotherapeutic interventions. Early on, Kogan was considered one of *Yonie's* brightest investigative stars, and he quickly climbed the ranks. Eventually, he became less involved in actual laboratory work, and was responsible for more administrative duties. Five years ago, he was named the Director of The Oncologic Pharmaceutical Division. For this role, he was well paid, but disappointingly, Kogan became completely separated from any hands-on research. He missed the lab and the work he did there. In the administrative world, Kogan never felt comfortable nor confident in his duties. He always felt he was a researcher, but the financial compensation in his new administrative role was good for Kogan, his wife, and two young children. As the costs of living in the northern Chicago suburbs were rising, the extra cushion of added financial compensation was welcomed. Kogan learned to live with the dull bureaucratic responsibilities and did his job.

Kogan was a purist. As a research scientist first and foremost, and someone committed to efforts to improve people's lives through his investigate work, the decision to halt further chemotherapeutic research was an affront to him. Brutal negotiations ultimately led to Kogan's resignation, and although he was given a significant severance—enough to continue to live the lifestyle of which he became accustomed—it was a disappointing end to his career at *Yonie Pharmaceuticals.* The *Yonie* lawyers clearly delineated that given Kogan's knowledge of their confidential investigative direction and research, he would be prohibited from ever working in the pharmaceutical industry again. He would be allowed to teach, do research, or work in any business, but he would be in violation of his termination agreement if he did any work related to pharmaceuticals—private, academic, or governmental—again.

Per his agreement, Kogan quietly removed all of his personal effects from his office. He turned in his ID badge, pulled off his automobile decals, and handed back to security a pocketful of keys and access fobs—all collected over his 25 years of employment. However, for reasons he still cannot recall, just before shutting off his computer for the last time, Kogan did something he knew would be a violation of his termination agreement. Perhaps it was out of anger, or perhaps it was out of instinct knowing he might need some leverage in the future. But the man who was labeled a *Boy Scout* by his colleagues felt the wolves at the company would soon be taking over. Kogan did not trust where the new aggressive *Yonie* executives were headed. As the Director of the Oncologic Pharmaceutical Division, Kogan had access to every file of current research data in his division. Kogan had one thing in his pocket he did not return to security. Kogan inserted the 16-Terabyte-SSD flash drive into his computer. When the red light on the device extinguished—indicating the download of his now ex-division's research files—Kogan removed it and slid it into his breast pocket. He then shut down his computer, shut off the lights, and closed the door to his office for the last time.

CHAPTER 4

Glenview, IL

Everything in life seems to have a hierarchy. Whether you are 5 or 50, someone in your group of friends or business associates takes the lead. Often, he or she gives the most directives and is the most verbal or most aggressive in the group. Others follow; some with their own ambitions to subsequently climb the ranks, and still others, simply take up the rear and go with the herd. But the ones who sometimes do the best work may also be the quietest in the group. At the *Yonie* Oncologic Pharmaceutical Division, one of the most dedicated scientists was a gentle, quiet man, named Shamus O'Donnell. Shamus was nearly 70 years old. He had previously worked at several biotech start-up companies and was heavily recruited to *Yonie* nearly 20 years ago. His expertise was in cell biology—the branch of biological sciences that studies the structure, function, and behavior of cells. More specifically, Shamus's research was aimed at trying to improve cancer therapy by applying principles of stem cell biology to understanding tumor development and progression.

Stem cells are cells with the potential to develop into many different types of cells in the body. In a sense, they can be thought of as a repair system for the body.

Shamus was working on a means to utilize stem cells to create an army of antibodies with the capability of immobilizing the progression of cancerous cells. His ultimate goal was the production of a line of stem cells that would aggressively respond with the immediate recognition of abnormal cells at very early stages of abnormal cell differentiation. In other words, Shamus was working at the heart of developing an anti-cancer vaccine.

"Good morning, Shamus," blurted Amy Kelly, as she looked up from her workspace in Shamus's lab and saw her boss walking toward his office.

"Good morn to you as well, Amy," responded Shamus in his thick Irish brogue. "Do you have those reports I asked you about yesterday?" Shamus asked, as he walked from the lab doorway towards his private office—a small, cluttered room adjacent to the main lab. Shamus unlocked his office door and threw his briefcase onto his desk. Shamus's lab was nearly 5000 square feet and located in the main research building on the *Yonie* campus. Large, black, granite-topped work benches were filled with the latest in advanced laboratory electronics, centrifuges, and microscopes. Above them, shelves were packed with books, laboratory guides, and binders full of collated data.

"Yes, Shamus, I do," Amy replied, anticipating that would be his first of many inquiries throughout the day. Amy pulled away from her microscope, removed her latex gloves, and sifted through the piles of papers next to her. Satisfied she had pulled the correct folder, Amy walked to the small office with Shamus O'Donnell, Ph.D., etched on the door's wooden plaque.

The office looked as though a windstorm had hit. The small room was mostly occupied by a desk that was nearly as wide as the room. A dual computer monitor was on one corner of the desk. Books, journals, and dozens of loose papers were strewn across the desk with no apparent order. The surface of the desk was probably last seen when it was delivered a decade ago. The floor was littered with piles of stacked papers interspersed with crumpled sheets and small post-it notes. A bookshelf located directly behind the massive desk was packed with books of every size. There was no available space for anything else to be placed in the office. Amy tiptoed between the piles of papers on the floor and deposited the requested file on Shamus's desk. Shamus looked up as she placed the manila-colored file in front of him. He quickly opened the file and skimmed through it.

"What do you think of the data?" Shamus asked Amy as he flipped through the file.

"Umm.... I think we would do better to continue our work on trial number 32," Amy replied slightly sheepishly. Amy was a bit intimidated by Shamus, who had an international reputation in the small world of stem cell regeneration and antibody production. Although everyone in the lab worked on a first-name basis, she rarely had the ear of the boss by herself. She was aware it was unusual to be the only person in the room when asked details of lab work. Amy had recently completed her masters in biochemistry and was thrilled to be working in the lab. She felt she needed work-experience in industry before applying for a doctorate program. Amy's advisors and professors at Emory thought she was a tremendous student and could advance directly into any academic program of her choice. However, they certainly couldn't dismiss the advantages she would gain by working with the well-known Doctor Shamus O'Donnell. Shamus lifted his head from the file and looked at Amy inquisitively.

"What about number 37?" he asked.

Amy shifted her weight and stood upright as she tried to appear confident. "I believe the difference in outcomes between those trials would be nullified if we had an effective cytotoxic T cell. If we were to try to build our own utilizing a synthetic mRNA vector—"

Shamus put his hand up informing Amy to stop speaking.

mRNA or messenger RNA is a molecule that contains the instructions for cells to make specific proteins. When the mRNA is given as a vaccine, it gives cells that take up the vaccine directions to produce specific proteins that may stimulate an immune response against these same proteins when they are present in the future. The immune response involves an extraordinarily complex cascade of events, and the development of antibodies and T cells (a type of white blood cell that is essential to the immune system response) are among the stimulated defenders of the body. The stunning success of the development and application of the mRNA COVID-19 vaccines has accelerated research on mRNA vaccines for cancer. And no mRNA cancer vaccine has yet been approved. Until, perhaps now...

Shamus sat very still for a moment. He lowered his hand and considered the opinion of his young assistant. Then, very slowly, Shamus nodded in agreement. "Yes, if we could just find the right T cell antigen receptor (TCR) for activation! Yes, well, thank you Amy…I agree that would be the key to our objective." Amy nodded. She also understood his gaze away from her and back to the files as her cue to leave. Amy left quickly and closed the office door. She obviously did not realize the full impact of what she had just stated, but realized by Shamus's reaction that she should memorialize what she just said to him. Upon leaving Shamus's office, she went immediately to her computer to enter the details of the conversation.

Shamus stared at the data in front of him. He clearly understood what he needed to fulfill *the objective.* He needed a specific molecule—a *specific mRNA* molecule that would allow him to complete the protocol necessary to develop the elusive prostate cancer vaccine everyone in the pharmacologic world wanted. Shamus knew that if he developed this vaccine, his status in the field of cell biology would become stratospheric. If he was successful, *Yonie Pharmaceuticals* would increase its value to its shareholders by multiples Shamus couldn't even begin to calculate. He then tried to estimate the value of his potential bonus options. After recovering from his momentary daydreaming fantasy, Shamus had to remind himself of the value to humanity this work would serve. He scolded himself at his selfishness. Then again…Shamus went back into the world of his imaginary success. Finally, Shamus shook it off and returned to the file. *Yes*, he thought. He knew exactly what he needed! After considering his options, Shamus also thought he might know where to get it.

Shamus quickly scribbled down his newly developed algorithm. And then…Shamus raised his head and looked around his office. Good, he noted, the door was closed. The room was dead silent. Shamus stared at his notes as though he were memorizing them for life. He looked at his newly conceived method to incorporate the specific mRNA molecule he needed into his protocol for effective vaccine development. And then, after closing his eyes to assure he could see the algorithm in his mind's-eye, he grabbed a black marker from his container of writing utensils. Shamus blackened the entire page, and then placed it into the paper shredder next to his feet. No one else could know what he now understood as the method to create what had eluded him, and everyone else for that matter, for so long.

Shamus needed that precious mRNA molecule to complete his efforts in developing the vaccine. *Yonie* had immense resources, both financially, and with its sprawling campus of multiple labs and personnel. However, *Yonie* didn't have a lab that could manufacture the specific type of mRNA that he needed. Shamus also knew that to make that particular molecule *de novo* could take *years* of experimentation. He understood that the only way to get the molecule he needed would be to obtain it from another pharmaceutical company which had done extensive work in this area. Purchasing this molecule would likely result in the need to divulge the reasons for its use. Given the molecule's potential value, nobody was going to sell this product without demanding an astronomical price. Such a transaction could also lead to having to share the rewards. Not only would a business deal be prohibitively expensive, selfishly, Shamus reasoned that he didn't want to have to share his concept for development.

CHAPTER 5

Glenview, IL

Shamus O'Donnell returned to his office the following morning more distracted than usual. He was exhausted; not so much from work, but rather from the constant anxiety over the past 24 hours, knowing he was about to violate standards of professional ethics.

In the scientific community, work is generally shared. Historically, scientific journal articles were published so colleagues could learn what new ideas, plans, or findings had been identified or developed. Conferences were held so discussion, debate, and the comparison of data and findings could be communicated openly. However, in 1992, a group of students and researchers at the University of Illinois developed a sophisticated browser they called Mosaic. Mosaic is often described as the first graphical web browser—a means to retrieve information from other parts of the connected internet web of computers and servers. It was instrumental in leading to the Internet boom of the 1990s. Scientists and researchers now had another tool with which to share their findings and discoveries. Indeed, the nature of scientific study has been for the betterment of mankind—to share information and prompt growth and learning. But then big business entered the scientific arena, and money was to be made.

Shamus needed a specific *T cell receptor (TCR)-engineered T cell* to complete the development of the prostate cancer vaccine. To create that T cell, he needed a particular mRNA molecule. There were a number of companies in the world involved in this specific molecule production. Unfortunately, many had their headquarters based in China. Navigating through that logistical nightmare would be enough to nix any reasonable means to obtain it. In North America, there were a handful of companies working with the specific mRNA molecule Shamus needed. In the United States, there was one company Shamus set his sights on—*Harris Therapeutics*—and fortunately, it was based just outside of Chicago! This small, boutique, pharmaceutical start-up company had what Shamus wanted.

Reviewing on-line reports about *Harris Therapeutics*, it appeared as though the company was in negotiations with a number of investors interested in its products and research developments. The company's current value was just *north* of a billion dollars; easily obtainable by any number of large pharmaceutical behemoths such as *Yonie*. Shamus felt his heart rate increase at the thought of *Yonie* acquiring *Harris*. That would open new doors to his research and all but assure access to the prized molecule. But as a research scientist, Shamus understood what he didn't know: was the purchase of *Harris Therapeutics* even possible? He impulsively grabbed the telephone and dialed the campus operator.

"Yes, kindly connect me with Administration," Shamus blurted out quickly.

"Who specifically would you like to speak with?" the operator asked with a touch of boredom.

"Hmm.... well, I don't rightly know offhand...who should I speak with regarding acquisitions?" Shamus asked.

"Sir, can I direct your call to someone specifically? I'm an operator, not an advisor," the telephone attendant responded with an edge to her voice.

Shamus had no idea of whom he needed to speak with, or which department the person would be in. He was a damn scientist, he thought. He didn't know if he was more upset with his ineptness in locating an administrator, or the obvious disparaging attitude of the phone operator. Before speaking again, he calmed down and took a deep breath. "Okay, Miss, can you just connect me to...ahh... the finance department?" Seconds later Shamus heard clicking over the receiver as the operator obliged him with the connection to the requested department. Shamus's ineptness with navigating inside the company, but outside of his little world, was painfully obvious to him.

"Finance," the perky young female voice on the other end of the line stated.

"Oh…ahh…good morn to you Miss," Shamus said in his nicest voice. "I'm trying to locate someone to discuss…well, I mean…I'd like to know who I should talk to regarding an idea to purchase another company."

"I'm sorry…may I ask with whom I'm speaking?" the friendly but now suspicious voice asked.

"Oh, yes…I'm sorry, this is Dr. Shamus O'Donnell. I work in… I'm a researcher here at *Yonie*. I have a project I'm trying to advance, and…well…to do it will require the assistance, well, really the product of another company." Shamus was embarrassed by his difficulty in articulating who he was and why he was calling. *This is too damn difficult!* Shamus thought to himself–almost saying it out loud.

"I see," said the receptionist. "Have you thought about just trying to buy the product you need? I'm happy to connect you with the purchasing department."

Shamus smiled as he listened to her naivety. "Well, I don't believe that would be possible. You see, they are a competitor of ours… anyway…do you know of someone I could discuss this issue with?" Shamus could feel his patience wearing thin.

"Give me a moment, please," the now, less-than-perky voice replied. The woman put Shamus on hold. The repeated music-loop on the line became annoying to Shamus, and after what felt like an eternity, a new voice was now speaking.

"Good morning, Doctor O'Donnell." My name is Rick in accounting. "I understand you want to speak to someone about some sort of a…large purchase? Am I correct?"

Shamus sighed and repeated his story to "Rick." "I see, sir. Okay, I'm going to transfer your request to one of our administrators in the Finance Department. This matter isn't really something we take up in accounting." Shamus's phone extension was requested, and he was informed someone would get back to him shortly. The call was then abruptly disconnected. Shamus felt he was getting an education on how the bureaucracy of corporate structure functioned—or didn't. Fine, he would sit tight on this for now. Shamus decided to forget about how he just spent the last 20 minutes on hold, and then wasting his effort with low-levels who were clueless about what he was trying to accomplish. He would go back into the lab and deal with this nonsense later.

By the end of the afternoon, no call had come back. Shamus had enough of this waiting, and his patience for stupidity was gone. He decided to take a walk over to the main administrative building—a building he hadn't visited once during his entire 20-year stint at *Yonie*. Besides, after reconsidering what he was about to discuss, Shamus felt a discussion of this importance shouldn't be done on the phone. Unsure if he was appropriately dressed in jeans and a tee-shirt, Shamus decided to leave his white lab coat on and make his way out. He walked the four blocks to the front of the campus, and stepped inside Building Number One.

As he pulled open the heavy glass door, Shamus was stunned at what he saw. The foyer of the building looked like one of the fanciest hotels he had ever visited. Not that he traveled that much—*what on a salary of a researcher?* Shamus mumbled to himself. The marbled floors glistened from the chic, overhead, LED lighting. Shamus strained his neck looking upwards and noted the power cables must be fifty feet in length, as they extended down from the ceiling to the bright lights. Nearly full-grown trees, and even a small babbling brook built inside the building foyer gave the appearance of a small tranquil forest. *So, this is where the money goes?* Shamus thought, as he shook his head at the opulence of the space. Shamus continued his gawking until a security guard approached, asking if he was lost. Shamus presented his ID and stated that he wanted to go to the administrative floors to discuss his *business proposal.*

"But you don't have an appointment?" the large, muscular guard asked.

"No sir, I do not," Shamus replied—perhaps a tad too defensively. He was quickly fatiguing of the barriers he had to go through to try to advance his proposal for his own company's benefit!

"Okay," the skeptical guard stated. "Wait right here and I will make a call." Shamus stood as instructed and watched the guard talking on the telephone. He appeared rather animated and would point occasionally in Shamus's direction. After what appeared to be an eternity, the guard returned.

"Okay, Doctor O'Donnell, I need you to sign in on this clipboard... followed by the date and time," the guard explained patiently. He took a *Yonie Pharmaceutical* pen from his shirt pocket and handed it to Shamus. Shamus completed the requested tasks and returned the pen. "Take the elevators over here to the 12th floor, and inform the receptionist who you are. They will take you from there." The guard pointed Shamus in the direction of the elevators and returned to his work station. Shamus followed instructions and walked over to the stainless-steel elevator bank. Just as he pushed the *Up* button, a group of six women were exiting the adjacent elevator car. They appeared to be laughing and enjoying themselves. As Shamus watched the highly-perfumed group move on, he noted one was more beautiful than the other. With their attractive figures and heavy makeup, Shamus deducted they were probably company pharmaceutical representatives. The drug reps were always the prettiest in the room, he conceded. Shamus just smiled at the silliness of this stereotype, but he knew well-enough that the attractive rep would be the one to get through the doctor's office doorway—whether man or woman. It's just the way the world worked. Shamus pushed the 12th floor button, and after a gentle ring, the elevator doors closed. Shamus noted the elegance of the bamboo floor and tiled walls of the elevator. *All the money made from work done in the research buildings is on full display on this side of town,* he thought. Within half-a-minute, Shamus reached the 12th floor. The elevator control panel released another gentle ring alerting the rider of the arrival to his or her destination.

"Good afternoon, Doctor O'Donnell." Shamus turned and noted yet another beautiful woman walking towards him. He noted she was wearing high heels and was also in full makeup. He wondered how the company acquired so many model-like employees on this end of the campus. Over on the research side, high heels would be a liability on the smooth cement floors. And makeup? The last time he saw a woman this coiffured was at a wedding six-months ago. Shamus smiled weakly at her, astonished how her beauty disarmed him so quickly.

"Please take a seat over there," she stated, pointing to a group of chairs. "Someone will be with you shortly." Shamus nodded as she walked away. He wondered how long it took her to perfect her seductive stride.

Shamus noted the well-cushioned chairs near a window and sat down. He then considered, *What was the protocol on this anointed floor? Was he a visitor, or an employee?* In this unfamiliar environment, Shamus felt out of place. He missed the familiarity of his lab, and wasn't quite sure of his status in these hotel-like surroundings. Despite the beautiful accoutrements, the room felt oddly cold. As Shamus waited, he observed more model-like ladies moving about; everyone seemed to have a focused mission. There was no chit-chat, no wasted movement. The room seemed to hum with extraordinary efficiency. Shamus understood exactly what this administrative floor of *Yonie Pharmaceuticals* was: a well-oiled machine.

After a few minutes of his observing the business side of *Yonie*, a well-dressed man quietly walked up to Shamus and introduced himself. "Doctor O'Donnell, my name is Greg Olson, one of the assistants to Neil Goodall." His sudden presence shook Shamus out of his observational trance. Olson extended his hand to shake.

"Oh…yes…Good afternoon, Mr. Olson." Shamus lifted his hand and shook Olson's. Shamus noted Olson used a weak grip–one that Shamus's grandfather described as a "fish grip." Shamus recalled his old Irish grandfather telling him once, "When you give a man your handshake, make sure its memorable and not some weak fish grip." Shamus never trusted anyone after a less-than-satisfactory handshake. He was also turned off by the smell of the man's overbearing aftershave. Shamus assessed that everything on this floor reeked of superficial efforts to impress.

"Won't you come with me, sir? I understand you wanted to discuss some potential business concepts with us?" Olson stated, with a mouthful of perfect teeth. *Were those suspenders under his suit coat,* Shamus wondered? He really was in a world completely different than the constant predictability of his scientific lab. Shamus followed Olson for what felt to be a hundred-yard walk down a busy hallway. More well-groomed, fragrance enhanced, young men and women paced the long corridor all with the same look of determination on their harried faces. *Welcome to Corporate America,* Shamus thought, as he realized none of the racing assistants looked relaxed or even mildly enjoying their work.

The duo finally reached their destination: the office of Neil Goodall. As they entered, the secretary acknowledged their presence by quickly nodding and pointing in the direction of Goodall's private office. She continued to talk loudly and quickly into her telephone headset. Upon entering Goodall's massive office, Olson closed the door behind them. Shamus noted the office had absolutely no resemblance to his own. Unlike his cramped space with papers and books occupying every free inch of space, the office of Goodall was as sterile as an operating room. Brazilian cherry hardwood floors against gray cement walls gave a rather cool, contemporary look. His large, quad-computer monitor arrangement was mounted neatly to the wall adjacent to his glass desk. The bookshelf behind Goodall's desk was filled with sports memorabilia—signed footballs, basketballs, and baseballs. Some of the game balls were in acrylic cases while others were left to endure the environment without protection. No overflow of books or bound journals were noted in these confines. An odd-shaped, steel sculpture, complete with overhead halogen lighting, filled one corner. As Shamus scanned the room, he was drawn to the large bank of computer monitors with colored lines, dashes, and flickering numbers. The office resembled more of an upscale financial boardroom than an academic workplace.

Oblivious to their presence, Goodall had his back turned to his visitors while he continued to stare at the flickering numbers. He typed rapidly into his keyboard, and one of the monitors changed the information being displayed. Whatever Goodall was doing, Shamus took note of his complete focus. He admired the man's undivided attention to his work. After a few moments of silence watching Goodall type feverishly, Olson gave a forced cough. Goodall looked up at the monitors, and then turned in their direction.

"Oh…I didn't hear you come in…I'm sorry." Goodall stated with an insincere apology. He stood and faced Shamus while extending his hand. "Neil Goodall…nice to meet you, Doctor O'Donnell." Shamus smiled and shook Goodall's hand. Shamus noted this was no fish grip—the handshake was firm and solid. Many hours spent by Goodall at the gym were evident. Goodall was not one to waste time on pleasantries and got right to business. He pointed the men towards the beautiful black, leather, Mies van der Rohe chairs facing his desk, and sat back down. With a quick touch on his keyboard, the monitors went into sleep mode and were now displaying an array of twisting colors and shapes.

"So, Doctor O'Donnell…" started Goodall

"Please…call me Shamus. I insist everyone working in my lab do the same." Shamus stated with a smile.

"Fine…Shamus…" Goodall started out. "Please tell me what brought you from the…ahh…I like to jokingly call them the… dungeons…to over here in the castle," Goodall stated with a smirk. Although intended as a joke, both he and Shamus both knew that was exactly how he really felt about the research labs—grunts working away so the *real business* of the company could be accomplished in the high tower. From Goodall's perspective, that *business* was making money—and lots of it.

Shamus stared at Goodall for a long moment. He wasn't sure he was talking to the right person, or if he should be talking at all. Goodall and Olson simply stared back waiting to hear what Shamus had trekked over to discuss. Shamus felt cornered. He now felt obliged to discuss his possible cancer vaccine proposal. The fact that he considered it *science*, and they considered it *business*, was ever present in his mind. Then again, Shamus considered, how would he get all those financial options he daydreamed about if it *wasn't* a business? Shamus took a deep breath and decided this is what he came here to do.

Shamus leaned forward, and in a soft, almost whispered voice began. "Let me start by first explaining what it is that I do…I think this will be the best way for you to comprehend what I'm about to say. In basic terms, my expertise is in cell biology—my work here is involved in developing vaccines. More specifically, my research is engaged in understanding the means to create an anti-cancer vaccine." At the sound of the words *cancer* and *vaccine,* the bored expression on Goodall's face dissipated. He leaned in a bit closer to hear Shamus's now even quieter voice. Given his thorough understanding of the financial implications of what Shamus was beginning to describe, Shamus had gained Goodall's full attention. Shamus continued, knowing he had achieved success in keeping his audience engaged so far.

"Now, for a vaccine to help prevent future infection, it needs to be able to mimic disease. In other words, it must induce the body's immune system to become activated against the same antigen or foreign invader it is pretending to be. The vaccine may be a weakened strain of, say, a particular viral agent, or perhaps it is a specific segment or part of that virus. But cancer cells are not foreign, and therefore they may replicate without attack or interference from a patient's immune system. So..." Shamus raised his voice and pointed his index finger in the air to emphasize his next statement. "The real trick is how to get a patient's immune system to attack its own cancer cells which have the same DNA as their normal cells. This is the crux of the matter: How to make the cancer cells which *genetically* look the same, but obviously behave so differently, become the only target of the immune system. This is not easy to do."

Shamus took a moment to let that concept sink in before going on. Goodall and Olson were like school boys waiting for the teacher to continue. "Now, there are numerous theories being propagated by investigators as we try to answer that question: How to achieve selective *immunoactivation* without damaging the host itself. So, let's dive into this a little deeper…" Goodall's phone rang. Given the men's intensity of focus, the sound was startling.

Goodall grabbed the receiver quickly and brought it close to his mouth. "Whatever it is, it can wait!" he yelled, and then slammed the receiver back into its cradle. "I'm sorry, Shamus…please continue."

Shamus wasn't sure if he was impressed or frightened by how quickly Goodall's temperament switched gears. He refocused on the subject and continued. "Some viruses known as oncologic viruses may be tools for directly killing cancer cells. We think they work by triggering a specific immune response in the body against the cancer. For instance, when an oncologic virus infects a tumor cell, the virus replicates itself until the cell bursts. Certain tumor antigens may then be released that allow the cancer to now be recognized by the immune system. The virus acted as a means to make the cancer cell visible to the body's immune defenses. This theory was shown to be true. It was put to use in developing the first oncologic virus to receive FDA approval. It was a treatment for melanoma. However, another direction to create an anti-cancer vaccine could be through an mRNA vaccine, which actually doesn't contain any virus at all. Remember, mRNA was used to create the COVID vaccine. mRNA vaccines work by telling the body to produce proteins that look like certain parts of the virus. The immune system will react to these proteins in a similar fashion to a full viral infection. With prior mRNA vaccination, the immune system will recall how to recognize these proteins quickly when exposed to the real infection in the future."

"Now…and here is the important part." Shamus spoke slowly and carefully, "Through gene-mapping or sequencing technology, we can identify certain mutations or changes found on a patient's cancer cells. These mutations are called neoepitopes—and they can help the immune system distinguish cancer cells from normal cells. If we could create a vaccine that encodes for these specific mutations and then incorporate them onto an mRNA molecule, we would have a very powerful anti-cancer weapon. We inject the newly created mRNA into the patient, and it has the ability to direct the patient's cancer cells to express the neoepitopes. It makes the cancer cell stand out from normal cells, and the immune system more able to destroy it. Where we hit a roadblock was identifying a specific protein… umm…a molecule, that would activate the immune system to the specific neoepitope. But, just recently we isolated it!" Shamus was now more animated with the scientific description of his work. He was now speaking more quickly and loudly. "So…the good news is we now know *exactly* what we need to advance this technique for making an anti-cancer vaccine. More specifically, an anti-cancer *prostate* vaccine. But the problem is, we don't have the molecule." Shamus stopped. He felt as though he gave them a compelling scientific review of the situation in his lab.

Goodall sat back in his chair. They could all hear the squeaking of the rich leather under his weight. "So, the real problem is obtaining this…this…mol-e-cule…" Goodall stated with some hesitation, "to activate the immune system to the neo…epi…whatever. Do I have this right?" Goodall asked while slowly rubbing his chin.

"Yes, that's it." Shamus stated rather excitedly. "That is basically the crux of the problem."

"So, why don't we just make the molecule we need ourselves?" Goodall asked.

"Ah, yes…well…that would obviously make the most sense." Shamus explained. "*The* problem is that we don't have a laboratory here at *Yonie* that is set-up and capable of doing this." This explanation was followed by a moment of complete silence. All three men stared off in different directions as they contemplated what was just discussed. They were all trying to come up with a solution to the problem.

"Well," started Goodall, "why don't we establish a new lab to develop this needed molecule so we can then complete the vaccine?"

Shamus smiled. "Yes, that would be ideal…but it takes years to put together the right combination of required assets to do this. The needs of the lab and required personnel, specific equipment…just assessing the costs and then creating a multi-year production budget…it can all take so much time…and time is not on our side." Shamus explained. "As you are aware, anti-cancer vaccine development is now at the forefront of pharmaceutical oncologic advancement. I believe the companies that are able to advance in this arena will be the most successful. I think the days of using chemotherapy…treatments that may be effective only *after* a patient has a cancer diagnosis, are certainly necessary–but not on the frontline. We want…we *need* to be on that frontline."

Goodall unconsciously found himself nodding in agreement with what Shamus just described. He knew that despite *Yonie*

Pharmaceutical's size and global position in the marketplace, the company always had to stay at the forefront to remain relevant. Today, there are so many biological-industry start-ups that any pharmaceutical company could get overtaken if not at the forefront of innovation and discovery. Whether by their own internal research or by buying out these aggressive new startups and their technologies, Goodall knew Y*onie* had to find a way to remain relevant. *Yonie* would not remain sustainable based on previous drug-product developments. *Advance or die* was the business model Goodall applied to make *Yonie* the competitive force it was. The business of medicine was a challenging battle to be in these days.

"Yes, it would take years to create a new lab for this need," Goodall acknowledged. "So, what are our alternative options?" he asked.

Olson perked up for the first time in the conversation. "Well, does anybody, or any company make this molecule? And if so, why don't we try to work out an arrangement with them?"

Goodall and Shamus both glared at Olson. Shamus had had enough of this assistant with his fancy clothes, pungent aftershave, and smug attitude. Shamus looked at him directly and stated, "Son, to your point, yes, there is a company that makes the molecule. But nobody is going to just let us waltz in and then share it with us."

Goodall jumped in and looked at Olson while stating, "We're talking about the potential for tens of billions of dollars of revenue if this thing flies. Nobody is going to work with us unless we pony up a fortune. Once they get wind we want their product, I don't think there will be an easily negotiated *arrangement*, as you stated. Whatever company has this molecule in their product line, they will ask for the moon. And if we disclose what it's for, others will follow suit and we will lose our edge in this. No, I don't like the idea of trying to buy this…if what Shamus states is true, we could be looking at a landmark new vaccine. One that is not only used for prostate cancer, but potentially for a myriad of other cancers as well. We need to be smart about this." Goodall stood up and started pacing the room. "So, Shamus…we can't make it, and we can't buy it…so where does that leave us?"

Shamus looked directly at Goodall, and then at Olson. He realized they were stuck. "Well, I could go back to the lab and see if I could determine another possible means to make the vaccine effective..." Shamus offered.

"How long did it take you to get this far in your research?" Goodall asked.

"I would guess, about 4 years," Shamus stated, while shaking his head. "It took a long time, and...a lot of money. This was a very challenging project...one that I don't want to throw away." Shamus looked directly at Goodall waiting for his response. Goodall stared back at Shamus and then started pacing the room.

After a few laps around the room, Goodall spoke up. "Shamus, what company produces the molecule we need?"

"I think our best chance of...procuring the molecule would be with *Harris Therapeutics.* There are several others that have that particular protein in their product line, but *Harris* would be our best bet," Shamus responded.

"And what makes *Harris* more attractive than the others?" Goodall inquired.

"Well, most of the other companies are abroad...China to be exact. *Harris* is not only in the U.S, but it's also not far from here... it is headquartered with its research labs in the southwest suburbs. In Wheaton, I believe." Shamus replied. Upon hearing the name of the company, Goodall was in his chair and *waking* his computer up before Shamus even completed his sentence. Goodall typed quickly on his keyboard. Shamus, who *pecked* one letter at a time at his computer, was astonished at the ease and efficiency Goodall displayed while looking up *Harris Therapeutics.* Goodall worked with the same intense focus Shamus noted when they first entered his office. Goodall appeared oblivious that anyone else was in the room. After a few silent minutes as Olson and Shamus simply acted as observers, Goodall pushed himself back from his desk. He swiveled in his chair and looked at them.

"*Harris* is like an ant compared to us," Goodall stated arrogantly. Obviously, we don't want to tip them off or this will raise their price and their company value considerably. That billion-dollar company will be worth 10-times that overnight."

"So, what is the harm in paying 10 billion if we can make triple that?" Olson again tried to interject. He was still trying to use the business-degree mentality his parents had paid for.

"No way," Goodall responded. "I won't let a small-turd biotech startup take advantage of us." He shook his head. "No way." Goodall repeated. "We take it."

Shamus squirmed in his chair as he wasn't quite sure he felt comfortable where this discussion was now going. When he was thinking about the financial gains of this project at his desk, it was more of a fantasy. But now, Shamus realized that Goodall wasn't fantasizing at all. This was potentially becoming a reality, and the stealing of another company's work didn't settle well with Shamus. Shamus was thinking, *tens of thousands, maybe hundreds of thousands of man-hours had been spent by how many researchers over how many years in an effort to isolate and then develop that molecule? And what if Yonie did acquire it? The researchers at Harris would eventually learn of their loss. Then what?*

"Listen…Mr. Goodall, I don't think stealing that molecule is the most appropriate thing for us to do…I agree with Mr. Olson. We make an offer to buy it," Shamus explained, almost pleading.

Goodall looked at Shamus with darkened eyes, "Doctor O'Donnell, I appreciate your effort to bring us your laboratory findings. I also appreciate that you work in *our* lab." Goodall stood and stated rather menacingly to Shamus. "You can now go back to the lab and let us take it from here." Goodall was eager to get this lab rat out of his office *now*. Goodall didn't leave Shamus any room for continued discussion as he walked over to his closed office door and quickly opened it. Shamus was about to speak. He was about to open his mouth, but instead decided the better of it. Shamus shook Goodall's extended hand and exited. Shamus thought to himself as he heard the door close abruptly behind him, *What have I done?*

CHAPTER 6

Glenview, IL

Behind his closed office door, Goodall spent the next several days scanning the available data he could find on *Harris Therapeutics.* He reviewed all the relevant published financial information, as well as researched the biographies of all the lead administrations at *Harris.* Just as he expected, *Harris* was a relatively young company—one of the many biotech startups trying to find its own space in this era of rapid biological innovation and development. With the ability to become a new company with little more than a good idea, eager young scientists, and a modest financial investment from friends and family, many of these startups wouldn't amount to more than an expensive trial-and-error.

On occasion, funds for a startup would come from a federal grant, a convinced venture capitalist group, or from a wealthy *whale* who had a vested interest in either the people at the new company, or the actual science they advanced. Often, even many of these sponsored enterprises would ultimately fail; how long the process took was simply a matter of how long their finances would last. On rare occasions, a small, new company would make a base-hit in the competitive world of entrepreneurial science. It was not only a matter of whether their product was relevant, desired, fiscally competitive—and marketable—that determined if the company would survive. It was also a matter of good fortune that they had the right product at the right time—seen by the right people. If all the business and science variables aligned, success could be achieved. The successful new company would grow and have its product purchased, or the company could be absorbed into another. From what Goodall could determine, *Harris Therapeutics* did have success in their research. Fortunately for *Yonie*, much of their work was still in early-stage development and was just under the radar for a major buyout.

Cancer vaccines are based on tumor antigens expressed in the context of what is referred to as the Major Histocompatibility Complex (MHC). These molecules are able to elicit a strong tumor-specific response which may result in the killing of tumor cells and eventual cancer regression.

Despite their relatively new company formation, eager and clever investigators at *Harris* had created the mRNA molecule which would stimulate the specific MHC activity that Shamus determined would be necessary to complete the complex cascade of events necessary to cause prostate cancer cell destruction identified in his lab. For Goodall, it wasn't just a matter of how to obtain that molecule. Having a limited quantity of a needed product, or in this case, the mRNA molecule, would hamper drug development and production significantly. Goodall understood that if he were to be successful in having *Yonie* have unlimited access to the molecule, what he really needed was the *methodology* to create it. The primary question that needed to be addressed by Goodall was assessing the best means to procure that formula.

Given his determination not to buy the protocol used to create the molecule, Goodall reached the conclusion that there was only one option remaining: to steal it. The secondary issue he confronted was how to keep secret *Yonie's* use of it once it was obtained. Goodall decided that the secondary concern would somehow be managed and controlled, just as it has in the past when an investigation is undertaken. He has been down this path before and has always found a way. Goodall's arrogance—both in intent and consequence—had gotten him in heat before, but he always found a way to slither out of it. This situation would be no different.

Goodall understood *Yonie* could buy the protocol and go into production with *Harris*. There would be plenty of profit to go around. But the competitor floodgates would open, and *Yonie* would no longer be in command of the market. Goodall smelled blood in the water, and he wanted to now proceed in this manner more out of his sense of privilege, rather than out of need.

Goodall reviewed the math. If his numbers were correct, given the incidence of prostate cancer and the scientific and social desire for a means to prevent it, this could be the financial boon he so desperately wanted. This could be his ticket to the riches he always felt he deserved. Goodall lifted his head from the files laid out in front of him. "The hell with them!" he said out loud. Goodall decided he would not advance his decision to obtain the molecular protocol up the food chain at *Yonie*—the fewer individuals involved, the better. At this point, Goodall considered that only himself, the new twerp, Olson, and Shamus had any knowledge of what could occur. From Goodall's perspective, those two were easily expendable once the production of the vaccine was underway. Goodall was so ignorant of the fact that arrogance and greed were a combination that seldom succeeded in the long run.

CHAPTER 7

Wheaton, IL

Harris Therapeutics Inc. was founded by its current CEO and president, William Waters. Waters was an affable fellow from Boston, who was always seen with a smile, an easy nature, and somehow, he always found a way to deliver a kind remark. Waters loved to tell clever jokes, yet he just couldn't stop himself from laughing while telling it—even if it was for the 20th time. He dressed in tee shirts and jeans, and often appeared as though he slept in both (most likely, because he did). Typically, Waters would let his beard grow for a week or so before he shaved, and he was rarely seen in anything other than a variety of tennis or cross-training sneakers. His choice of clothing resembled his personality—easy going, confident, and colorful. His good-natured appearance was genuine, but underneath, he was driven to always achieve excellence. Despite his family's wealth and the associated opportunity to do absolutely nothing of significance with his life, Waters had lofty goals. His education and work background was impressive. He first obtained a bachelor's degree in molecular biology from Duke University. Unsure what path to take, Waters then obtained a Master's in Public health, thinking he could make a difference in health care delivery. After working for two years as a mid-level hospital administrator, Waters realized he could be more productive in health care as a scientific investigator. He returned to Duke and obtained a Doctorate in Molecular Toxicology. His post-doctoral work was in drug research at *Kenner Pharmaceuticals*, a small boutique company outside of Indianapolis where *Kenner* was engaged in vaccine development.

While working at *Kenner,* Waters attended a research symposium in Chicago. At that meeting he was intrigued by the work of one of the keynote speakers. From that experience, Waters had an invigorated mind-set about what he could potentially achieve in drug development. He decided during the four-hour drive home the time had come to no longer work for anyone else. Waters now had ideas of what to achieve for himself and how to do it. He had his trust money available to survive, but now he needed to initiate a plan to give him a sense of fulfillment. The following day, Waters gave the requisite two-week resignation notice to his lab director, and three weeks later he was sitting in the office of the speaker he met in Chicago. There, the two had a lively discussion about the direction of vaccine development—particularly as it related to cancer prevention. Taking advice from his new friend and esteemed research colleague, Waters carefully laid out his calculations to initiate a new company.

Traveling back to his alma mater in Durham, Waters sought out graduate student acquaintances with whom he had stayed in contact. Luckily, many had secured jobs locally, and he was able to make a series of appointments and meetings to catch up with those who had the expertise he sought. One of Waters's greatest strengths was his awareness of what he didn't know—and, perhaps more importantly, a willingness to accept his lack of experience and knowledge. Waters met with friends and acquaintances in business, patent law, and finance. He spent the next three months meeting and interviewing a slew of potentially recruitable scientists from both academic institutions as well as the private sector.

Critically, Waters traveled back to the New England area and had multiple discussions with his closest uncle, Edward. Edward and William had nearly grown up together with only 15 years separating them. They were always friends first and relatives second. Edward had been extraordinarily successful in the card-printing business, and was delighted to be able to give his brilliant nephew the non-interest loans his accountants determined would be necessary to begin the new start-up biotech company.

With finances secured and a list of willing young scientists hand-picked for their work and work-ethic, Waters returned to the Midwest. He spent the next six months meeting with a variety of real estate developers, financial managers, and federal, state, and local regulators involved in creating his new company. Meetings with the FDA felt like a mud fight in slow motion, but after multiple rounds of challenging and often frustrating negotiations, he finally received the approval he needed to proceed. William Waters assembled his board, his scientific staff, and secured a refurbished facility in Wheaton, Illinois, a western suburb just outside of Chicago. The $50 million he *borrowed* from his uncle and other equity investors was finally being put to use, and five years after he conceived of what and how he wanted to spend his life-efforts accomplishing, Waters launched his new company. In honor of his beloved father who died of pancreatic cancer, Harris Waters, William Waters came up with the name of his new company: *Harris Therapeutics Inc.*

Michael J. Young, M.D.

CHAPTER 8

Security

Pharmaceutical and biotech company security is paramount to the company's survival. Theft and counterfeiting are their top security concerns—not only for the profitability of the company, but also for the end-users of their products and medications. The security risks are complex, and they require the involvement of governmental and international regulation.

The concerns begin in the physical realm; these companies require protection from actually being robbed of devices or drugs. The physical barrier protection a facility must incorporate into its campus is obvious; there must first be perimeter security to prevent any unauthorized access. This fortification would include fences, walls, guards, and surveillance. Entry and exit locations would require authentication measures. These may include security personnel, ID badges, and any of a variety of biometric scanners. Throughout the physical grounds, video surveillance and alarm systems—both obvious and non—must be present.

Perhaps even more important today is the need for advanced cybersecurity. As the world is now connected through the Internet and private electronic interfaces, including Bluetooth and Wi-Fi systems, protection from intruders—both from outside and within—is paramount. All computer systems require protection from malicious actors that may cause unauthorized information disclosure, theft, disruption or misdirection of services, or damage to the internal hardware, software, or data. Sophisticated hackers can do more damage to a company with just a few moments of properly sequenced keystrokes than could ever be accomplished with a weapon and physical force. As the value of the data increases, so will the methods of intrusion.

Gaining access to another's locked computer without permission—hacking, can be performed in a number of ways. To do so requires a password, a code, or PIN (personal identification number). The degree of difficulty encountered with hacking into someone's computer depends upon many variables. For instance, a home computer may have a simple password sign-on or PIN. Educated guessing could be considered one method of breaching this computer. To be successful, this technique often mandates intimate knowledge of the user or owner. Consequently, without such information, the process can be tedious and often unsuccessful. Many computer users are relatively unsophisticated in using dates or names that belies the security they require. We are all aware of the nuisance of maintaining password hygiene. We generally find it insulting to be mandated to change our passwords regularly. Often, this process is associated with having to add more letters, numbers, special characters, or capitalization, often in a sequence that is challenging to remember. This necessitates our creating a new record and storage of the changes. Failure to record the change, and then not remembering it, can be infuriating when we are in need of the information. Consequently, many of us will continue with our original password with just a slight variation. Not an ideal situation for maintaining security in any system. Given enough time, opportunity, and a modicum of owner knowledge, an experienced hacker can usually find his or her way into a simple PIN or password protected system.

As simple as it sounds, perhaps the easiest method to obtain a password is to just ask the user for it. Naive users will share passwords indiscriminately. In a low-complexity work environment, such behavior is more likely to happen. As the value of the information on any computer system increases—whether it is a personal computer, a highly sophisticated integrated network within a company, or even governmental—so will the sophistication of user password protection and identifiers needed for access. Even with these systems, colleagues may lower their guard and share privileged password information. Finally, a hacker could pretend to be an authentic internet service provider or colleague. Often referred to as phishing, the intruder impersonates a trusted contact and sends the victim fake emails. Unaware of this, the victim opens the mail and clicks on the malicious link or attachment. By doing so, the hacker can gain access to confidential information or install malware.

Another means to identify security passwords and codes is to use a keylogger program on the computer the hacker seeks to enter. Keystroke logging is the action of recording the keys struck on a keyboard. Hardware keyloggers are physical devices that record every keystroke, but they require physical access to the computer. Software keyloggers are more cryptic, as they don't require physical access to a device. Typically, the program is installed covertly with downloaded malware, and the user is unaware his or her actions are being monitored. Data can then be retrieved by the individual operating the logging program.

More sophisticated means to identify a user's password can be accomplished by password cracking programs. A hacker can crack the password using brute force or dictionary attacks. A brute force attack uses trial-and-error to guess login information. Basically, the hacker is calculating every possible combination that could make up a password. There are 94 numbers, letters, and symbols on a standard keyboard. These algorithms can generate about two hundred billion, 8-character passwords. Computer programs used for brute force attacks can check anywhere from 10,000 to 1 billion passwords per second. A dictionary attack is a method of breaking into a password-protected computer or network by systematically entering every word in a dictionary as a password. Additionally, an intruder could discover a vulnerability in the network's application and bypass authentication.

Perhaps one of the most difficult types of intrusion into a company's data that is challenging to prevent is an insider threat: the potential for an insider to use their authorized access to harm an organization.

The Internet of things (IoT) describes physical objects with sensors, processing ability, software or other technologies that connect and exchange data with other devices and systems over the Internet or other communications networks. In other words, the IoT refers to the collective network of connected devices and the technology that facilitates communication between devices and the cloud, as well as between the devices themselves. In the most basic of terms, it is a system of interrelated computed devices.

IoT devices are physical objects that sense things going on in the physical world. They contain an integrated central processing unit (CPU), network adapter and firmware, and are usually connected to a Dynamic

Host Configuration Protocol server. Most IoT devices are configured and managed through a software application. There are over 20 billion active connective devices in the world today. In our personal lives, IoT devices are our Amazon Echo, our Google Home voice controller, our doorbell cams, and our smart locks. The basic advantage of IoT is that it doesn't require human-to-human or human-to-computer interaction to fulfill any intermediate process. These devices enable an increase in productivity and efficiency in our lives and businesses.

In the pharmaceutical industry, IoT has evolved into a significant role. These systems monitor and control the machinery, regulators, environmental conditions, and other complicated and detailed processes engaged in the extraordinarily specific requisites of medication production. It tracks and controls material use and inventory. These sensors and computers also maintain the quality and speed of medication production, and manage packaging and tracking of drug batches. Post drug production, IoT connected devices will be involved in clinical trials and monitoring of the effects of medication in real-time management. It is the very fact that these devices are devoid of any need for human interaction which makes them potentially vulnerable to unnoticed or unmonitored activity. Perhaps their strength of efficiency is also their weakness should nefarious activity become involved.

There are multiple vulnerabilities to the IoT. One of the largest risks is basically insecure communications. Data transmission between devices is potentially susceptible to interception by third parties. Such breaches could obviously allow access to sensitive information. Another vulnerability is insufficient authentication and password hygiene—meaning, the device lacks adequate measures to verify that users are who they claim to be. Despite the most complex security system design, if there are inadequate measures to limit or control who can gain access to data or information, security of that data is at risk. Authentication methods (e.g., two-factor authentication), biometrics, rotating or changing passwords, and secure centralized infrastructure access, are all potential means to help maintain system security. But IoT devices may individually have simple operating systems, and consequently, the system as a whole could be compromised if access though a weak portal or non-responsible user occurs. What is ultimately the weakest link in any of these highly sophisticated systems is also the most difficult to manage and control: people.

CHAPTER 9

Chicago, IL

Lucifer Ashwood was a peculiar man. He had no living family, and few friends. Labeling the few individuals he occasionally drank with as *friends* was probably an overstatement. Basically, he was a loner. He lived by himself in a small two-bedroom apartment in the part of Chicago known as Wrigleyville. It is a neighborhood on the near-north side of Chicago best known for one thing; it is the neighborhood that surrounds the famous old baseball field for the Chicago Cubs: Wrigley Field. The Chicago *Greystone* began appearing in neighborhoods in the 1890's. These townhomes got their name from the locally sourced Bedford limestone, which was grey-ish in color, and many of the old Greystones in the Wrigleyville neighborhood were built coinciding with the opening of the ballpark in 1914. A Greystone located near the intersection of Sheffield Avenue and Irving Park Road was as ordinary as they come. There was nothing particularly outstanding about this building. The brick walls surrounding the inconspicuous, tri-level apartment building were worn down and blackened from dirt. This was the end-result of horrible Midwest winters, and over a hundred years of wind blowing in from Lake Michigan. The short cement staircase leading to the weathered front door similarly revealed its age by the many cracks in the structure. Weeds were growing in the deep crevices despite the many efforts to pull, or poison them. The building was one of hundreds in this neighborhood that looked un-strikingly similar. They were all built on the same design, at the same time, and with the same construction materials.

However, on the top floor unit of this particular building where Ashwood resided for the past 30 years, there was a difference from all the surrounding buildings that looked the same—there were no windows in this unit. A person passing by on the street probably wouldn't give it a second thought as block by block, the neighborhood looked pretty much the same. The monotony of the townhomes and apartment buildings would simply numb someone interested in looking for structural differences. As much as one may desire ample sunlight and fresh air in their living space, Ashwood had other needs that mandated complete privacy.

Ashwood did not want to be seen through a window, or have peering telescopes pointed in his direction. Similarly, the door to his unit was reinforced, and all the walls and covered windows were modified. His home functioned as a SCIF (Sensitive Compartmented Information Facility)—a secure location that shields against electronic surveillance and prevents data leakage of sensitive information. From an electronic perspective, a SCIF must have access controls, intrusion detection systems, and secure data communications. The SCIF must also use metallic barriers to block radio frequency signals and electromagnetic emissions, as well as filter the power coming into the room.

Ashwood converted the second bedroom into an office. On one long table were four linked Falcon Northwest Talon Desktop computers. Additionally, there was a wall of connected modems and routers. A Wi-Fi Pineapple, Alpha USB Wi-Fi adaptors, and a shelf full of new Raspberry pi and Arduino devices were stacked in a pile. Electronic gadgetry and paraphernalia were strewn everywhere. LED lights in a variety of colors and shapes blinked continuously. Given the lack of sunlight, the small, darkened office appeared to resemble a computer lab residing in an industrial technology company.

Lucifer Ashwood was a contract hacker; he made his living breaking into computer systems. His fee structure was simple: He would first hack into whatever computer system or network for which he was hired. Whatever effort he expended would then be reflected in what he would ask for in compensation. No final cost was ever determined upfront given the variability of potential security breaches encountered, and the amount of time and effort required to complete the job. All clients were, however, required to provide a $100,000 cash deposit before any work commenced. Once the final cash payment was made, and only then, would Ashwood deliver whatever data or information the purchaser requested.

Over the past 10 years, Ashwood made over 20 million dollars in *service fees.* Over this time period, Ashwood hacked into perhaps three dozen private company computer networks—they were his bread and butter. With mostly innocuous security systems, he could enter them without so much as breaking a sweat. Whatever inter-company feud that was settled or made with the data he stole didn't interest him in the least. But it was the big fish; large, multimillion-dollar industries and governmental agencies that he was asked to retrieve information from—that got him excited. He loved the challenge of breaking the codes and stealing the precious *secure* data their cybersecurity experts protected. Ashwood's service fee was significantly higher than others in the same line of work, but so often, so was the value of what he retrieved.

Time was rarely a factor for Ashwood. He played the long game, and was never in a hurry. Ashwood was meticulous with his work and would always carefully cover his tracks. And, despite his reputation for being slow, nobody complained; no one he ever worked for could remember the last time he failed to deliver.

Ashwood was quietly reading an article from the magazine, *Wired,* when his encrypted cellphone vibrated. Despite all of his security protocols, Ashwood still limited his telephone conversations to the bare minimum. Nothing incriminating was ever discussed on the phone or via text. He always preferred to meet in-person. Ashwood felt the least likely means to have any eavesdropping take place would be in a public space. Mindful of the use of potential noise-filtering equipment and the use of long-range listening devices, he still wanted any unwanted listeners to have to work at it. Before any unverified, in-person conversation, he would electronically scan his visitor to check for any bugs or listening devices. Hacking someone at a minimally protected home or office was easy for Ashwood, and the likelihood of getting caught was minimal. Illegally entering a foreign nation's network or a highly sophisticated, highly valued, industry computer system was a significantly different situation. Severe punishment or retaliation would be inevitable should he be caught.

"I would like to schedule a meeting," the voice stated. It was obvious the buyer on the other end of the line was versed in maintaining a cryptic profile.

"Text your code," Ashwood stated flatly. Anyone who hired Ashwood in the past was given a code number to use for all communications. Moments later, a 6-digit number appeared on his phone. Ashwood hung up, now knowing who was calling. Ashwood would now dial the caller as another means to additionally assure a secure communication.

"2 p.m. tomorrow. Meet at the bench next to the Foster Beach concession stand." Ashwood stated quietly. He always liked meeting near Lake Michigan. It was an open location and allowed Ashwood to observe his visitor as he approached.

"That would be fine." The voice stated and hung up.

Ashwood continued to listen to the line for a few moments, and then closed his phone. He put down his magazine and pondered for a moment what Neil Goodall wanted this time.

CHAPTER 10

Chicago, IL

As per his usual routine, Ashwood arrived at the meeting point well ahead of schedule. He positioned himself at one end of the bench assuring others who came to sit would most likely position themselves at the opposite end. People were like birds on an electrical line, he reasoned; they will spread themselves out evenly. Ashwood brought along the same copy of the magazine *Wired* that he was reading the day before; he kept one eye on the article that interested him, and one on the oncoming foot traffic. Having worked with Goodall in the past, Ashwood didn't expect any surprises. He recalled that Goodall was a total asshole, but the man paid his previous fee promptly and without any issues or complaints. Ashwood also recalled Goodall to be in the pharmaceutical industry, where the money came from deep pockets. The last job he did for Goodall netted over a million dollars. Ashwood smiled to himself as he thought about the previous job—*Big Pharma was run by idiots.* They are in a constant battle to be king. If they collaborated together rather than spending fortunes in competition, there would be more to go around, and plenty for everyone. *Whatever,* thought Ashwood; their war among themselves is his gain. While contemplating that thought, Goodall appeared, walking briskly towards the bench. He seemed anxious. Fortunately, the park bench remained empty.

"Good afternoon, Mr. Ashwood," Goodall stated, his large mouth filled with perfectly white, capped teeth. The contrast between his tan and his teeth was striking.

"Good afternoon, indeed, Mr. Goodall. What can I do for you today?" Ashwood inquired. Always mindful of time, he wasted none and got right to the point. Goodall was not his friend and Ashwood had no interest in anything the man did or why he did it.

"Ahh…right to the point, as usual, I see." Goodall stated with a false smile. "Well, let me get right to it. At *Yonie*, we are working on a new project…"

Ashwood raised his hand in a motion to inform Goodall to stop talking. "I don't care about your new project. I don't care what you are making or selling. Just tell me what you need." Ashwood stated firmly.

"Yes…yes…of course…" Goodall stuttered. "There is a biotech startup in Wheaton, Illinois, called *Harris Therapeutics.* They make a protein…ahh…a molecule that we need. More precisely, we need the methodology…the process, or formula, they use to make it."

"How large is the company?" Ashwood asked.

"Well, it's a new startup…they really don't have much in the way of size…from what I can ascertain, there are less than 50 full-time employees. But, there is a biochemist who works there…his name is Gene Cortes." Goodall stopped speaking and reached into the breast pocket of his tailor-made suit. He pulled out a photograph of Doctor Cortes and handed it to Ashwood. Ashwood looked at the image. He saw a strong man with clear blue eyes and long, black hair looking back at him. He appeared to be young, confident…perhaps in his early to mid-forties. Ashwood took the photograph and put it into his own jacket pocket as Goodall continued. "Anyway, he is the lead investigator in the lab that produced this molecule. I don't need him, and I don't need the molecule. I just need to know how they make it. I need the recipe."

Ashwood looked out towards the shimmering, smooth water on Lake Michigan. Without any breeze, and no waves, the surface reminded him of a pane of glass. After a silent moment, he looked back at Goodall, who was staring intently at him.

"No problem." Ashwood stated. "Drop off the deposit tomorrow—same as before. I'll let you know what the balance is once I have what you want." Goodall knew it was as *good to go* at that point. He relaxed and smiled. He shook Ashwood's hand and got up from the bench. As Goodall walked away with a new bounce to his step, Ashwood simply observed the fool walk away. Ashwood turned his attention back to the water. The games these idiots play, he thought.

CHAPTER 11

Chicago, IL

Ashwood prepared to perform his due diligence. As with any new job, before getting into the actual work he needed to understand what he was up against. Ashwood needed to understand more about the company he was going to hack into, the individuals who may hold the keys to whatever data he sought, and of course, the security systems he would need to circumvent. Ashwood actually enjoyed this part. He was a planner, someone who acted methodically and rarely made a mistake. He also knew to accomplish any task efficiently required the requisite upfront work; studying, planning, and understanding. The actual solution or accomplishment of the work will then flow downhill. When it was time to actually execute the hack, Ashwood knew it would then proceed seamlessly and undetected. As much as he desired to fulfill his work obligation, he also did not want to get implicated. Some of the jobs he did in the past were against rather unsavory individuals. They could and would take the law into their own hands. *Get in, get out, get on,* was Ashwood's personal motto for survival in the hacking business.

Ashwood would spend the next month learning about *Harris Therapeutics*. He was impressed with the accomplishments of William Waters. How this privileged man turned his back on what could have come easily and worked at what he believed in, was testament to his voracity. As much as Ashwood tried to do his work devoid of emotion, he found himself feeling envious of a man who was so determined to accomplish what was important to him. Despite efforts to suppress such feelings, Ashwood knew that what Doctor Waters was doing with his life was admirable. The more he read about the man, the more Ashwood knew all of Waters's efforts were expended for all the right reasons. Ashwood was also impressed with the résumés of the scientists brought into the fold at *Harris Therapeutics*. Despite performing exhaustive background checks on everyone at *Harris*, Ashwood could not find a single researcher who had anything other than altruistic goals as the purpose for his or her work. Ashwood worked hard to suppress his emotions, and repeatedly reminded himself that he had a job to do. He reprimanded himself for losing perspective. He was reminded of his mantra: All these companies were dishonest—perhaps he just hadn't identified the underlying root of their evil. He implored himself to plod on with his background work.

After reviewing all the key employees and board members, Ashwood was surprised to learn that *Harris Therapeutics* was surprisingly, financially secure. Unlike most startups which were beholden to any number of banks, lenders, or venture capitalists—all of whom expected some type of compensation for their investment—*Harris* was under the basic *ownership* of one man, Waters's uncle. And Edward Waters, who *loaned* the money for getting the company going, did so because of his belief in their work. This was not only most unusual, but it also prohibited applying a financial pressure point. Once again, Ashwood found himself a bit uneasy by what he discovered about this young, bold company. His concerns were amplified as he dug into background research of the company's security systems.

Ashwood understood that as any entity increased its size and complexity, the potential for employee disenfranchisement, increased physical and cyber backdoor entryways, as well as the potential for more functional mishaps or mistakes occurred logarithmically. The larger the company, the hierarchy of procedural steps needed to accomplish nearly every task always became more complicated. In essence, the larger the company, the easier it was for Ashwood to enter and exit without detection. It was simple mathematics; more things could go wrong as a company expanded its footprint. But, *Harris Therapeutics* was a tight ship.

Ashwood was impressed by the planning and expenditure involved in the perimeter security. Its physical plant was simple and elegant—

the 200,000 square-foot structure was constructed of limestone, steel, and glass, and built in a secluded area. Ashwood's study of the building's construction and development identified numerous, unusual contractors involved. The landscape architect wanted open space around the ultra-modern design. Not only would this allow the building to standout, but the 20 acres of grass surrounding the building acted as a security buffer. He identified a company involved in the installation of underground pressure sensors. Underneath the large acreage surrounding the building, the underground sensors could measure mechanical impulses induced by a pedestrian intruder or vehicular activity. The presence of impulse time delay and amplitude would allow exact identification of any such activity. The outer wall surrounding the property similarly appeared mundane, but was anything but. Not only were there visible and (most likely) non-visible cameras mounted every 10 feet on the top of the twenty-foot limestone wall, but cameras were also directed at the face of the entire structure. Ashwood stopped calculating how many cameras this entailed, as he had no idea how many were hidden. He also suspected in all likelihood, thermal photo imaging and acoustical monitoring would also be present. But all this hardware really didn't matter, as he would not be scaling any walls or crawling on the grass.

Based upon what he identified, Ashwood suspected the building itself would be as secure as Fort Knox. More out of curiosity, he continued his research using both publicly available as well as previously used, more cryptic methods, to access the major companies involved in security system design and construction. There were limited access points to the building. By law, all work spaces required a minimum number of exits based upon occupancy. Given only 50 or so employees, the *Harris* building did not need many. Similarly, it only had one loading dock. All of the entry points were guarded by two heavily-armed security officers at multiple locations. The guards were not from any known security agency or company. They were hand-picked, rotated regularly, and were highly compensated. Entry into any one of the outside doors required the visitors to go through a holding area, separated by entry and exit doors controlled by the guards. No doors opened automatically without *both* guards activating its electromagnetic locks. All the access doors were glass-clad polycarbonate—also referred to as bulletproof glass. Once inside the door holding area, all employees and visitors were required to pass through a high-resolution millimeter wave imaging scanner, as well as physical search. Additional scanners were used for all personal items. The guards were expertly well trained in espionage techniques, and knew what to look for. Any unexplainable material or devices, physical or electronic, was likely to be identified. At the end of each workday, all employees and visitors went through the same rigorous routine upon leaving the premises. The process was tedious and time-consuming, but everyone knew the rules, and no unauthorized entry or exit of personnel or material was ever likely to occur.

No doubt, all the computers and data storage equipment on the premises had highly sophisticated, anti-theft measures installed. USB or other external data storage device use would be electronically impeded and any attempt at downloading would be detected.

Ashwood realized he was not likely to bypass the number and complexity of *Harris's* security systems—at least, by any physical methods. He felt it would be impossible to enter and leave with the needed data; even with a well-hidden, electronic data storage device.

After his very detailed, but disappointing, analysis of the company's operational and physical security, Ashwood now turned his attention to how *Harris Therapeutics* conducted its business via the Internet. As Ashwood now appreciated how disciplined the company and its employees were with its physical security protocols, Ashwood realized he would be left with only one option to obtain the requested information: hack remotely. But his growing pessimism about the effectiveness of obtaining the data in this manner was also realized as he continued his research. Unlike most companies, where security was considered an adjunct to their work, it appeared that *Harris Therapeutics* was constructed with security as a prime directive. Ashwood wondered what security advisors assisted the company during its pre-construction planning. Whoever it was, this security was tighter than anything he had ever encountered—certainly in the civilian sector.

Pouring himself his 3rd cup of coffee one night, Ashwood opened up a series of Internet activity scanning profiles. Although the data was impenetrably encrypted, he was able to assess a particular pattern within the data-packet transmissions. Reviewing the information he could access, Ashwood suddenly slammed down his coffee cup, and pushed himself back from his desk. "Damn it!" he said, out loud. Ashwood realized *Harris* had a time-locked, Internet access web filter. He noted the company *opened* itself up to Internet activity for only 30 minutes every 4 hours. That severely limited how much data transmission could occur at any one point in time—but *Harris* was not in any race. The company employees were patient with their work and would accept that limitation. However, for Ashwood, this meant that any malware or other intrusion efforts he might use would be hard-cut after 30 minutes.

No malware program Ashwood possessed could invade, modify, and then retransmit the volume of information needed in that short of a time span. To properly and cryptically hack into an advanced, protected, network can be a painstaking effort; one that mandates patience. More importantly, patience has the requisite of *time*. Time that he wouldn't have. Ashwood's thoughts raced as he considered alternative hacking options. *Could he parcel the transmissions?* Meaning, could he segment any instruction codes to misdirect the network, which could allow him to subsequently retrieve the requested data? Ashwood sat motionless for several minutes as he went over different scenarios of intrusion in his mind. None came to him.

"Unbelievable!" Ashwood shouted as he realized the futility of his potential hacking options. He had never come across a company, let alone one in the private domain, with such secure cyber protocols in place. He would have to go to plan B—gain access physically, and then try to obtain the passcodes to obtain the required molecular synthesis protocol. Ashwood understood he couldn't physically overwhelm any of the many barriers and security mechanisms. He would have to gain access by being clever and preying on human weakness, or less likely, someone's sloppiness at *Harris,* to achieve this mission.

CHAPTER 12

Chicago, IL

Ashwood reconsidered his predicament. He had agreed to and deposited a 100G to obtain a specific file of highly-protected pharmaceutical data of a molecular synthesis protocol. And, despite his evolved skills of Internet espionage, he understood the target of his potential attack was equally sophisticated in its defense. That was often not the case in his many years of hacking. Ashwood had several options to consider: He could return the money and walk away from the job. As a consequence, he would most likely never receive another referral from Goodall and his company. More importantly, Ashwood was concerned a leak of his inabilities would surface among his clientele. None of them would understand or care that the intended target in this job appeared to be ultra-prepared, and constructed and managed in a manner to prevent electronic intrusion. They would not understand the nuances or details—only that he was not the dependable resource they counted on for their dirty work. Ashwood realized his reputation would take a hit, and his ego would not allow that. He also understood he did not have the skill set to waltz into a company and coerce or manipulate anyone for passcodes. Ashwood understood he was not a spy; he was a hacker—someone who worked from afar while being protected by layers of electronic firewalls and misdirection. His strength was not in his interpersonal skills of deceit. On the contrary, Ashwood knew he was socially inept, and would probably be caught in a nanosecond. He had accepted a job and needed to see it completed. For this, he needed help. After considering his options, Ashwood picked up his phone and contacted Goodall.

"Good afternoon, Mr. Goodall," Ashwood began.

"Do you have what I need?" Goodall responded quickly.

"I do not. I have run into some…challenges. *Harris Therapeutics* is run like a military operation. I do not see any electronic means for successful penetration. Which leads me to my next question," Ashwood stated slowly.

"Go on." Goodall responded tentatively.

"To obtain the data you are requesting will require a different type of intrusion," Ashwood began. "It will require someone who has the capability to get in close and…use his *coercive* skills to…well, let me state this appropriately…to *encourage* someone to give us what we want. I know of someone with this ability."

"I'm listening." Goodall spoke with a quiet calm.

Ashwood continued, "I suspect during the process of retrieving what you want there will be…" Ashwood paused for a moment to carefully select the appropriate words, "I think there will casualties along the way. But, I assure you there will be no traces of our… intervention. The fee schedule will remain the same. I will personally compensate this associate…as a reflection of my reliability in completing the job."

Goodall was quick to reply, "My only concern is obtaining the molecular synthesis protocol. I honestly don't care how you fulfill the requisites of our agreement. I have no interest in what you need to do, but I expect results. And, if there are casualties, as you said, along the way, well, so be it. Just make sure the job is clean, and can't be tracked back to us." After a long pause, Goodall continued. "Anything else?"

"No…understood." Ashwood disconnected the call.

Ashwood went to his desk and logged onto his computer. Given his own password authentication steps, it took several moments for his contact list to populate. Ashwood found the name he was looking for and then dialed the number.

The other end of the line picked up, "Yes?"

"Good evening, Mr. Burksdale, this is Lucifer Ashwood."

"It's been awhile, my friend. Shall we meet at the same location?" Burksdale replied.

This caught Ashwood by surprise. He had to jog his memory in order to recall where he met Burksdale nearly two years ago. He paused for a moment before responding.

"Yes…ahh…yes, that would be fine." Ashwood replied, as he suddenly remembered. *This guy doesn't forget a thing!* Ashwood thought. "Excellent…how about tomorrow at noon?"

"That would be fine." Replied Burksdale. The line disconnected.

CHAPTER 13

Chicago, IL

At precisely 11:45 a.m., Ashwood sat down on the park bench across from the basketball courts at Foster Avenue and the bike path. He watched a few people who were untethered from work on this beautiful afternoon, shooting hoops. Ashwood recalled doing the same when he was younger; somehow his world became more complicated, and he now missed those carefree days. Today, his life was shrouded in secrecy as he tried to evade detection while staying hidden in the shadows. Ashwood's moment of self-reflection quickly departed as he observed the outline of Burksdale making his way up the path.

Other than the few individuals playing basketball, the lakefront was empty, and nobody was within earshot of the park bench. Ashwood, however, felt the need to walk. He got up from the bench and waved as Burksdale neared. The two men approached one another and shook hands. With Ashwood leading the way, they walked along the bike trail slowly. Their conversation was lively and collegial. An uninformed observer would think two old friends just ran into each other and were catching up. But the conversation occurring was that of two professional criminals reminiscing about how the past two years treated them—both had done well. Apparently, there was no shortage of employment in the world of deceit and manipulation. Perhaps, there never was—just newer ways of doing it had evolved. Ashwood brought Burksdale up-to-speed with what roadblocks he ran into, and detailed what was needed to complete the job.

CHAPTER 13 – *To Cure Or Kill*

"So, tell me about the lead researcher...Cortes," Burksdale stated.

"The guy's a genius," Ashwood began. "But he's a private citizen who I'm sure doesn't want any trouble. He has no reason not to be forthcoming if properly approached. I must say, its impressive how disciplined everyone is at *Harris.* Every morning and evening, they go through the same search routine by the guards. I suspect these people are just as compulsive and careful in their lives outside of work."

"That's probably correct. The question is really how dedicated they are to the company boss, Doctor Waters, and the objectives and mission of *Harris Therapeutics*." Burksdale answered, as they continued their slow journey up the trail. "I really don't think it will be difficult to extract the formula from Cortes. He's a damn scientist, not some hero. But if he feels whatever they are working on is the holy grail of medicine, then he might put up a fight."

Ashwood stopped momentarily and stated, "It's possible there are others in the lab who also know the protocol we want. It might be worthwhile to go after them first. Should anything *happen* to them, it might send a message to Doctor Cortes that we're playing hardball."

Burksdale considered what he just heard, and then responded, "We can't kidnap or trap someone from the lab and then threaten them for the protocol. Neither one of us is skilled or experienced in interrogation techniques. If they don't know or have access to what we need, we let them go? That will only bring tighter security around Cortes and the company. The protocol will go dark, and the situation will become public." Burksdale calmly remarked while staring at a large schooner traversing Lake Michigan. He was impressed by the boat's speed. "No...to do this correctly will require a coordinated strike."

"Meaning?" Ashwood asked.

Burksdale looked directly at Ashwood and stated, "Meaning...we will identify two, maybe three, specific lab associates of Cortes. They must all be confronted around the same time, and we won't need to ask them anything or threaten them. If we were to question them and get misinformation, what use is it? And how would we know what they gave us was valuable until after we gave it to Goodall and he had it tested. They would then need to be eliminated. And if they do know useful information, we still have to find a way to retrieve it. We are going to be exactly where we are right now. And that's assuming they know and tell us everything. Again, in that case we would still have to eliminate them. No, we take them out—no witnesses. What we need to do is use their *misfortune* to make it crystal clear to Cortes to give us the protocol. Once Cortes is made aware what has occurred to his lab associates, he will be incentivized to give us what we want. This way it is handed right to us directly from the person who created the protocol. I'm not going to waste any effort negotiating—Cortes will comply. Once we have what we need and it is tested and verified by Goodall, then we can take care of Cortes."

"You're right…we need to do this cleanly. All at once," Ashwood stated, as he shook his head in the affirmative. He wanted to give a good front, but was becoming concerned with the evolving complexity of the situation. Ashwood understood if this job was botched there would be hell to pay.

Burksdale understood his associate's frustration. He nodded forward, and the two started walking again. "Obviously, we need full reconnaissance of these individuals. We're not going to move until we have everyone completely analyzed and understood. We need to know their habits, how they live, and when it's time to tighten the noose, we'll be ready. I'll do my homework, and we'll get the information we need."

"Yes. We will get what we need," Ashwood stated in a quiet whisper, as though he was trying to convince himself. He did not feel comfortable that this job was now out of his hands. He initially became less confident in a successful outcome when he realized he didn't have the requisite skills for the job. He now had to rely on Burksdale—who was good at what he did, but had a tendency to be overly aggressive. The successful completion of the agreement Ashwood made with Goodall was now out of his control. Burksdale could sense the apprehension in Ashwood's demeanor.

Burksdale stopped walking and looked directly as Ashwood. "We will leave no witnesses and we will get this done."

"No witnesses." Ashwood reiterated firmly. He could feel his confidence returning.

The two men continued to walk in silence for a few more minutes. They made arrangements to meet again in two weeks. In the interim, Burksdale would familiarize himself with those who worked in Cortes's lab. But he wouldn't just study what each worker did in the lab. Burksdale would scrutinize their lives.

CHAPTER 14

Chicago, IL

Jonathan Burksdale had many talents. Along with his extensive medical background, he was also an excellent researcher. He had a knack for being able to find important details others would easily miss. But aside from knowing what was important, he also had a keen sense of where to find information. As Burksdale began his review of associates that worked in the lab of Gene Cortes at *Harris Therapeutics,* he first did the obvious: going onto the website of the company. Although the company was using its website for self-promotion; discussing where its research was headed, philosophies of its work, etc., it was quite cryptic in articulating the details of what research it was actually doing. The various company interdepartmental heads were shown with polished biographies and photographs. When Burksdale tried to access more information about each lab, he was linked to a boilerplate web page requesting visitor information: 'Leave your contact information and *Harris* will contact you'. "I don't think so," Burksdale said out loud as he logged off the site.

Going onto *Facebook, Instagram* and *LinkedIn,* Burksdale was able to discover many of Cortes's friends and work associates. Most of the photographs were also name-tagged, making his cross-referencing task easier. Performing a *Med-Pub* search, he then researched scientific publications from Cortes. The publications were completed with his co-investigators' names attached. Additional *Google* searches filled in more of the blanks. It was just a matter of performing additional well-directed online searches, and Burksdale was able to assemble a list of the names, addresses, and photographs of the five individuals who were the primary associates in Cortes's lab. It is frightening how much personal information is available online. With time, finding what one wants can easily be accomplished. It requires an understanding of how to navigate within the Internet, and knowing how to cross-reference the information from a variety of sites. With little more than time required to finish a double scotch on the rocks, Burksdale had the information he needed.

Burksdale performed a similar type of online review for each of the individuals in the lab. When that was completed, he performed a different search—but one in which he wasn't looking for data. Burksdale didn't need demographical information; he already collected that. What he wanted to find out now was more about the personality of each of the individuals selected. As so many technology savvy individuals are prone to these days, they *had* to have social media interaction. It was easy for Burksdale to go onto any number of these websites and see who these people associated with—what they did, where they did it, and with whom. Family information, photographs, even what they ate at various restaurants was posted. Burksdale shook his head in dismay each time he did this type of background review. How pathetic that so many people felt the need for affirmation and attention.

There was a particular Cortes associate whose name appeared most often in his publications. She was frequently named behind Cortes in authorship, but she also had a significant number of lead-author publications as well. Her name was Rebecca Sunnis. Sunnis had an academic profile that would be acceptable as a professor at any university. With a Ph.D. in molecular biology from Tufts, Sunnis's work focused entirely on genetic mapping sequencing. Her role was vital to the development of the protein molecule desired by Goodall. As Burksdale studied her work, he wondered how far up the hierarchy at *Yonie Pharmaceuticals* this plan went? Did the higher-ups honestly think they could keep a wrap on pilfering another company's intellectual property? Obviously, they must have thought this through, but the competitiveness of this endeavor seemed way out of line. Burksdale shook off his lack of focus, and continued exploring the habits of Rebecca Sunnis.

Unlike most of the scientists Burksdale came across, Rebecca Sunnis was definitely unique. Along with her academic achievements, she had formal training at a culinary school. Many of the scientists

Burksdale came across in his career were often socially *challenged.* Few had interests such as gourmet cooking—which generally mandated a significant amount of time and effort—effort that few expended outside of their work. None appeared to have the patience required to learn, let alone properly plan, shop, and prepare gourmet meals. At one point in her life, Sunnis even had a small catering company specializing in desserts. Burksdale admired her interests, but was more impressed with the discipline she must have to organize and develop expertise in areas outside of her research endeavors. Looking at her many posted photographs, Burksdale suspected she was quiet and reserved; perhaps she was a loner. She often appeared by herself in the on-line images. With her long brown hair and bright blue eyes, Sunnis was also quite easy on the eyes. A distorted, mischievous grin appeared on Burksdale's face as he reveled in what lay in store for her. So be it, thought Burksdale, she was a stepping stone to achieve his objective. He didn't really care who or what got in his way—he would get the damn formula.

Before moving on to the next profile for review, Burksdale took a break. As he poured himself another scotch, he questioned the need to study more. Why expend energy when it might not be needed? He decided to focus on Sunnis. If she was able to deliver the goods then his work will be done. If not, well, then he would continue to peck away at others. Whether it was the effect of his third scotch, or just his own self-confidence, Burksdale felt he could control the task in front of him.

Burksdale looked up Sunnis's address again. She lived in Naperville, a rather large city west of Chicago, and close to *Harris Therapeutics* in Wheaton. He located it on *Google Maps* and laid out a plan to find out more about where the target resided and her daily habits. Burksdale anticipated his ability to observe would not be difficult on someone like Sunnis. She was untrained, unsuspecting, and most likely, too preoccupied with other interests to notice she was being surveilled. Burksdale felt a rush of excitement knowing what was coming.

He finished his drink and went to bed. As he turned off his bed-stand light, he reviewed the next days' itinerary. Tomorrow, the hunt will begin.

CHAPTER 15

Chicago, IL

At 5:30 a.m., Burksdale's alarm clock buzzed. He shot out of bed, took a quick shower, and hurriedly ate his breakfast. Knowing he had close to an hour drive on the Eisenhower Expressway commute to the western Chicago suburbs, he didn't want to waste any time. Traffic on the expressway can be brutal during rush hour, and getting off late would be a miserable waste of time. Weaving through the heavy traffic, Burksdale let his car's navigation system get him near Sunnis's home address. Naperville was ranked one of the safest cities in America. It's also a very wealthy community; one of the wealthiest in the Midwest. But, in a single-working household with employment as a scientist, the large homes and estates were way out of her reach. Rebecca Sunnis lived in a modest apartment complex just a few blocks off the Naperville Riverwalk. It was a perfect location for her: safe, accessible, and close to parks and recreational facilities. She took her ballroom dance classes within walking distance to her apartment, and a slew of new, unique restaurants were nearby. Sunnis had a close circle of friends with whom she enjoyed her foodie-dining experiences.

Upon his arrival, Burksdale did a drive-by and noted the absence of any entrance gate into the apartment complex. He parked his car two blocks away and walked back. The complex was large: twelve separate, 5-story brick buildings surrounded a pond with a fountain in the middle. The structures appeared new—perhaps ten years old at most. There were small planted trees on the property, many with supporting rods and ropes, which gave away the complex's young age. Surrounding the pond was a running track, and despite the early hour, a dozen or so dedicated athletes were pounding the pavement as walkers on the outer lanes took their time on the track. Walking alongside the track, Burksdale was able to see the various building addresses posted in large numbers. He located Sunnis's building. Fortunate for Burksdale, there were numerous benches located on a small playground adjacent to her building entrance. He easily slid onto one of the benches and was able to inconspicuously observe the entranceway to her building. After waiting over an hour, Burksdale chastised himself. He failed to look at the rear of the building, which faced the owner's parking lot. *You idiot*, he murmured to himself as he realized his folly.

It was now after 9:00 a.m., so Burksdale could only suspect that Sunnis had long ago left for work exiting through the back. Despite his error, all was not lost. He decided he would follow her morning routine another day and would assess her apartment today. Waiting for someone to enter or exit her building, Burksdale remained on the bench and watched the complex's hyperactive children play on their rubberized protected playground. The children's multi-tasking parents worked on their laptops or spoke with exaggerated hand gestures on their cellphones while occasionally observing their kids. Burksdale wasn't sure which irritated him more—the kids or their parents. He noted an elderly couple exiting the building and Burksdale shot up to hold the door open for them.

"Such a nice young man," the woman noted to her husband, who nodded in agreement.

With his best smile, Burksdale helped guide the couple towards the short flight of stairs in front of the building, while keeping his free hand on the door handle. Once inside, he took the staircase up to the third floor and located unit 3C, Rebecca Sunnis's apartment. Burksdale knocked and waited. Then knocked again. With no answer, he pulled out a lock-pick set from his jacket and within seconds, Burksdale was able to disable the flimsy door lock. He entered the unit quickly and closed the door behind himself. Burksdale stood motionless for several moments as he listened carefully for any noise or movement within the apartment. The only noise he heard was from the squealing children on the playground. He could hear the refrigerator's condenser fan kick in. Burksdale slowly walked through the modestly appointed one-bedroom unit. He knew cheap when he saw it; the quality of the appliances in the kitchen and the shoddy furniture, all reflected someone on a limited budget. Burksdale smiled and reminded himself that crime *does* pay. He quickly walked through the entire unit and opened every closet door. He spent the most time in Rebecca's kitchen, going through her cabinets, the pantry, and refrigerator. He noted what foods she seemed to have a preference for, and what type of alcohol she kept in stock. He noted only red wine in a small rack near the living area. The rack contained twelve bottles total, and they were all variations of Cabernet Sauvignon. A bit odd, Burksdale surmised, or perhaps she really liked that type of wine. He continued his evaluation of the small living room. There was the standard layout of a couch and two chairs surrounding a small, glass coffee table. A cheap wall-unit was filled with a variety of books and collectibles. A 40-inch flat screen television and a small stereo receiver was on one of the shelves. There was nothing unusual or even interesting in the small room.

Burksdale entered her bedroom. The room was also small—perhaps eighteen feet by fifteen— with an adjoining bathroom. Next to the bed was a small desk with a laptop computer. He assumed this was her personal computer and suspected she most likely carried a work laptop to *Harris Therapeutics* every day. The bed was made, and no clothes or other items appeared out of place—everything was neat and tidy. The bathroom was also orderly and clean. All of Rebecca's grooming instruments and makeup appeared to be in an allocated spot without clutter or disorganization. Burksdale reminded himself that this was the home of a scientist. Everything appeared purposeful, and there was no redundancy or excess. As he was about to exit the bedroom, Burksdale noted a series of framed photographs on the window sill. He bent down to examine each one carefully. Odd, he thought; none of the framed images in front of him revealed a consistent mate. And although she was seen smiling in all of the photos, Burksdale thought he caught a glimpse of sadness in her face. As he approached the door to the bedroom, he turned around and looked one more time. There were no posters, paintings, or hung photographs on the walls. The light blue walls were completely barren. How odd, Burksdale reflected. There was something amiss in this scientist's life.

Before leaving the apartment, Burksdale went back into the kitchen and opened the trash container. With his hands still gloved, he tossed around the contents. Nothing appeared unusual; just empty jars of food containers and a lot of carry-out boxes. Something again struck Burksdale as out of place…this woman was a foodie. She loved eating out and cooking exotic meals, but he didn't find evidence of that in her trash or cupboards. With her background training in the culinary arts, it was surprising to Burksdale not to find evidence of that in her home. Had she given up on that aspect of her life? Burksdale also found a few empty wine bottles near the bottom of the trash container—all were Cabernet Sauvignons. Burksdale made a final look-around the rather boring, sullen, apartment and then listened to the door before opening it. He quickly exited, making sure to re-lock the cheap, flimsy door before going back outside into the bright, mid-morning sun.

Retracing the two-block walk to his parked car, Burksdale reflected on his findings. Rebecca Sunnis obviously lived alone in a rather simple, boring environment. From what Burksdale assessed, this target would be a chip shot. That was too bad, he thought. After reviewing her online profiles, he was hoping to have a more exciting target to stalk and then eliminate. *I guess that's why it's called work,* Burksdale chuckled to himself. As he started the engine, Burksdale decided there would be limited usefulness to continue to track Sunnis's daily routine. When he was ready to go after her, Burksdale felt he had all the information he needed.

CHAPTER 16

Chicago, IL

Burksdale got home earlier than he anticipated, as the drive back during the noon-hour was painless. Rather than look into the details of other lab associates that may also be of use, Burksdale elected to focus on what would be the most appropriate intervention for Rebecca Sunnis. He knew she would be an easy target to take down, and would be an example to Cortes what would happen to him if the information was not given. In a sense, this made his job easier, as Burksdale knew he didn't have to camouflage this death. The death could be viewed as accidental, initially, but that wouldn't help put the squeeze on Cortes. Cortes would have to know *why* Sunnis died. That would become apparent to Cortes only after other events occurred. Burksdale had to start somewhere, so it might as well be with this easy target.

The question Burksdale now wanted to answer was, *What was the most appropriate technique to use on her?* From what he gleaned on his visit, Burksdale was sure the woman was most consistent in her taste for red wine. So, what paired well with that? he mused. Burksdale poured himself a healthy-sized scotch and went to his desk to review some information.

Arsenic is one of the most interesting elements of the periodic table. Its use as an intentional poison has been known for centuries and has been referred to as the King of Poisons because it had been used to poison royalty, and therefore alter who should ascend to the throne. It is also known as a silent killer, because, dissolved in water, it is colorless, odorless, and tasteless. Consumed in its most toxic form, it can cause a rapid and violent death. Arsenic is a naturally occurring element that is toxic to humans in only certain forms, and it is readily absorbed if ingested or inhaled. It is typically found combined with other elements, and it is so endemic to our environment that the EPA allows drinking water to contain no more than 10 parts per billion of arsenic. But people can get exposed to higher amounts of inorganic arsenic through contaminated water, food, or from various industrial processes. In wine samples, the average arsenic quantity is 24 parts per billion, a tolerable amount that would not cause disease or injury. However, if exposed to a high enough amount over an extended period of time, arsenic can lead to a variety of toxicity related symptoms.

Given arsenic's natural occurrence in wine—particularly red wine—Burksdale thought this would be the perfect method he needed; not that the wine would camouflage the arsenic as much as he wanted something *poetic.* This desire to torture and kill his victims with methods that were intimately related to their personalities was another reflection of the sociopathic tendencies of Burksdale. He enjoyed toying with and taking advantage of other's weaknesses and habits. Although he had used arsenic in the past, he wanted to refresh his memory about some of the nuances of this chemical.

Arsenic's similarity to phosphorous means that it can substitute very easily for the substance in many fundamental chemical reactions in biological systems. For example, phosphorus helps cells generate adenosine triphosphate (ATP), which is the main source of energy in all known organisms. By chemically disrupting energy production, multiple organ failure can occur resulting in death. In high enough doses, arsenic can, in effect, interfere with cellular respiration. Onset of the poisoning may begin within 24-72 hours, but if consumed in large amounts, it can kill a person rapidly.

The character of post-mortem appearances depends very largely upon the quantity taken and the period which has elapsed before death. As a result of inorganic arsenic's direct toxicity to the lining of the gastrointestinal tract, profound gastroenteritis and hemorrhage can occur from within minutes to hours after ingestion. In acute arsenic poisoning, death is usually due to cardiovascular collapse and hypovolemic shock.

Again, Burksdale came back to the same question: Did he want Sunnis's death to be identifiable or not? Would an undiagnosed death be less intimidating to Cortes? He knew by exposing Sunnis to arsenic over time, she would become quite ill, but a large dose at once would lead to an ugly death—potentially more obvious to Cortes and *Harris Therapeutics.* A gruesome death could send the very message he wanted. Burksdale took notes as he continued his review.

The fatal human dose is about 1-3 mg/kg. Even with modern autopsy and analysis techniques, many cases of poisoning may remain undiscovered. Similarly, arsenic is not likely to be detected in blood specimens drawn more than two days after exposure because it becomes integrated into non-vascular tissue. As with so many other disease states, to detect poisoning requires consideration of it as a cause of death.

As much pleasure as Burksdale derived by considering techniques to camouflage Sunnis's death, he understood what was needed was to have Sunnis's death set an example. On the other hand, Burksdale also knew that if the cause of her death was too obvious, it could set off warnings from the police and *Harris.* If that were to occur, the future targets could become more protective or behave less predictably. That would not help his cause. No, Burksdale had to come up with the right balance in Sunnis's death to eventually cause suspicion in Cortes, but not instigate difficulty in proceeding with their plan.

From past medical experiences, Burksdale could make a well-approximated estimate of her weight. He had plenty of online images and available information to make this assessment. Burksdale went into his hidden storage area under the floor boards in his bedroom. The arsenic he had available was more than sufficient. All Burksdale needed now were two simple things: a bicycle pump and a nice bottle of Cabernet Sauvignon.

CHAPTER 17

Chicago, IL

Today, the foil surrounding the top of a wine bottle is purely for aesthetics. The foil was originally invented as a means to keep insects and rodents from damaging the cork while a wine was stored. As more wineries are now corking their bottles without foil, which is also more environmentally friendly and cost effective, Burksdale had no difficulty researching various wineries of Cabernet Sauvignon to deliver his arsenic. He made a list of wines bottled in this manner. Knowing Rebecca to be a wine connoisseur, Burksdale had some difficulty in choosing which of the chosen labels she would be most inclined to drink. Burksdale did not want to fall into the trap that undermines many unsophisticated wine drinkers; the more expensive wines are always better. Price did not necessarily correlate with quality. What variables would be the best bait was a problem, as Burksdale knew knowledgeable wine drinkers could be finicky. And if price wasn't a good determinate, what was?

Burksdale decided the best answer to this dilemma would be to discuss this issue with someone in the wine business. Should he go to a small family-owned wine shop for this inquiry and purchase, or would he have better success—and anonymity—at a large, retail chain-store? After considering the issue, Burksdale felt a smaller shop would have a less sophisticated security system. He also didn't want to buy the wine in any suburban shop, as those establishments tend to have locals as customers and an outsider would stand out. Burksdale *Google-searched* family-owned wine shops in Chicago. The list was significant. He chose one that was accessible downtown—but slightly offbeat, and probably used to non-repeat customers. Burksdale made his way to *The Barducci Bros. Wine Shop,* est. 1922. Having been around for over 100 years, Burksdale suspected they must be knowledgeable enough to have survived the onslaught of the big-outlet as well as the budget liquor stores.

After parking his usual two-blocks away, Burksdale approached the small establishment in the Old-Town neighborhood in Chicago. He smiled as the small bell atop the door jingled when he opened the heavy wooden door and entered. The sound of old, creaky floors and the scent of wood—probably from wine crates being cracked open, leaving wood-packing shavings everywhere—was also familiar. The long display shelves were stocked with bottles of every shape and color, all carefully nestled in natural wood shavings. There were no signs demarcating red from white, or which region or country the various products were from. No, that knowledge came from the staff—staff that was older, experienced, and interested in understanding the palate of each customer. They were not in a hurry to move anyone along. The store resembled more of an old bookstore than a retail liquor store. Here was a wine store that sold wine not by quantity, but by what a buyer needed. Within several minutes of opening the door, an elderly man wearing jeans, a wrinkled, white linen, button-down shirt, and a stained-denim apron approached Burksdale. An older woman also appeared from a back room and went up to sit near the register.

"May I help you? My name is Stephen." The man extended his hand and smiled.

Burksdale responded. "Great…I'm *Tom*…nice to meet you." As Burksdale shook the nice fella's hand, he explained he was interested in a unique Cabernet Sauvignon for a close friend's birthday. He took out his list, but soon realized it wouldn't be useful; the small store would have what it had. Burksdale decided to just ad-lib it and see what he could find. Stephen walked slowly towards the back of the store and led Burksdale over to the selection of Cabs. He pointed out several that he liked, but then he stopped talking and inquired more about *Tom's* friend's taste.

Feigning a rather fumbled description of what his friend liked, Burksdale stated, "I believe she likes Cabs that are bold, with a hint of cherry…well, perhaps she likes something that is more *earthy,"*

Burksdale continued. He rambled a long description of nearly every possible palate combination. Stephen stared at him intently, wondering what in the hell his friend liked to drink. Rather than ask anymore, Stephen pointed out several bottles he thought the man might consider, who apparently had no clue what he was looking for. As Stephen was speaking about his selections, Burksdale spotted a foil-less bottle on an adjacent shelf. He picked it up quickly and read the name aloud. "*Jurdesson Napa Valley Red, 2018*—any good?"

Stephen stopped his descriptions in mid-sentence and stated, "You picked out an extraordinary bottle there, Tom. That bottle would satisfy most any wine drinker. It has a lovely…"

Burksdale stopped Stephen in mid-sentence. He didn't give a shit what it tasted like. "How much?" He was losing his patience in the charming store. Burksdale now wanted his wine, and he wanted to leave.

"Why, that bottle is also quite expensive…it would run…" Stephen stopped, slowly put on his reading glasses, and pulled out a yellowed sheet of paper with hand-written notes. "That bottle would cost… three-hundred-thirty-five dollars…perhaps you would prefer…"

Again, Burksdale stopped Stephen in mid-sentence. "That will be fine. I will take it." Burksdale could feel a sense of anxiety creeping in. Sweat was forming on his temples…he wanted—he needed to get out of the store as quickly as possible. He had lost patience with the old man, getting the wine, and hearing about all its glory.

"As you wish, *Tom*." Stephen shuffled over to the register and took the bottle from *Tom's* hand. The woman shopkeeper stayed seated on her stool, but watched with interest as this peculiar man appeared to suddenly be in a hurry. She noted a bead of sweat emanating from *Tom's* brow. Stephen punched a few keys on the register, passed the bottle over the in-counter barcode scanner, and placed the bottle into a brown, paper wine bag. "With tax, that will be three-hundred-seventy-eight and thirty-two cents. How would you…"

Burksdale quickly took out four crisp $100 dollar bills and laid them on the counter. Stephen stopped speaking and looked at *Tom* quizzically. He took the bills, looked at them carefully, and placed them under the money tray in the register. He then handed the change back to *Tom*. Feeling a bit uneasy with this odd individual, Stephen too, wanted the transaction concluded. He gave *Tom* the bagged bottle and wished him well. "I hope your friend enjoys her present." He stated with the best smile he could manage.

"Thank you…you've been most helpful." Burksdale stated, as he bolted out the door.

Stephen stared at the closed door. *What an odd guy*, Stephen thought as he shrugged his shoulders and went back into the recesses of the store. Well, he's seen all types, he recalled as he slowly shuffled back.

Burksdale took a deep breath as he exited the store. He could feel the buildup of sweat on his back. He took a moment to close his eyes and focus on calming himself. Burksdale knew he was prone to these panic attacks but still couldn't get a grip on what brought them out. After letting the moment settle down, he walked back to his car, clutching the bottle. He recapped the series of events. After considering what transpired in the store, Burksdale came to the conclusion that ole' Stephen—in this dilapidated old wine store—wouldn't pose any issues.

He pulled out of his parking space and went back home. Burksdale looked forward to what he had to do next.

Upon arriving at his home, Burksdale went into his bedroom and located the bottle of arsenic under the floor boards. The hidden compartment in the floor had a long history of illegal use. Burksdale's old home was built in 1889. Apparently, during Prohibition in the 1920's, the owners of the home created the compartment to hide their illegal liquor. It was cleverly made and without prior knowledge of its existence, it would be nearly impossible to detect. Burksdale was pleasantly surprised when he was casually told about it by the real estate agent who sold him the property. It was probably that compartment more than anything else about the home that prompted the sale. The large cryptic area could hold a significant amount of drugs and chemicals that Burksdale prided himself on having and knowing how to use.

Burksdale removed the old wooden boards and retrieved the arsenic bottle. He went to his workshop area, donned a mask and latex gloves, and carefully measured out the lethal quantity of arsenic needed. Burksdale went into his closet, took out his bicycle pump and attached an inflation needle one would typically use to inflate a football. He then inserted the needle just inside the bottle's glass mouth adjacent to the wine bottle's cork top. By slowly pumping air into the bottle, he effectively increased the pressure within the wine bottle. With continued insufflation, the cork started to rise up, and it could then be pulled out by gently rocking it out of the top of the bottle. Keeping a clean rag adjacent to the bottle top to catch any spillage, Burksdale poured out a tablespoon of the wine. He dissolved the measured amount of needed arsenic powder with water, and added the solution to the wine bottle. Burksdale placed the wine bottle firmly on a table and tilted the cork slightly. In one motion, he twisted and pressed down on the cork. Using the heel of his hand, Burksdale continued to press the cork back into its original position into the brown-tinted bottle. No spillage occurred. Burksdale looked approvingly at his completed effort: the bottle, cork, and label all looked perfect.

Burksdale's next consideration was determining when and how to get the wine to Sunnis. He would need to coordinate this with the still-to-be-determined plans for other workers of Cortes's lab. Getting Sunnis—and only her—to then drink the wine will be another challenge. As he put down a large swig of scotch, the events of the day started to slip out of focus. Tomorrow, he would get to work on another employee in Cortes's lab at *Harris Therapeutics*.

CHAPTER 18

Chicago, IL

Bob Margolis was the type of guy everyone wanted just to be with. He triple-lettered in high school sports and later went on to play golf at Northwestern—while pursuing an undergraduate degree in biophysics. He was bright, affable, and driven, but most importantly, he was a nice person. With his good looks, self-confidence, and obvious intelligence, Bob could walk into any room and just light it up. The women adored him and the men wanted to be him. After completing his undergraduate education at Northwestern, he matriculated to the University of Chicago and pursued his Doctorate in Molecular Biology. He then completed a Postdoctoral Fellowship in Viral Immunology. With his background in virus-based immunological diseases, he was a perfect fit for Cortes's lab at *Harris Therapeutics*.

Jonathan Burksdale went through the online information about Doctor Margolis. Unlike Rebecca Sunnis, who lived in relative solitude, Bob Margolis was the exact opposite. The man lived a life of adventure. On social media websites Margolis posted images of his many travels across the country, playing golf at numerous resorts, and photographs taken at frequent dinner events with a variety of friends. Always with a broad smile, Margolis appeared to be the life of the party. As expected with someone of Margolis's personality, nothing was hidden. The man appeared to live large, and he wasn't shy about putting it on display. Without much difficulty, Burksdale found Margolis's address through the on-line white pages. The man lived in Chicago in an upscale apartment in the *hot* Fulton-Market neighborhood. Given this location, Margolis would have to commute nearly forty-five minutes each way to *Harris Therapeutics.* How a researcher who probably earned the same as Rebecca Sunnis lived so much more extravagantly, implied he had other sources of income. Burksdale set out next to investigate this aspect of Doctor Margolis.

It only took a matter of some simple online cross-referencing for Burksdale to learn that Bob Margolis was the grandson of Richard Margolis—a real estate mogul who made his fortune investing in the development of none other than the expensive Fulton-Market neighborhood. Richard Margolis also developed the West Loop neighborhood. These newly renovated areas were highly sought after, and were doing exceptionally well as desirable places to live in the Chicago area. Having his grandfather develop, build, and own the building he lived in, Burksdale could now understand how Margolis was able to enjoy living where he did. Burksdale also understood that Margolis's family lineage could make his own job more challenging. Any questionable or suspicious misgivings that happened to the scientist could lead to more scrutiny than usual. The investigative strength of the law was supposed to be equal; it was simply more equal for some. Burksdale was mindful of what he was up against, and he welcomed the challenge.

Continuing his review of *Harris Therapeutics'* website, Burksdale came across a posting regarding an upcoming company golf outing. The event was an effort to introduce the company and its research in antibody and cancer therapeutics to potential investors. As much endowment as the company already had, it was apparently seeking more. The event was also advertised to regional hospitals and medical centers. Given the entry fee of $700 dollars per player, it would obviously entice only the most serious of golfers. The event was to be held in about a month at *The Richie Country Club*, in Aurora, Illinois. This club was relatively new and was an attractive venue to hold this type of outing. Burksdale felt that given Margolis's love for the game, as well as his previous collegiate playing history, it would be most unusual for him *not* to be involved. Continuing his review of the website posting, Burksdale's assumption was verified as he noted at the bottom of the site that Bob Margolis was, indeed, the chairman for the event. *Outstanding*, Burksdale thought. Given Margolis's lifestyle, there would be little opportunity to get to him alone. Living in a bustling Chicago neighborhood in a modern, busy, apartment building, there would undoubtedly be passersby and CCD cameras Burksdale wouldn't be aware of. However, an open golf course meant the man will be separated from others for extended periods of time. It was a golden opportunity for Burksdale to take advantage of.

CHAPTER 19

Chicago, IL

Jay Yamp could hardly contain himself. As the Head of The Department of Urology at University Hospital, his days were consumed with administrative meetings, surgery, patient office-appointments, and his own research commitments. Over the years of this intense grind, he felt as though he had allowed his own needs, both physical and emotional, to take a back seat. On this particular summer Sunday, Yamp woke up as usual before the sun was up. Years of early-morning patient rounds and surgery had prevented him from ever sleeping in. After dressing quickly, Yamp located towards the back of his desk drawer one of his infrequently-used key rings. It was packed with numerous keys to a variety of locks and doors. He shook his head in mild disgust as he realized none of the metallic objects appeared familiar to him. Keys which he obviously needed and saved, were oddly no longer a part of his overly busy life anymore. He made a mental note to re-learn what each of them opened, and to try to return to using whatever they unlocked. For his own survival, Yamp knew he had to get back to the life he once controlled as opposed to his current nonstop schedule. He quickly grabbed the heavy ring of forgotten keys, almost forgetting to pick up his current key chain, as he sprinted out his doorway. Yamp impatiently waited for his slow condominium elevator to arrive. He tried to pass the time by recounting how many times he pushed the button to call the ancient elevator car. He tried to remember where in his storage room he had buried what he now needed. The elevator doors opened revealing four others crammed into the small space. He felt it odd on an early Sunday morning so many others were also ready to go about their business. Had he been so focused on his own world that he somehow learned to tune everyone else out? After what felt like an eternity waiting for the others to reach their floors, he finally reached his destination. Yamp made his way down the poorly lit hallway noting how awful the carpeting looked on this storage-room floor. Didn't the building's housekeeping personnel tend to things like this? Yamp made a mental note to bring this issue up at the next condo board meeting.

He tried several keys before finding the right one to open the slightly stuck door. Yamp realized it must have been at least a year since he last deposited some other wanted, but not imminently needed, object to join the others in store-room perpetuity. He remembered where the light switch was located and illuminated the room with a fluorescent light fixture that flickered several times before staying on. There, up against the wall in the far corner, he found what he sought: his old set of golf clubs. Between multiple tables, chairs, old lamps and boxes, Yamp performed what felt like an Olympic gymnastics routine to finally pull the black bag away from the corner. Excitedly, he lifted the heavy bag up and over the boxes to a perfect landing. Yamp was pleased with his early morning accomplishment—he found the keys and was able to get what he wanted without tearing apart the entire storage unit.

Turning off the light and re-locking the door, Yamp took his prized clubs back to his condo unit. He put the bag down in the middle of his living room and looked it over. The clubs looked so very familiar, yet when he picked up his beloved 7-iron, it felt odd in his hand. The grip had wear-marks where he repeatedly placed his hands so many thousands of times. But that was years ago—long before he had accumulated the many responsibilities he now spent so much of his time and effort developing. Yamp gently squeezed the grip on the 7-iron and took a slow swing. Hearing the *swish* of the club as it arced through the air brought a smile. Yamp swung a bit faster, and then again faster. With the increased swing speed, the sound of the club *swooshing* in the air became more audible—it was all good.

Yamp dragged the bag of clubs into his kitchen. He turned on the faucet and proceeded to clean the club heads and the grips one-by-one. It was almost meditative for him. Completing that task, Yamp went through each of the many pockets on the golf bag. He discarded old protein bars, gum, and score cards. Yamp threw away the six or so old golf balls he located, knowing they were long past their prime. He noted the blackened mark he made on all of his golf balls with a *Sharpie* to identify them in the fairway. Looking at the many tees, ball markers, and other paraphernalia he pulled out of the old pockets, Yamp recalled how much joy the game had brought him. He decided it was time not just to prepare for the upcoming *Harris Therapeutics* golf event, but to recommit to the game he loved so much. He had a week to get ready.

Yamp went to his desk and reviewed the golf event welcoming letter. It was a generous gift from the higher-ups at University Hospital to have him play and represent them in this event. And, although it was an opportunity to play golf on their dime, Yamp also understood his responsibilities. As the Chairman of the Department of Urology, and as an active researcher himself, he was intrigued by the publications that came out of *Harris Therapeutics'* labs. They were at the forefront of some of the most innovative research in oncology he had seen in years. Yamp was amazed with their unique approach and innovative concepts; this company still flew beneath the radar. Yamp felt *Harris Therapeutics* would soon be a major player in the oncologic pharmaceutical world. Perhaps this golf outing will be its launching pad.

Yamp examined the invitation. He reviewed the names of the other players who would be in his foursome. Although he quickly looked at the other players' names when the invite first arrived in the mail two weeks ago, he now had time to check them out. And as much as the golf outing was advertised as *entertainment*, in reality it was a means to do business. It was a chance for *Harris* employees to integrate with the regional users of their research—the people and institutions that would potentially *buy* their products. Unfortunately, *medicine* had become business—big business—and everyone involved understood that.

Yamp looked at the players he was assigned to spend four hours with in the outing. As was his routine for most everything, preparation was key to success. Whether it was bringing out his clubs to the practice range, or studying who he would be with on the golf course, Yamp was always one to plan. He read the short bios of the players. Two of the players were administrators from other medical centers. He suspected they would be as exciting as burnt toast. Nothing bored Yamp more than listening to the administrators at his own institution complain about the financial benchmarks and expectations for the hospital. Yamp was a surgeon; he didn't want to deal with the administrative issues. He understood the need, but simply didn't want to waste his time listening to their complaints.

Yamp reviewed the name of the fourth player in their upcoming group: Bob Margolis, Ph.D. Yamp was intrigued to read Margolis was the second-in-charge of a group of researchers studying a molecular antibody development project. Apparently, this project could have a significant role in future oncologic cancer applications and perhaps be needed in an upcoming research project Yamp was considering as well. Equally important to Yamp, he also learned that Margolis played golf in college. This was all the more reason he needed to get his game into shape. Perhaps the foursome—despite the presence of the hospital administrators—will be more interesting than he previously anticipated.

Yamp put the invitation back on his desk. No time like the present, he reminded himself, as he looked out the window and acknowledged it was a beautiful Sunday afternoon. Yamp grabbed his keys, his clubs, and his golf shoes. Time to head out to the golf practice range.

CHAPTER 20

Chicago, IL

Burksdale sat back in his favorite rocking chair nursing a scotch on the rocks, while contemplating his upcoming mission. The question he now faced: What chemical agent to use on Bob Margolis? First off, he wanted to use Margolis's death as a means to intimidate Doctor Cortes. With the tragic death of two of his trusted associates, Burksdale thought Cortes would become a willing volunteer to hand over the molecular synthesis protocol. Burksdale suspected Cortes would never give up his research findings and methodology unless threatened with such extreme events. Cortes needed to know he was in danger. He would be fearful for his own life and release whatever is requested. Burksdale again decided there was no need to camouflage the death of Margolis; the more obvious, the better.

Planting the agent of choice into, onto, or in proximity to Margolis was going to be a challenge. As each chemical poison had its own unique means of delivery, uptake, and symptomatology, finding the right agent for the task was mandatory. Burksdale needed a poison he could get to Margolis while he was alone on the golf course. The chemical's delivery would be less likely observed if given in this manner, and tracing it back to himself would consequently be more difficult.

Burksdale stopped rocking for a few moments. He didn't move a muscle as he focused. "Novichok", he said out loud. "Yes, Novichok," he reiterated. Burksdale took a long sip of his scotch and started rocking again, this time more vigorously.

In human neurological function, neurotransmitters are chemical substances that are released at the end of a nerve fiber by the arrival of a nerve impulse. Essentially, neurotransmitters are molecular messengers whose function is to carry chemical signals from one nerve cell to the next target cell—which could be another nerve, a muscle cell, or a gland. By diffusing across the synapse or junction, the neurotransmitter causes the transfer of the impulse. One of the main neurotransmitters in our bodies is called acetylcholine. Once the acetylcholine has performed its function, it is degraded by a specific enzyme known as acetylcholinesterase. Novichok is a group of nerve agents developed by the Soviet Union and Russia, and they function by inhibiting the normal breakdown of the acetylcholine. The increased concentration of the acetylcholine will cause involuntary contraction of all skeletal muscles.

The effect from Novichok can take seconds, to minutes, to hours, depending upon the route of administration and dosage. It can enter the body by inhalation, injection, or by contact with the skin. The initial symptoms may include blurred vision, sweating, nausea, and difficulty breathing. Eventually, it will lead to continuous convulsions, and eventually, loss of consciousness. Respiratory and cardiac arrest can occur as the victim's heart and diaphragm muscles no longer function properly. Death from heart failure or suffocation can also occur as fluid secretions fill the lungs. Should a victim survive, the Novichok may also cause lasting nerve damage, resulting in permanent disablement.

"Yes," Burksdale repeated quietly to himself, "this will work." He decided a transdermal approach would be appropriate. The question he now contemplated was where and how. Burksdale was not a golfer, but had hit golf balls in the past. He understood the rules of the game, but he didn't understand why anyone would want to play it; the game took all day, had limited physical activity, and from what he could tell, it rarely led to an afternoon of enjoyment. From Burksdale's warped perspective, the people who played golf were nuts, which was all the more reason for him to take this opportunity to intervene.

Burksdale thought about how a golfer would navigate around the clubhouse and course. He closed his eyes and imagined himself being a player in the upcoming event: *He would be received at the bag drop, leave his clubs with the attendant and then go to park his car, or, if available, have it parked with a valet service. Burksdale would then be directed to the locker room, see another attendant who would get him settled into a locker, and show him the available amenities. As a player, he would then change into his golf attire, probably visit the restroom, and stop at the sinks to wash his hands and apply sunscreen. He would then go to the event check-in area. Typically, this is composed of a group of welcoming and enthusiastic individuals associated with the outing's organization or sponsor. The volunteers at the check-in are usually seated at a long reception table and they check-off the incoming participating players with their event list. At this time, they will inform the player from what hole he or she will commence the game. Tee-gifts are given out at this step of the check-in process. Depending upon the size and cost of the event, the participants receive any number of tee-gifts. Sometimes, the gifts are lavish—golf clubs or other expensive equipment. More often, a gift bag is simply handed out. Each bag has the player's name on it, and the gifts generally include some type of athletic apparel, perhaps a personalized item, and always a collection of golf paraphernalia such as tees, event-sponsored imprinted balls, or ball markers. Generally, the golfer would then be directed to a large ballroom to enjoy a buffet and open bar. The golfer would probably sit and meet with other participants for about an hour, and then go back to the locker room to drop off the newly acquired gifts. He would likely put some of the balls and tees in his pockets. The golfer would find his way to the practice driving range, which sometimes required the use of a golf cart. He would spend 30-60 minutes or so working on his golf swing. If the player was highly motivated, he would practice his short-game, and then proceed to work at the all-important, warm-up on the putting green. Burksdale anticipated there would then be an announcement for all of the participants to proceed to a staging area, where they would meet the other players in their group and get settled in. Most golf outings are played in a manner that is referred to as a* shotgun start. *Meaning, all of the foursomes are assigned to begin on a different hole on the golf course. Shotgun starts begin with all of the foursomes following an orderly procession onto the course to their assigned starting holes. All the groups would tee off at the sound of the shotgun (typically a horn of some type) and begin their round. With this type of event format, all of the foursomes will finish playing at the same time.*

Often, each foursome would also have an assigned forecaddie. This is typically a young man or woman who will run ahead on the fairway of each hole and do his or her best to locate each player's ball after it was struck. If the golf group is composed of talented players, the forecaddie's job is significantly easier. If the group is made up of duffers, *those who play infrequently or are simply not very good golfers, the forecaddie's job is considerably more work as balls will end up flying in all directions. On rare occasion, however, a duffer's shot might actually go in the direction of the hole they are aiming for. The caddie's job is to locate balls, clean the balls, repair divots, tend to the flag, rake sand traps, and, if possible, make the player's day as enjoyable as possible. At the conclusion of eighteen holes of golf, the players will drive their carts back to the clubhouse. Their clubs will be cleaned by attendants and put onto a rack for the players to pick up at the end of post-round showers, drinks, and dinner.*

So, where to intervene in this process was the question Burksdale had to answer. He understood the Novichok liquid must be handled cautiously and is an oily fluid. Considering this, Burksdale thought the poison might be best camouflaged as something resembling liquid soap. The thought of putting it into a ball washer on the course came to mind. But then it would be difficult to get the solution only on Margolis's hands without affecting others. Another thought occurred to Burksdale; one that preyed on Margolis's gregarious personality and vanity. Would Margolis not be inclined to use a new cologne if it were given to him? Some colognes were oil based and could be the perfect medium to carry the Novichok. Knowing what Burksdale read on the online posts about Margolis made him confident Margolis would try it sooner than later. It would be a simple matter of putting a cologne bottle into Margolis's gift bag when he checked in for the golf outing.

As Burksdale was thinking through the scenario, it occurred to him that nearly everybody rummages through their tee-gift bag upon receipt of it. Often one participant and then another will open up the bag to see what is inside. Burksdale realized it would appear odd if only Margolis received the bottle of cologne. Others would probably complain—bringing attention to the solitary cologne bottle. Burksdale smiled and shook his head as he considered all the participants at these outings make plenty of money and pay handsomely to play in these events. But if you deprive them of a freebie, they will go nuts. Burksdale knew he would need to find out ahead of time how many participants were playing, and get the cologne bottles into the gift bags. Burksdale suspected the gift bags would be prepared a day or so before the event. Regrettably, he also realized he would need to spend a fair amount of money on probably over a hundred cologne bottles just to spike one. After continued assessment, Burksdale thought it was a workable plan. He wrote down what he needed and went to bed. Without difficulty, Burksdale fell asleep in minutes.

CHAPTER 21

Aurora, IL

Burksdale was able to contact the Public Relations Department at *Harris* ahead of the golf event and was informed 120 golfers would be participating—a large number of participants, but certainly doable at a venue like *The Richie Country Club*. He found an online boutique site that would sell him 125 3oz. bottles of a new cologne from *Redont*—a new company trying to break into the market of men's grooming products. At the negotiated price of nearly $90 per bottle, it was an expensive gamble. Burksdale thought this plan was subtle, yet enticing, for the more stylish participant to indulge himself. Burksdale knew Margolis was part of that crowd.

As the lunch was set for noon and the shotgun start to begin promptly at 1:30 p.m., Burksdale anticipated golfers would begin to show up around 10:00 a.m. Dressed in khaki cargo shorts, a *Richie Country Club* cap, and a polo shirt—complete with a pin with the name *Tom* engraved on it—Burksdale pushed the trolley carrying the heavy box of cologne bottles to the reception area around 8:00 a.m. He was greeted by the event coordinator from *Harris Therapeutics*.

"Good morning," Burksdale stated with his warmest smile. "I have some gift-boxes to add to your player goodie-bags."

The event coordinator looked puzzled. "We already made up the bags last night...hmm...I don't recall having additional products to add..." She trailed off as she looked quizzically at her to-do list on the clipboard.

"Oh, not to worry," Burksdale chimed in. "I heard this was a last-minute donation...anyway, I can help you put these boxes in the bags...its really no big deal." Burksdale, then added, "I've been doing this for so many years...there's always another thing that's supposed to go into those bags...and the players love this stuff. Besides, I think this is some top-end cologne or something."

The coordinator paused for a moment. She had so many more important issues to tend to that morning that adding more crap to a gift bag was hardly worth her time. "Fine...sure...go ahead...the bags are stored in the white minivan over there." She pointed in the direction of a van parked near the bag-drop area.

"No problem...happy to help out." Burksdale announced as he started rolling the trolley in the direction of the van. "We're pleased to have you here," he added while walking away. The event coordinator was then distracted by a call that came in on her walkie-talkie, and she soon forgot about *Tom*.

Once at the minivan, Burksdale opened the side-door and found the 120 pre-filled gift bags. They were each labeled with an adhesive sticker bearing the name of the participant. Quickly, Burksdale threw the small black boxes of cologne into each bag while checking the names as he proceeded. Fortunately, the bags were in alphabetical order, and with little effort he identified the one he was looking for: Bob Margolis, Ph.D. Burksdale took the Novichok-laced cologne out of his cargo shorts pocket and placed it into the bag destined for Dr. Margolis. He continued placing his cologne boxes into the remaining bags and closed the van door. Burksdale then returned the trolley to the bag drop area. The young boys who were hired to assist for the day didn't so much as give him a second look. Burksdale then proceeded to the large parking lot. He removed his hat and name tag, started his car, and left. It was now 9:00 a.m. in the morning. As Burksdale drove out the front gate, he looked up at the sky through his windshield. It was a beautiful summer day for a golf outing.

The gift bags were alphabetically placed behind the check-in desk and the receptionists were ready with their participant lists. As anticipated, shortly after 10:00 a.m., golfers started to arrive. There was always a great deal of joviality at these events. Everyone had taken the day off—the invited doctors had their calls held or forwarded, the financiers and administrators who were playing had an excuse not to wear a suit and tie, and the event planners had a day in the sun. Everyone was anticipating a day of fun, food, and drinks. Around 10:45 a.m., Bob Margolis arrived wearing color-coordinated golf attire and looking as though he just stepped out of a GQ ad. With a warm smile, he approached the check-in desk.

"Well, good morning, Doctor Margolis," the excited young receptionist clucked, as she brushed her hair away from her face as she spoke. She had a small crush on the handsome researcher, and always tried to look her best when she saw him.

"Good morning, Marjorie…good to see you. This sure beats sitting in the office, doesn't it?" Margolis said with his perfect teeth and smile.

"Yes…it does! I hope you have a great time today," she stated while crossing his name off a list. Margolis started to walk away and her eyes followed him. "Oh…I'm sorry…I almost forgot…here is gift bag for you, Doctor," she stated rather clumsily. Marjorie nearly knocked over the table as she extended her reach towards him.

Margolis smiled, and graciously accepted her apology. He knew she was smitten, but he kept his social distance from anyone at work. Margolis took the bag and quickly proceeded to the luncheon. Given he came dressed in golf attire, he decided to skip the locker room. Upon walking into the extravagant ballroom, he was immediately greeted by other participants and co-workers from *Harris Therapeutics* who knew he was the company chairman for this event. Many came up to congratulate and thank him for the effort he put into making this event happen. Margolis was his usual gracious self, and accepted their good wishes and committed to work on the event next year. Although he knew the guest-list reasonably well, there were many in the event he had neither met or knew. Margolis was pleased with the turnout, and could palpate the excitement in the room. After searching for a place to sit in the noisy, bustling room, he finally located a vacancy at a nearby table. Margolis put his gift bag down on the empty seat and then got into the queue line for the lavish buffet. It was obvious Harris spared no expense for the spread. The line moved quickly as the hungry golfers loaded their plates with freshly carved roast beef, turkey, and ham. There was an impressive salad bar, and more types of pastas than he had ever seen. The desert table was mobbed. The longest lines he noted were, of course, for the two open bars. Looking at the line for drinks you'd think these players walked two miles in the desert to get here.

Margolis picked out his lunch, got a beer, and made his way back to the vicinity of the table where he left his gift bag. Somehow, he lost track of where he put it down. Well, no matter, Margolis thought. He knew if he lost his bag he would just get another. Eventually, he found another seat at a table with a vacancy.

"Hi there, I'm Bob Margolis," he stated while extending an open hand.

"It's a pleasure to meet you. I'm Jay Yamp." Yamp stated as he stood from his seat to shake Margolis's hand. "I believe we are playing together today. I'm very much looking forward to learning about your work and the work at *Harris Therapeutics*."

"Please, Doctor Yamp, please sit down." Margolis stated as he shook Yamp's hand. "Let's leave the work discussion for later. We need to stay focused for our game today!"

"Absolutely…the shop talk can wait. And please, call me Jay. I insist." Yamp stated with a smile.

"I will, Jay…thank you." Margolis replied. "We have plenty of time to talk business later." Margolis pulled his seat forward in preparation to eat and he felt his left foot kick something hard. He looked down and realized he had hit a gift bag with his toe. He suspected it was the sleeve of golf balls he knew was in the bag that his big toe found. Margolis bent down and pulled up the white plastic bag. "Hmm… John Tannenbaum, do you know who that is?"

Yamp shook his head and answered while swallowing a piece of the roast beef. "I don't...why do you ask?"

"Well, I misplaced my gift bag after I came in...this one belongs to someone by this name. I hope I find him. Inside each bag is a golf polo with the *Harris Therapeutics* logo embroidered on it. That's why we asked each participant to give us their shirt size when registering." Margolis stated while looking around the room. "Well, if not, hopefully he and I are the same size." Margolis stated with a smile.

The two men continued to enjoy each other's company while having a rotating conversation about golf, science, more golf, and then a slew of jokes. The jokes were concluded with equal laughter from both the teller and listener. It was obvious Yamp and Margolis respected and admired each other. The foundation for a solid friendship was evolving. Shortly after they finished eating, an announcement was made for those who wanted to hit a few balls or practice putting should do so, as the shot-gun start would begin in thirty minutes. With that, Yamp bolted upright and gathered his gift bag. "Golf awaits, sir!" Yamp stated with a big smile.

"Indeed, it does! I'll see you out there, Jay." Margolis also stated with a big grin. As Yamp left, Margolis looked around again for his gift bag, but it was not to be seen. He decided to take the bag of John Tannenbaum and hopefully exchange with him later in the day...if only Margolis knew who Tannenbaum was.

CHAPTER 22

Aurora, IL

Shotgun golf outings were always a great deal of fun for the participants. Because they were usually organized to benefit or promote a charitable cause, there was usually a sense of congeniality among the players. And, although the golfers may be *competing* for certain prizes such as the longest drive, who could putt the ball the longest, or hit the ball closest to the flag, the outings were always played with camaraderie and in good spirits. The ultimate beneficiary of the *Harris Therapeutics* event was cancer research, and everyone involved in the outing understood the value and need for medical and scientific research; these were the people engaged in it. It was also understood and accepted that *Harris* benefited from the opportunity to advertise itself. Still, it was good to have an afternoon of fun together despite the corporate affiliations that came with the business of medicine. All the players wanted to spend time with one another, while sharing both their love and frustrations for the same organizations they worked both with and for.

Jay Yamp's and Bob Margolis's perspectives of health care—its direction and needs—were on the same wavelength. They shared a golf cart and looked forward to an afternoon of forgetting the painful sides of their jobs and just enjoy the time out on the course. According to the tee-sheet, which assigned each foursome the hole on which they would start, as the chairman of the event, Margolis, et al., started on hole number one.

The first hole at *The Richie Country Club* is a beautiful, par-4 golf hole with large sand bunkers on either side of a broad, slightly downhill fairway. As the chairman of the event, the honor to tee off first in the group went to Bob Margolis. He smacked a beautiful, high-arching drive 260 yards down the center of the fairway. His swing resembled that of the collegiate player he once was; it was textbook. He and the others in the foursome watched the ball soar in the air, and they let out a collective sigh at the ball's flight. Yamp was next, and undeterred by his new friend's impressive start, got up to the tee and without hesitation, belted one almost as equally impressive. The ball wasn't as high, but it had a lovely draw and landed about 240 yards away. When he picked up his tee, Yamp looked over at Margolis and just winked. They were going to have fun, indeed. Neither Yamp nor Margolis had much to say to the other two players in the group. They were administrators who wanted to talk shop with each other and were less interested in how well they actually played golf. It really didn't matter, as each player was there for his own reasons, and although cordial to the two administrators, Yamp and Margolis pretty much stayed together during the round.

By the time the foursome reached the18th hole, it was obvious the administrators had accomplished their goal—to consume as much of the free alcohol as possible and still manage to drive the golf cart. Yamp and Margolis on the other hand, had an enjoyable round of golf mixed in with good natured competitiveness. As the last ball dropped into the 18th hole, handshakes were shared as everyone seemed to have had an enjoyable afternoon. The group headed for the clubhouse to shower and have their banquet dinner. While changing in the locker room, Margolis became aware of a new scent in the air. It appeared many of the players had opened their gift bags and found the bottles of cologne. He liked the smell of the light fragrance, and thought he would put it on as well. But he was distracted as he remembered he had to give a brief presentation after dinner and wanted to spend a few moments reviewing his note cards. Soon, the players assembled into the large ballroom to start their pre-dinner round of drinks.

Margolis spotted Yamp and walked over to him. "I've made an executive decision," Margolis stated.

"Yeah, Bob, what's that?" Yamp inquired.

"I think next year, we would save a lot of money by forgoing the golf and just have an open bar. I think most of the guys are here just for the drinking!" Margolis said with a grin.

"Yep…that's pretty much how these things go, isn't it?" Yamp replied while smiling.

Margolis shook his head and stated more somberly, "Unfortunately, I'm supposed to sit at the adult table in the front. I have to introduce some of the key players at *Harris Therapeutics* and then give a talk about what we are trying to accomplish there. I would much rather just eat and leave."

Yamp replied, "Well Bob, you've done a great job with the organization of this event. I like what I've heard about *Harris* and what you guys are trying to accomplish. I'm looking forward to learning more. I think some of the research going on at University Hospital may have a new partner with *Harris Therapeutics*. Let's play again together in a few weeks and see what we can do to forge a collaborative partnership. Really, Bob, it has been a pleasure to make your acquaintance. I'm so glad we had this opportunity to play today."

"The pleasure is mine, Doctor Yamp." Margolis stated as they shook hands.

The two men exchanged contact information. Yamp then retreated to the back of the room to join others he wanted to see. Margolis made his way to the front to sit with the *Harris Therapeutics* group.

After dinner was served, Margolis went up to the podium. The lights were dimmed, and he started the *Power Point* presentation about *Harris Therapeutics*—its origin, its mission, and where the company was headed in oncologic research. The talk was well-prepared and delivered. It was obvious *Harris Therapeutics* was going to be a significant player going forward in oncologic pharmacological therapeutics. It was just a matter of time before they developed a significant pipeline of interventions. There was no doubt in the minds of the audience that *Harris* was on the forefront of developing a major breakthrough in the near future. When Margolis finished, there was a standing ovation for the innovative research and anticipated treatments that would stem from the work being performed at *Harris*.

Following Margolis's presentation, a brief awards ceremony was held for those participants who, by luck or by skill, hit the ball closest to the flag, had the straightest drive, or made the best score on a few select holes. The event concluded with a large round of applause and handshakes all around. Best wishes were given to old and new friends as the event participants gradually made their exit. Margolis looked around, but couldn't find Yamp, who knew it best to leave promptly, lest he wait forever for the valet boys to get his car. Margolis went down to the locker room and retrieved his gym bag. His golf shoes had been cleaned by the locker room staff, and were neatly placed into a plastic shoe bag hanging by the locker-door handle. Almost forgetting his gift bag, Margolis grabbed it and went outside to the long line as golfers waited in the queue for the parking attendants to retrieve their cars. While patiently waiting, Margolis struck up a conversation with the man next to him. The man thanked Margolis for the wonderful event, and promised to follow-up with his administrators to facilitate a future meeting.

"That would be wonderful," Margolis stated. "I look forward to having the opportunity to explore a collaborative relationship. By the way, what is your name, may I ask?"

The pleasant man extended his hand and stated, "My name is John…John Tannenbaum."

Bob Margolis started to laugh.

"What did I say that was so funny?" Tannenbaum stated with a quizzical look.

Margolis lifted the gift bag in his hand. He then showed Tannenbaum the sticker on the bag with his name on it. Tannenbaum looked at it and then looked back at Margolis.

"I'm embarrassed to say I never even looked at the name on the bag after I sat down for lunch," Tannenbaum stated. Tannenbaum now bent down and lifted his bag, only to see the name *Bob Margolis, Ph.D.* on his. "I assumed I had my bag all day in my locker. Stupid me, I had yours. My apology." Tannenbaum stated with a slight blush as the two exchanged gift bags. "I was told there was a nice bottle of cologne in there…I was thinking I would give it to my nephew for his 16th birthday next week."

"Sounds like a great idea." Margolis said with a grin. "I think I'll put it on next time I go out on the town."

"Well, here's my car, Bob." Tannenbaum stated as he saw the valet approaching with his car. "Good thing we found each other…I wouldn't want your cologne!" Tannenbaum said jokingly.

Margolis wished him well, and looked for another valet who might have his own car. While waiting, he thought about the silly gift bag, and how fortuitous it was that the last person he met that evening was the proper owner of the bag he had been carrying. Margolis then paused for a moment and recalled that he didn't remember any cologne being on the gift-list discussions while planning the event. Well, it must have slipped his mind. Margolis got into his car and felt a bit of relief knowing the event was successful. As he buckled his seat belt and started to pull away, he recapped the day's events. *Yes, it was a successful outing.*

CHAPTER 23

Naperville, IL

Understanding Rebecca Sunnis's solidarity and introverted tendencies was important, just as knowing Bob Margolis's lifestyle and outgoing nature allowed for a stress-free delivery of the tainted cologne. Burksdale now needed to deliver the wine bottle to Rebecca Sunnis. Considering how she lived, all he really needed to do was to get the bottle to her front door. Burksdale went back into Sunnis's social media posts. Without much difficulty, he was able to find her announcement on *LinkedIn* when she was hired by *Harris Therapeutics.* She even disclosed the date when she was 'thrilled' to start working in Gene Cortes's lab. Either date was good enough for his needs—he could easily manufacture a reason for the wine *gift* to her.

Burksdale walked the eight blocks from his home to the *U-Haul* rental center. Although he didn't need anything out of his storage bay, he was always impressed with the number of shipping and storage products they had. Burksdale was also pleased that in the post-COVID world, he could wear a facemask and gloves and it wouldn't raise an eyebrow. He purchased with cash a box designed for sending a variety of items. It was tall and narrow—perfect for sending a bottle of arsenic-laced *Jurdesson Napa Valley Red, 2018.* Burksdale carefully wiped down the bottle before inserting it into the box—more out of habit than need. Burksdale then walked into a stationary store and found an appropriate gift card and wrapping paper. Using a clerk's pen, he carefully wrote out his note:

Rebecca, thank you for everything you have done to advance our lab.
Congratulations on your six-month anniversary with us. Enjoy!
Best, Gene Cortes

The friendly stationary store clerk was more than happy to wrap the box with the purchased paper. Burksdale got into his car. Luckily, it was still morning and expressway traffic would be light. Burksdale knew that sending the bottle in the mail would be risky. In the unlikely event the bottle broke in transit, his efforts would need to be repeated. Similarly, if the bottle was found tainted with arsenic, the situation would be investigated and possibly the addressee protected. Not concerned with who else might inadvertently get exposed to the spilled arsenic, Burksdale was more focused that future attempts to get to Sunnis would be more difficult. Burksdale drove the forty-five minutes back to her apartment complex. Robotic-like, he parked two blocks away, walked to the bench near Sunnis's building's entrance and waited for an opportunity to enter. It took nearly thirty minutes before anyone approached the building. As soon as a pair of painters walked up to the short cement staircase, Burksdale was right beside them. He wanted to assist the men as they had to carry a short ladder and supplies.

Once inside, Burksdale walked up the stairs to Sunnis's apartment and carefully placed the beautifully wrapped box against the door jam. He exited the building and walked back to his car. Burksdale was pleased with himself. All his effort was now completed. He would now follow the social media sites and online news outlets for updates. Burksdale now set his sights on how to best contact his final target, Gene Cortes. With the tragic death of his associates, Burksdale felt it was just a matter of going to Cortes's home and making a simple request: give up the molecular synthesis protocol, or die.

CHAPTER 24

Chicago, IL

"No, Paul, that's not how you hold the knife," Jay Yamp looked at the trembling hands of the young surgical intern about to perform a varicocelectomy—a surgical procedure most often performed to treat male infertility. "I want to see you hold the scalpel in the palm of your hands…here let me show you again." Yamp patiently repeated the proper way to handle the sharply bladed instrument. "Here you go…try it again," Yamp stated calmly as he handed the scalpel back to the surgeon-in-training. "Please…try to calm down and relax…there is nothing you can do here that I can't fix." Yamp stated with such confidence, that it apparently inspired the intern. He took the scalpel from Yamp, palmed it as instructed, and made a clean, one and one-half inch incision in the inguinal region of the anesthetized patient. "There you go…well done! Now, next time, let's try to get through all the layers of the skin in one stroke." Yamp said enthusiastically. The frightened intern nodded his head—he had no idea Doctor Yamp was being instructive and teasing him at the same time. Yamp just sighed quietly to himself as the humor of his remark was lost on the intern. *Well, this is what I do*, he thought to himself. *Another budding new doctor to teach.* Yamp refocused and continued to guide the *learning new hands* though the procedure. An hour later, Yamp pulled off his gown and gloves and let Paul apply the dressings. "Well done, Paul…please write the post-op orders while I go talk to the patient's wife. Thank you everyone." Yamp left the room as the scrub nurse, circulator, and anesthesiologist all said their goodbyes.

After returning from the family waiting room, Yamp went to the locker room and changed out of his scrubs and into street clothes. He noted on the shelf of his locker the small black box containing the bottle of cologne from the golf outing. He forgot he brought it over last week with some other toiletries. Yamp decided, *why not.* He opened the box, took out the bottle, and was about to give himself a spritz when his pager went off. He recognized the number immediately as the surgical recovery room. Instinctively, he put the cologne back into his locker and grabbed his phone. It was the nurses notifying Yamp of some details about his patient. When he disconnected the call, Yamp forgot about the cologne. He sat down on the metallic bench in front of the lockers and opened up the contact list on his phone. He looked up Bob Margolis's email and sent him a note:

From: jyamp@uh.edu
To: rmargolis@hti.com
June 30, 10:52 a.m.
Hey Bob, its Jay. How's your schedule looking? I'm hoping we can get together in the next couple of weeks to play—it's on me. Just let me know. Jay

Yamp went to the mirror to put on his tie. Within a minute of sending his email, he received a text message back.

From: Robert Margolis, Ph.D.
To: Jay Yamp, M.D.
Great! How about in three weeks...does Saturday, July 22, work out?

From: Jay Yamp, M.D.
To: Robert Margolis, Ph.D.
Perfect...I'll call a great course in Wheaton. I'll let you know as soon as I confirm.

From: Robert Margolis, Ph.D.
To: Jay Yamp, M.D.
Sounds good! Just let me know. Thanks.

CHAPTER 25

Naperville, IL

Rebecca Sunnis got into her car after an exhausting but productive day. Mindlessly buckling her seat belt, she recounted the day's events—starting with the initial panic when she could not locate the printouts of yesterday's lab run. After running around for twenty-minutes, she discovered them in an odd location above one of the lab's refrigerators. Relieved, Rebecca found out a new housekeeper started the night before and must have moved them. The day just seemed to present one challenge after another as staff meetings were unusually contentious and additional expectations were placed on Rebecca regarding an upcoming drug trial. But the pinnacle of her day occurred when her sister called hysterically while Rebecca was having a meeting with her boss, Gene Cortes. The timing could not have been worse. As Rebecca and Cortes were discussing upcoming time-line goals for the development for a new drug, her sister needed to unload about an issue with their mother. Rebecca had neither the time nor patience to listen to the details. Rebecca subsequently got into a fight with her sister about the ill-timed call. She decided she would call her sister back tonight after she had dinner, took a warm bath, and wound down from the day's events.

Without focusing on the drive home, she soon found herself in her complex's parking lot. Rebecca was so preoccupied with the day's turmoil, she didn't even recall driving. Entering her building through the back entrance, she proceeded to the mailboxes and picked up her mail and a few advertisement fliers left on the ground. Rebecca walked up the staircase thinking about what she might have in her refrigerator. She realized with all of the turmoil going on at the lab, she barely ate that day and was now starving. As she separated out her apartment key from the others, Rebecca noted a nicely wrapped box placed next to her door. Embarrassingly, she looked around the empty hallway wondering if this was really for her. As Rebecca knelt down and picked it up, she could feel the weight in the box and heard the slight gurgle of fluid movement within a container. She smiled, as she knew it was a bottle of liquid—probably alcoholic. *The timing couldn't be better*, Rebecca thought to herself. Maybe it was from her sister to make up for the argument. But there is no way her sister could have had this delivered…*what…during the day? And how did it get here without being left near the mailboxes…was it from a neighbor? It obviously wasn't delivered via a standard courier.* The presence of the nicely wrapped box was now more of a dilemma than a delight. Rebecca quickly got the key into the door, stepped inside and turned on the light switch. She tossed her mail, purse, and the fliers onto the small kitchen table. Rebecca then sat down at the table and curiously looked over the beautifully wrapped box. She found an envelope taped to the multi-colored bow and carefully peeled it away. Rebecca always kept bows and she didn't want to damage it in haste. She opened the envelope slowly as she did not to want to tear anything. Being a sentimentalist, Rebecca anticipated keeping whatever note was inside. She quickly read the enclosed note:

Rebecca, thank you for everything you have done to advance our lab.
Congratulations on your six-month anniversary with us. Enjoy!
Best, Gene Cortes

Rebecca read it again, and then, again. Tears started to swell as she looked at the congratulatory note for a third and fourth time. Wiping them away, Rebecca excitedly tore open the wrapping paper. She opened the box and pulled out the bottle. It was a beautiful bottle of a Cabernet she wasn't familiar with. Rebecca reached into her purse and pulled out her cellphone and opened the *Vivino* app. It was her *app* of choice when looking up wine reviews and prices. The review was outstanding.

"Holy Shit!" Rebecca spurted out loud. "It's over three-hundred dollars!" Rebecca read the review of the celebrated wine she held in her hand. She smiled and made a plan: have dinner, get into the bath, light some candles, and drink the very thoughtful gift from her boss. The fatigue from the day suddenly vanished as she now felt rejuvenated. Rebecca went into her bedroom, undressed and put on a robe. She returned to the kitchen and opened up one of her favorite drawers—the one with the corkscrew in it. Rebecca knew a wine like this must have a chance to breathe before tasting. Sitting down at the table, she placed the corkscrew precisely in the middle of the cork. Making sure she had a firm grip on the bottle, Rebecca carefully turned the screw and pulled out the cork. She considered, but then decided not to get her decanter. Rebecca reached up to her cupboard and brought down a rather large wine glass. She then nearly filled the entire glass with the burgundy colored fluid. Rebecca placed a bottle stopper in the top of the wine bottle and put the remaining wine into the refrigerator. While the refrigerator was open, Rebecca pulled out a leftover salad from the day before. She sat down and quickly consumed the food.

Excitedly, Rebecca went into her bathroom and drew a steamy hot bath. She added her favorite bath oil, and lit the large, scented candles located throughout the small room. After turning off the room lights, Rebecca returned to the kitchen for her prize. Holding the large glass with both hands, she entered her bathroom, carefully placed the glass down on the edge of the tub and let her robe fall to the floor. Rebecca entered the hot bath slowly, letting the heat creep its way up her legs. She then submerged herself completely. Within a few moments Rebecca could feel the day's tension slip away completely. She sat quietly in the tub for a moment, and then realized she forgot to turn on music.

"Shit." Rebecca scolded herself. She reluctantly pulled herself out of the water, dried herself, and quickly walked naked into the living area of her apartment. Rebecca turned on her stereo—a gift from an old boyfriend. She found a CD of *The Brandenburg Concertos* by Bach and put it into the now antiquated CD player. She also hit the replay button as she wanted it to play continuously. With the volume adjusted, Rebecca padded back to the bathroom and lowered herself into the tub. After settling back down, Rebecca felt it was now time to indulge herself with the wine.

She brought the large glass next to her nose and swirled the glass ever so gently. She could smell the subtle odors of cherry and wood.

Rebecca smiled at the calming sensations of the music, the flickering candles, and the hot bath water. She closed her eyes and took a small sip of the wine. It was delightful. The wine was as advertised: flavorful—without being overwhelming, and so smooth. The rich aroma was accentuated by the wonderful taste; it prompted her to want to drink more. Rebecca took a large swig. She held it in her mouth for an extended moment before swallowing. Rebecca could feel the warm sensation of the alcohol as it coated the back of her throat. She took another large swallow. Rebecca looked at the half-empty glass and thought this may be the finest wine she ever had. She wasn't sure if it was the wine itself, or the fact that it was a gift from her boss that made it so good. Rebecca didn't really care, and she took another large gulp. Rebecca was suddenly quite aware of the effect of the alcohol—she felt slightly dizzy, but still cognizant of everything.

The protective blood-brain barrier, which has evolved over eons, provides a defense against disease-causing pathogens and toxins in our blood from entering this remarkable organ. However, it cannot block alcohol.

Without having eaten most of the day and consuming just a small salad for dinner, there was little in Rebecca's stomach to buffer the wine. The more light-headed she became, the more she drank. Within a matter of a few minutes, Rebecca had consumed the entire large glass of the gift.

Rebecca clumsily tried to put the glass back on the tub ledge. But with her loss of coordination, Rebecca missed the ledge and the glass fell onto the bathroom floor and shattered loudly. Through her dizziness she heard the sound of glass breaking, but couldn't assess what had happened. Rebecca could feel she was in a far greater state of drunkenness than she had previously experienced. Perhaps it was something other than being intoxicated. Rebecca now experienced the onset of a severe headache and became aware of an odd metallic taste in her mouth.

Suddenly, Rebecca noted the onset of a severe stomach cramp. She bent over and wailed in pain as the spasm in her left-upper abdominal quadrant was now exquisite. Rebecca couldn't think clearly as the fog from the wine was blunting her ability to comprehend what she was experiencing. Despite her intoxication, it was as though a primordial reaction was taking over and Rebecca now started to panic at how her body was reacting. The pounding headache became overwhelming. She thought to herself, *My god, what is happening?* Without warning, Rebecca suddenly had projectile vomiting. The vomiting wouldn't stop. *The pain…why is this happening?* kept repeating in her head. Rebecca then felt a sudden flutter in her chest and she couldn't catch her breath. Rebecca slipped under the surface of the hot water, but somehow managed to right herself and get her head above the surface and catch her breath. And then the severe pain in her abdomen reoccurred accompanied by another vomiting episode. Just as Rebecca tried to catch her breath between spasms of abdominal pain, she aspirated the vomit. Suddenly Rebecca couldn't get any air into her lungs. The dizziness, the pain, the inability to get a breath—Rebecca started flailing. Again, she slipped under the surface of the water. This time she did not get up. With hypoxemia setting in, her heart rate increased dramatically. And then it slowed. And then it stopped. Rebecca lay under the water's surface. Her eyes were wide open. Rebecca had a terrible day, indeed.

CHAPTER 26

Naperville, IL

When Rebecca Sunnis did not come into work the following day, calls and texts were sent to her phone. Rebecca was so fastidious in her work habits, it would be uncharacteristic for her to simply not show up. Certainly, she would call or notify those in the lab with whom she had project deadlines or scheduled meetings with. Her sister left a voicemail message apologizing for their argument the previous day. On the second day without a word from Rebecca, Bob Cortes suggested someone should go to her home and see if she was ill or possibly injured. Eddie Wong, one of the technicians who had given Rebecca a ride home in the past stated he would swing by her apartment on his way home from work. Numerous calls and messages were again left for her.

That evening, Eddie pulled into the parking lot at her apartment complex and walked to the front entrance. As it was locked, he sat down on the cement staircase and waited for another tenant to open the door for him. Fortunately, his wait was short as someone was exiting the building. The exiting elderly woman glared at him as he grabbed the closing door behind her, but she quickly went on her way. Eddie climbed the stairs and knocked on her door. He waited, and then knocked again—louder the second time. With no response, he started to turn and leave. But then, he thought he heard some quiet music emanating from her apartment. Yes, it was classical music. Eddie now pounded on her apartment door, thinking she couldn't hear him with the music playing. Eddie pulled out his cell phone and dialed Rebecca's number. He heard the dial tone on his phone, and then seconds later, he heard Rebecca's phone ringing in the apartment! *What was going on?* Eddie went from being concerned to now being frightened. Eddie called his boss, Gene Cortes, and explained the situation. As instructed, Eddie dialed 911, and reviewed with the telephone operator the situation. Eddie was told to remain in place until a squad car arrived. He waited by the window in Rebecca's hallway.

Within minutes a police car arrived and parked in front of the building. Two officers approached, and Eddie ran down to open the door and let them in. He explained who he was and why he was there.

"It is most unusual for Rebecca not to show up at work—she is very reliable," Eddie said excitedly. "I can hear music coming from her apartment, but she doesn't answer when I knock." The officers walked with Eddie up the staircase and also banged on her door.

"Ms. Sunnis…this is the Naperville Police…please open your door!" They banged again. The noise must have disturbed one of the neighbors who opened her door and poked her head out.

"I haven't seen Rebecca in a few days…maybe she's out of town?" the neighbor stated from her doorway.

"Well, that's possible, Ma'am…but this man works with her and states that she should have been at work the past two days but has been absent. There is also music coming from inside. Do you happen to know the number to the building manager?" one of the police officers stated politely.

"Yes…yes…I have it…give me a moment." The neighbor ducked inside and then came back out into the hallway with a yellowed sheet of paper. The officer took the paper and dialed the number on his cellphone. He explained the situation to the manager.

The officer looked at the neighbor and stated, "The apartment super will be here in a few minutes. You can go back inside, Ma'am. Thank you."

The building manager arrived looking a bit disheveled. He lifted a keychain with no less than 50 keys, and on the first try, inserted the proper one into the lock. Before turning the key, the manager knocked, and announced that he was going to enter. He then turned to the officer.

"It's okay that we enter—this is an emergency," the officer stated to the relief of the manager.

The door was opened and all four of them started to enter Rebecca's apartment. The officer turned and asked if the manager and Eddie could wait outside. They immediately complied and stood in the hallway as the police walked in. One officer went into the bedroom while the other was getting out a notebook and pen.

"Holy shit!" The officer in the bedroom shouted. He came running out, urgently stating, "The woman is in the bathtub…she looks like she drowned!" There is glass all over the floor…Call backup and the paramedic squad now!"

"Is there a chance she is alive?" the second officer stated just after he made the instructed call.

"No way…take a look…she's bloated…probably been in there a couple of days," the lead officer stated. They both walked into the bathroom. They were careful to avoid touching anything except the light switch. The water in the tub was a greenish, turbid color… material was floating on the water surface. "Is that stomach contents in the water? Did she throw up? What the hell?"

They could hear the sound of the approaching siren from the ambulance. Minutes later, two paramedics entered the apartment with a foldable gurney. They entered the bathroom, but then stopped. There was absolute silence in the room. There were no signs of life in the bathtub. One of the medics placed a gloved hand into the water to feel for a carotid pulse. There was none. The water was cold, as was the neck he just touched.

The second squad car arrived; and then a third and a fourth. The blue and white flashing lights atop the emergency response vehicles became more prominent as the evening sky darkened. Police personnel, both uniformed and non, entered and left the premises as they were informed of the details. Whenever an unexplained or suspicious death was identified, the major crimes unit was notified and the area is wardened off.

Susan Blight was a young new detective on the Naperville police force. She was made detective a year earlier and was tagged by the higher brass as an up-and-coming star. Although Naperville as a city did not have the size or crime rate to mandate a massive police presence, the force was sophisticated, and if necessary, it had assistance from the neighboring Chicago Police Department. Often, complicated cases did mandate inter-city departmental cooperation. Blight entered the apartment and did a cursory assessment. From the doorway, she was immediately impressed by how clean and tidy the apartment was. Blight had been informed the deceased was a biologist working on drug development at *Harris Therapeutics* in nearby Wheaton. In the apartment, everything was in its place. No loose newspapers or magazines were on the couch or coffee table. No clothing scattered about. The kitchen appeared well-appointed with numerous food-preparation gadgets and counter-top appliances. Blight opened the refrigerator with her gloved hands and noted plenty of produce—the milk was still fresh. An opened bottle of wine was in the door storage compartment next to some ketchup and salad dressings. The trash was half-full, but nothing out of the ordinary was seen. A wine bottle cork was the last thing that appeared to have been dropped into the stainless-steel trash container. Everything appeared appropriate to Blight's eye.

The bedroom was similarly immaculate. The bed was made and no dirty clothes or other evidence of disarray was seen. The bathroom was another story. Blight carefully entered the small room, asking the photographer to kindly step aside. The bathroom itself was organized and clean. Multiple remnants of extinguished candles could be seen. The candles appeared to have been large, as the frozen puddle of wax from each was nearly the size of a dinner plate. Most likely the candles continued to burn for the two days since she last reported to work. They only extinguished when the liquefied hot wax was the same height as the wicks. A bath robe appeared to be haphazardly dropped onto the floor in one corner. The white linoleum floor was covered by shards of glass. The stem of a wine glass was present among the broken pieces. Dried spots of a brownish liquid were seen on the floor; it was too thin to be blood, and not the right shade of red. It was probably the contents of the wine glass. Blight wrote down a question in her notebook: *Was the glass dropped or thrown?* Given the location and spread of the glass pieces, it appears to have struck the floor right next to the bathtub ledge—it was most likely inadvertently knocked, surmised Blight.

Blight looked at the dead woman in the tub. Remarkably, the drainage stopper was still watertight. Blight shook her head knowing she couldn't keep water in her own tub at home for the duration of a soak, let alone for two days. There appeared to be pieces of green material in the tub. *Was that a piece of lettuce?* Blight wondered, as she looked through the water. She recalled seeing a left-over salad in the refrigerator. Could the woman have vomited up her dinner while taking a bath and drinking some wine? Did she have a seizure, causing an accidental drowning? Blight confirmed with the forensics team that they scraped the fluid off the floor, taken samples of the tub water, obtained specimens of the glass, and fingerprinted the room. After having the photographer complete his recording of the room—including the deceased—Blight asked for assistance to have the tub drained and the body lifted out of it.

Rebecca's body was bloated from soaking in the water for over 48 hours. Her beautiful figure was now one of grotesque distortion. The wide-open eyes were a distraction for Blight, who realized she and the woman were probably the same age. There was no external bruising, and the woman's neck was clean without any marks or trauma. A thin gold necklace with a pendent was the only jewelry on the body. After a thorough field examination, no foul play was evident. What caused this young woman's death was certainly not obvious.

Blight went into the kitchen and sat at the small kitchen table. She pulled out her tablet device and started to type into it her findings and impressions. The police personnel were starting to file out as the coroner's team entered and began their evaluation of the scene. Shortly after, the corpse was placed into a black, plastic, body bag and zipped closed. When everyone but the officer standing watch at the apartment doorway had left, Blight was alone at the table, still entering her thoughts. She was known among her colleagues to be exceptionally slow and deliberate, even when the obvious was obvious. As she searched for the right words to convey her impressions, Blight noted a small envelope on the kitchen counter. Putting on a fresh pair of gloves, she opened it and found a small card inside:

Rebecca, thank you for everything you have done to advance our lab.
Congratulations on your six-month anniversary with us. Enjoy!
Best, Gene Cortes

Blight looked around the small kitchen. *What was the note accompanying? There was no gift box laying around. Was this note recent, or perhaps from a week or two ago?* She remembered the cork in the trash was on top of everything else. It was probably the last thing the dead woman threw in there. Blight took a photo of the note before putting it and the envelope into an evidence bag. She typed more questions into her tablet:

Was there a gift that accompanied the note card?
When did this unknown gift arrive?
What was it?
Who is Gene Cortes?

Blight wrote down to check on the employment date of Rebecca Sunnis. It was two days ago when she apparently didn't come in to work. *So, was three days ago the date of her six-month anniversary at work?* In celebration, would she have received and then opened the gift on that date? Blight went to the trash container again and looked inside. It was too tall and narrow to make out any details. She used the flashlight on her phone to illuminate the trash container. Blight identified a brown cardboard box and wrapping paper. Blight remembered the refrigerator. She looked around and spotted an open wine bottle with a glass stopper. She took off the stopper and carefully smelled the wine. The wine smelled unremarkable without any peculiar odors. She took a photograph of the wine label and returned the bottle to its original location. Blight went back to her tablet and added more questions to her list:

Was death accidental?
Does deceased have known medical problems?
Need toxicology screen.

Without any additional evidence or information to consider, Blight put down her impression:

Cause of death: probable accidental drowning.

CHAPTER 27

Wheaton, IL

Blight drove to the *Harris Therapeutics* facility. She flashed her badge to the attendant at the gatehouse and drove up the long road to the main building. The grounds were immaculate as everything appeared well maintained and beautifully cared for; all the foliage and flowers were manicured. She walked from the parking lot to the main entrance and introduced herself to the guard. Blight was then asked to go through the magnetometer after removing her firearm as well as a new-fangled scanning device she was less familiar with. The second guard examined her purse, and she was then accompanied to the reception area. Blight had never witnessed such an elaborate security protocol at a private company before. Everyone, she noted, was very pleasant and accommodating. After explaining the reason for her visit for the third time, Blight was finally brought to a room that appeared to be used for group conference calls or meetings. The room was beautifully appointed with cherry-wood paneled walls and deep burgundy carpeting. Large television monitors were mounted flush with the paneling, and microphones were suspended every three or four feet from the ceiling. A large white board was on one side of the room. On the other, an electric presentation screen was partially deployed from the ceiling and a back-wall mounted projector was facing it. Twelve chairs surrounded the matching cherry-wood conference table. The tan-leather, reclining, chairs were more comfortable than anything she had at home. Blight sat there for a few minutes and was offered a beverage. Minutes later, a handsome man, probably in his early 40's entered. He was wearing tennis shoes, jeans and a white lab coat. His embroidered lab coat read: *Gene Cortes, Ph.D.*

Blight stood up. “Good morning, Doctor Cortes, I’m Susan Blight. I’m a detective from the Naperville Police Department.” Cortes extended his hand and introduced himself as well.

“Good morning, Detective. After getting a report from my lab technician, Eddie Wong, I was expecting a visit from the police. Thank you for coming.” Cortes said somberly. “Rebecca was not only an outstanding researcher, but she was a friend. I can’t begin to tell you how saddened we all are with the news of her passing. What can I help you with?”

They both sat down. “Well, to begin, Doctor, can you tell me how long you’ve known Rebecca?”

Cortes looked up as he considered her question. “Well, I suppose maybe a year, give or take. No, maybe a bit less. I can get HR to get us a file on her employment. It will only take a moment.” Cortes got out of his chair and walked to the intercom panel on the wall and spoke into it briefly. “We should have that file shortly…I also told HR to make a copy of it, as I’m sure you will want that as well.”

“Yes, I would, thank you.” Blight had very good radar for liars, and she could not detect any effort by Cortes to hide or mislead. “So, you think Rebecca was here for less than a year?”

“Well, I’m just guessing… we should know exactly soon. I’m not great with dates and such, but yes, I worked quite closely with Rebecca as she was an integral part of our research team. In fact…” Cortes trailed off. “I really can’t recall not talking with her on a daily basis…I mean…” Just then the door opened and a smartly dressed woman entered carrying two manila folders. She handed one to Cortes, one to Blight, and promptly left the room. Blight opened the file and went through it as Cortes sat quietly.

“Rebecca worked here for nearly ten months, according to her employment records.” Blight stated. She carefully observed Cortes to see if there was any reaction. There was none. “My gosh, nothing but glowing assessments and work reviews." Blight commented as she continued to leaf through the employment file. "So, if you think she worked here for perhaps less than a year, and her employment records show she was here for about 10 months, why did you send her a note congratulating her on her six-month anniversary at *Harris?"*

"I didn't." Cortes stated with a quizzical face. "What are you talking about, Detective?"

Blight stopped looking at the file. She looked straight at Cortes. "You never sent Rebecca a congratulatory note about her employment?"

Cortes looked surprised and asked, "Why no…why would I? She was a great researcher and I knew we were making steady progress on a project we were very proud of…but I have never sent anyone I work with a…what? An anniversary card? I never sent anyone such a thing. Do you have a copy of it I can look at?"

Blight opened her phone and showed Cortes the image of the note. He looked at it and shook his head. "That's not my handwriting…and certainly not my signature!"

Blight looked at Cortes closely. "Maybe a store clerk filled it out… like when you order flowers for someone and they write the note."

Cortes looked at Blight with pleading eyes and stated quietly, "Look, Detective, I never sent…I never ordered any flowers for Rebecca…"

"Maybe something other than flowers," Blight stated, trying to catch Cortes in a lie.

Cortes replied quickly, "Detective…I haven't sent Rebecca anything…ever! I don't know what this is all about." Cortes was now visibly upset. "All I know is Eddie Wong called me last night and said that Rebecca was found dead…apparently drowned…in her bathtub. That's all I know. I am trying to help, but I don't know what you are talking about right now."

Blight looked closely at Cortes. She was quickly trying to reason through the known facts: *So, if Cortes didn't send the note that was signed with his name and maybe accompanied a gift…then who did? And why would he congratulate her on a six-month anniversary at the company if she was there nearly ten months? By using Cortes's note, perhaps someone was also trying to implicate Cortes. Or, was that just a muse to get Rebecca to open or do something?* Blight asked Cortes some additional questions and then wrapped up the meeting. Her instincts told her Doctor Cortes had nothing to do with anything in Rebecca's apartment on the day of her death.

Detective Blight then requested to speak with Eddie Wong. Eddie came into the conference room visibly shaken. He reiterated facts that Blight already knew, but she wanted to hear them from his mouth. After his interview, Blight left the building with more questions than answers. What was thought to be a possible accidental drowning was appearing to be much more complicated. Blight got into her car and opened her tablet. Some of her questions were answered, but others were created:

Cortes had neither a motive or desire to kill Rebecca. But it appears his name was placed on a note purposely. Was that merely to incentivize her to open whatever accompanied the note?

If she worked for nearly ten months at Harris, why would someone write six months…and wouldn't she know this? Perhaps she didn't care, or in her excitement of a gift, she overlooked this?

Blight closed the tablet. She sat in her car for a few moments trying to reconcile what she just heard and wrote down. As Blight pulled out of the parking lot, she realized, this was no accidental drowning.

CHAPTER 28

Naperville, IL

The autopsy performed by the Naperville medical examiner, Doctor Timothy Contrell, was expected to be routine. The body lying on the stainless-steel autopsy table in front of him was that of a woman in her mid-thirties. Doctor Contrell took a few moments to review the accompanying paperwork. Apparently, she had not shown up to work for two days prompting a work associate to check on her. The associate heard music emanating from her apartment, prompting his call to the police. The police report stated she was found without a pulse and was submerged in her own bathtub. The only description of anything out of the ordinary was a broken wine glass noted on the bathroom floor, but otherwise there was no suspicious activity reported at the scene. The impression of the investigating detective was this was possibly alcoholic intoxication leading to an accidental drowning. The deceased's past medical history obtained from her family revealed there was no significant underlying medical conditions, and they were unaware of any use of routine medications.

Doctor Contrell donned his gown, protective eyewear, and gloves; no mask was required. He uncovered the body of Rebecca Sunnis and examined her carefully. He stated her name and assigned case ID number into the microphone suspended above the table. There were no clothes to remove or examine. He looked at every surface of Rebecca's body, audibly recording the details of his findings. He noted she was in excellent physical shape—well nourished, developed, and without any obvious physical deformities or abnormalities. Rebecca's external examination was consistent with her stated age. There were no scars or evidence of surgical incisions. The deceased didn't have any tattoos or piercings. All of her fingernails and toes were painted a bright cobalt blue, but otherwise they appeared normal without any evidence of debris or blood under them. Her head, face, chest, and neck were completely normal. There was no evidence of recent sexual activity. Consistent with the police report, there was no evidence to suggest any external injury occurred prior to death—her external physical evaluation was completely unremarkable.

Doctor Contrell then proceeded with his internal investigation of her organs. He made a standard Y-shaped incision from each shoulder under her breasts down to the mid-chest, and then carried the vertical incision to her pubis. He cut the sides of the chest cavity leaving the ribs attached to the breastbone and removed the entire frontal rib cage. Using the Rokitansky method for his autopsy, Contrell removed the internal organs en-bloc as a connected group. He then proceeded to make a cut across the crown of the head, opened the cranium with an electric saw and removed the brain. Doctor Contrell then dissected each organ, weighed and examined each grossly, and took a sliver for microscopic examination.

Upon opening the gastrointestinal tract, Doctor Contrell noted acute ulceration of the stomach and distal esophagus. There was evidence of bleeding from these sites as well as remnants of Rebecca's last meal; both in her stomach and esophagus. It was evident she had a small meal, and it was consistent with lettuce and other small vegetables. A burgundy-colored fluid was noted in the dependent region of her stomach. Contrell used a pipette and extracted a sampling. Knowing the history of a shattered wine glass in the bathroom, he suspected the fluid would be consistent with wine she had consumed. Given the food in her esophagus and noting the ulceration, Contrell suspected she had vomited her dinner shortly before death. Some petechial bleeding—small capillary rupture—would be expected from regurgitation, but the amount of blood and the extent of the ulceration would indicate more severe or protracted vomiting had occurred. The previously obtained blood and urine samples will be helpful, but often determining if infected food in a body is causally related with pathological findings some forty-eight hours after death is difficult. Contrell spoke into his dictation microphone the need to evaluate for possible food poisoning. Doctor Contrell continued with his gross examination of the GI tract, including the liver, large and small intestines, and rectum. All appeared normal.

Contrell then proceeded to separate the heart and lungs from the attached organs. The heart appeared healthy without evidence of infection, disease, or acute changes. Opening the lungs, Contrell anticipated finding evidence of excessive fluid within the alveoli—the delicate part of the lungs where oxygen and carbon dioxide are exchanged during respiration. He examined multiple areas in both lungs looking for evidence to coincide with her apparent drowning presentation. Despite his intensified examination, he couldn't find evidence to support this. Similarly, her trachea and bronchioles—the branching tubes where air flows into and out of the lungs—were dry. Contrell put down his instruments and sat next to the eviscerated corpse for a few minutes as he collected his thoughts. This was very odd, indeed. He looked at Rebecca's face, as if she could help explain to him what happened; no answers came to him. Contrell stood up, and returned to his autopsy. Continuing his dissection, all the remaining organ systems, including his gross anatomical study of her brain, appeared normal.

Contrell was perplexed. He entered the autopsy facility expecting to find evidence of a drowning. What Contrell found was currently unexplainable at this point. But, what he did know, for sure, was that Rebecca Sunnis did not die as a result of drowning. There was no water in her lungs. The only abnormality he could find was evidence of vomiting. Doctor Contrell made a notation that he would await tissue microscopy and toxicology results before rendering any determination of the cause of death. Something was very much out of order here. Contrell took off his gloves and picked up the telephone. He dialed the number attached to the file.

"This is Detective Blight. Who may I ask is calling?"

"Good afternoon, Detective. This is Doctor Contrell from the ME's office…I understand you are investigating the Rebecca Sunnis case?"

"That is correct, Doctor…have you concluded your autopsy?" Blight inquired.

"Well, not completely. I need to wait for the tox screens and microscopies to come back. We'll have the pathology on the tissue back in a day or so, but the toxicology can take a while. I'll let you know when they come in," Contrell stated very matter-of-factly.

Blight cut him off, "Okay, Doctor…so why exactly are you calling me?"

Contrell began, "Well, Detective…there is an inconsistency between what was filed in your report and what I'm finding. The report revealed the woman's…err…Rebecca Sunnis's body was under the water in a bathtub. Apparently, there was no evidence of foul play… except a broken wine glass on the floor. The scene was noted to be consistent with a drowning…correct?"

"Yes…go on, Doctor," Blight stated slowly, as she was considering where the conversation was going.

Contrell began. "Well, with a drowning, there is often evidence of aspiration…of inhaling fluids into the respiratory tract. About 10 percent of drowning victims die without aspirating water. The presumed reason for that is the victim experiences laryngospasm or chest-wall spasm when submerged; thus, they die without taking a breath. More typically we see frothy foam in the nasal cavity and pharynx. Usually there is fluid in the paranasal sinuses, the trachea and main bronchi. And on gross exam, the lungs are typically… well…heavy due to the presence of excessive fluid. In this case, with the exception of aspirated food contents consistent with vomiting, there is no findings to suggest she died of drowning. I will need confirmation from the microscopic evaluation of her lungs, but from what I can tell at this time, she may have slipped under the water in the tub only after she died. I know this makes your case imminently more complicated. Now…I'm not suggesting anything just yet…but the gross pathological findings are not consistent with the cause of death as reported." Contrell took a breath.

After a long pause, Blight stated quietly, "Well, this is certainly interesting news, Doctor. Please keep me informed as soon as you find anything else." Blight disconnected the call. She reminded herself that her instincts after meeting with Cortes were correct—if it wasn't a drowning, whatever happened, it most probably wasn't accidental!

Blight wasn't going to wait for the additional testing before proceeding. She went back to Sunnis's apartment for another look.

Upon approaching Rebecca Sunnis's apartment building, Blight felt a pang in her stomach. Using the key given to her by the building management, she walked up the short staircase and into the building lobby. She continued up the stairs and pulled down the yellow crime scene tape outside the door. Once inside the quiet apartment, Blight could *feel* the scene of a crime. The apartment was darkened with the window coverings closed and the lights off. Blight turned on the wall switch and yellow light was cast from an incandescent bulb in an old lamp. The stereo was now off. The previously immaculate bedroom carpeting had dirty footprints everywhere from the police officers, EMT personnel, and crime scene technicians that went in and out when Rebecca's body was discovered. The powder used for fingerprint identification remained on the doorknobs, cabinets, and mirrors. The bathtub water had been drained, and all that remained was a rim of residue at the previous waterline. The larger pieces of the wine glass had been removed and taken as evidence after photographers captured their location. All that remained on the bathroom floor were some of the smaller glass shards left behind. Blight opened the medicine cabinet. Not a single prescription bottle was present; this woman was healthy, Blight acknowledged. Something was very off, indeed.

Blight sat down on the closed, white, toilet seat. She sat there quietly for a few minutes as she looked around the small bathroom—what she now felt was a *true* crime scene. Blight tried to imagine the scene: *The small room was darkened with the exception of the light emanating from the multiple flickering candles. There was a hot bath…a glass of wine. Rebecca had no idea what was going to happen to her.* Blight understood this was not a suicide, and it was not an accidental mishap. Blight stared at the bathtub. She now knew that *something* induced this healthy, vibrant, woman to die in that tub.

Blight got up and went back to the kitchen table. She remembered the note. The *apparent* note from Rebecca's boss, Gene Cortes. Blight pulled out her phone and looked at the image she had taken of it. Nobody gets a congratulatory note without something else…flowers or maybe candy. She thought for a moment…wine! Yes…the wine was the gift! Blight looked again at her notes. The wine cork was the top item in the waste basket in the kitchen! Blight quickly stood up and opened the trash container. Fortunately, it was still there. She took out a pair of latex gloves that were always with her and one of the evidence bags located in all of her jacket pockets, and carefully wrapped it around the cork before sealing it. Blight then remembered seeing the wine bottle in the refrigerator when she was first here. She turned to the refrigerator and opened the door. The bottle was still there with the glass stopper in place. Rebecca wanted to keep the wine…to drink it again—maybe even save the bottle when it was empty. It was a gift from her boss…or at least she thought so! Blight grabbed her phone again, but this time she took multiple images of the wine bottle and then she set it aside to take with her. She remembered the other contents in the trash as well: the wrapping paper and the box. She gathered these items as well. As Blight was just about to turn off the kitchen lights, she noted on the counter one more clue. Something only a sentimental woman would keep. Blight picked up the ribbon and bow. Blight understood this gift was important to Rebecca, as it represented more than a congratulation; it was an affirmation of her value. Whoever gave her this bottle knew she would drink it and not store it or give it away. Whoever gave her this gift knew a great deal about her.

Blight gathered what she had collected, turned off the lights, and closed the door. She looked at her watch and felt there was still time in the day to keep the investigation moving. Blight made her way to the Naperville Police crime lab knowing what she wanted. With cooperation from the Chicago Police Department, if needed, she felt they could find what she was looking for. She handed the paper goods, the cork, and the wine bottle to the intake clerk. After assuring all were properly labeled and logged-in, Blight walked through the maze of the lab looking for her friend, forensic lab technician, Joan Englewood. Blight had forgotten how large the lab was. It was certainly far bigger than the city of Naperville required, but the lab also served many of the neighboring communities. After recalling where her friend's workstation was located, Blight found Englewood looking through a microscope at fiber samples from another crime. Blight filled Englewood in on the case details and what she was anticipating they could determine.

Englewood decided to take a coffee break with Blight. The two women walked over to the small canteen, selected the *Keurig* coffee flavor-of-the-day and sat down. They drank their coffees in silence for a few moments thinking about the case. Englewood put her paper coffee cup down and looked at Blight. "Everything is pointing to something the decedent was given to cause her demise. She sounds like a very organized and predictable individual. She wouldn't have done anything or consumed something unless it was from a trusted source. From your description of the scene and your interview with Doctor Cortes, Sunnis apparently received a package that contained a gift from an unknown subject. That package contained the wine. We need to identify if, in fact, the bottle contains only wine and nothing else. We also need to see if we can trace the path that bottle took to get to Sunnis. The packaging you retrieved from her trash will probably be of little use, but we'll take a look and see if we can find out anything from it."

"What's your time-frame, Joan?" Blight asked.

"I think we can have your answers in less than a week," Englewood responded and got up from the table. "I need to get going, Susan. I'll give you a call as soon as we get an answer to these questions."

"Thank you, Joan," Blight stated with a weak smile. As Englwood walked away, Blight pulled out her tablet from her oversized bag. She opened up the *Sunnis* file and reviewed her notes. Other than the limited additional evidence she gave to the crime lab, so far the pathologist's preliminary report was all she had to go on. The only other link in the case was to Gene Cortes, who seemed completely blindsided as to what happened. Blight sat for a few moments drinking the last of her coffee as she reflected on the case. She typed only one word on the next line in her case file:

Why?

CHAPTER 29

Naperville, IL

Englewood retrieved from the crime lab clerk the evidence Susan Blight brought in. The wine bottle was the only significant item brought in from the scene. All of the other objects and articles brought in from the investigation were of no particular interest, and gave no information as to what occurred at the scene. Englewood re-read the investigative preliminary report which described that a woman apparently drowned in her bathtub. However, after hearing Blight's recounting of the scene, her discussion with the pathologist, and learning of the *gifted* wine bottle which was accompanied by a fictitious note, Englewood too, felt there was more to this story.

With gloved hands, the wine bottle was photographed and dusted. The only obvious prints were those of Rebecca Sunnis. As expected, nothing else was noted other than useless smudges. After measuring the amount of liquid still inside the bottle, an aliquot of the fluid was sent for chemical and biological analysis. Englewood then performed a diligent review of the wine label: the name and address of the winery of origin, the distributor, and what information the bar code revealed.

A barcode is also known as a UPC or Universal Product Code. More precisely, it is a Global Trade Identification Number, or GTIN. It consists of bars and spaces and is a machine-readable representation of numerals and characters. This label is on practically every item sold worldwide, and is there to assist retailers manage their inventory and speed up the sale process at check-out. It can't tell you who bought the item, but the barcode represents the company and product details. With that information, one can check the batch, and confirm from that company where it has been sent to find the seller details.

Englewood sent an email to *The Jurdesson Winery* located in Napa Valley requesting any information they could give regarding this particular wine bottle. Fortunately, this was apparently a rather exclusive wine, and the list of retailers who sell this product is limited. It did not take long for her to have the name and location of *The Barducci Bros. Wine Shop* located in Chicago. She forwarded the name of the retailer via email to detective Blight.

Blight had the compulsive habit of checking her emails every few hours, and was pleased to see the progress the lab was making on her case. Blight checked her watch. It was only 2 p.m. on a rather slow Wednesday. Knowing rush hour would soon begin, she quickly left her office, got onto the Eisenhower Expressway and made her way from Naperville to the address of the wine shop in Chicago using her phone's GPS. Fortunately, parking was never an issue with a municipal police car license plate. Blight entered *The Barducci Bros. Wine Shop* and noted the rich smell of the wood chips used in the bottle crates. Blight looked around the old shop and thought this is a place she needs to come back to when she is off-duty. She very much wanted to walk up and down the aisles and look at the wines and where they were from. Blight walked up to the store clerk, presented her ID, and asked to speak with the manager of the store. The woman stated she would get him and promptly left. While waiting, Blight again surveyed the store and then walked over to the entranceway. For some odd reason, Blight found herself intrigued with the detailed carving in the old heavy door and its doorframe. She was an antique collector in her spare time, and estimated the door was well over a hundred years old. While studying it, she noted an inconspicuous camera located above the door facing the register. It was hidden within a large green planter, and she appreciated that it was so cleverly placed that it would probably not be seen by a casual observer. After a couple of minutes, an elderly man walking rather slowly came out from a back room accompanied by the clerk. Blight quickly returned to the counter and introduced herself. Blight showed her credentials and pulled out her notepad.

"My name is Stephen…the manager is not on the premises. How may I help you?"

Blight began, "I'm working on a case where a bottle of wine was involved…and through our investigation, it appears the bottle was purchased here. I'm trying to find out if you might have some information about the buyer that could be useful to us." She flipped open her notepad and came to the details regarding the wine. "The bottle in question is a *Jurdesson Napa Valley Red.* Do you sell many bottles of this?"

Stephen perked up when he heard the name of the winery and that particular wine. As Blight was speaking, she could see his facial expression change as he was apparently trying to recall something from his memory about what she had asked. After a moment, Stephen returned to the present.

"Actually, Detective, we don't sell too much of that particular vintage. It's out of the price range of most buyers, and there are other comparable wines that I think are quite good and are half the price. Not that it isn't excellent…because it is. We keep a case in stock, and every now and then someone sees it and wants to indulge themself." Stephen stated. As he was speaking, Stephen shuffled over to where a few bottles from *The Jurdesson Winery* were located on the shelves. He picked up a bottle, brought it over to Blight and handed it to her. Blight recognized the label immediately as the one she took a photograph of at Rebecca Sunnis's apartment.

Blight then stopped looking at the label and turned her focus to the top of the bottle. She ran her finger over the smooth edge of the bottle's rounded lip. Blight then touched the cork.

"Where's the cork foil?" Blight asked.

Stephen smiled back at her, "Some wineries no longer use foil. It was originally used to keep rodents and insects from gnawing at the cork while the bottles were in storage. But with modern storage facilities, they probably aren't necessary and function more as a decoration. *Jurdesson* has chosen not to use foil for this particular wine."

Blight took some quick notes while Stephen was speaking. She made an asterisk next to her entry:

* *Why no cork on bottle given to Rebecca?*

Although she didn't understand *why* this mundane fact was so bothersome, Blight was curious by the lack of foil over the cork. She wrote down an additional note in her pad:

Does no foil on bottle have significance?

After looking at her notepad questions about the cork, Blight decided she would return to those questions later. She looked at Stephen directly and asked, "Do you recall selling this wine to anyone…in say…the last month or so?"

Stephen again appeared to be straining his memory when she asked the question. He appeared as though he knew the answer, but he just couldn't get the thought to surface. He stared up and to the left as he tried to recall. The store clerk who had remained quiet the entire time stated, "We have a barcode scanner at the register. Why don't we just check to see if a bottle was sold off our inventory?" Both Blight and Stephen looked at her realizing how obvious her response was. Blight chastised herself, *Why depend on the old man's memory when the computerized inventory list can give us the information?* In a few minutes, they were able to determine that, indeed, a bottle with its specific barcode was sold three weeks ago. Stephen suddenly appeared animated.

"Yes…now I remember…I do recall a rather peculiar man… Tom! That's it…he said his name was Tom!" Stephen blurted out. "This fella came in and stated he wanted a bottle for a friend's birthday…I remember now because he knew nothing about wines… yet when he saw this bottle, he picked it up immediately. Yes…he paid for it with hundred-dollar bills! How odd is that? Such an expensive bottle of wine…Yes…I do remember. He was also in a big hurry…funny how I remember those things!" Stephen stated while congratulating himself for his detailed recollection. "I just needed a little push to get things started," Stephen trailed off, satisfied that his memory was still intact.

Blight wrote down the date of sale and then looked at the store clerk. "Would your camera above the door have recorded the sale?"

Stephen re-entered the conversation. "Yes…our camera recordings are stored for a month and then new recordings go over them. I don't know how all of it works, of course, but I can call the company that services our equipment…you know…the register, the scanners and the like. I can ask if they can…"

Blight interrupted. "Not to worry, Stephen…we can handle that from our end. If you can just get me the contact information, we'll take care of getting what we need. You both have been tremendously helpful, and I appreciate your time. If we need anything more, I'll let you know."

Blight waited until she got the name and phone number of the security company that manages the store's video and bar-scanning equipment. She again thanked the clerk and Stephen and left the premises.

As was her routine, Blight sat in her car and opened up her tablet and paper notepad. She transferred her previous questions, and added some new ones to the tablet while reviewing what she had just heard and seen:

Get video of unsub.
Paid in cash-hundred dollar bills. Why?
Why this particular wine?
Is lack of cork foil relevant?

CHAPTER 30

Naperville, IL

"Are you serious?" Detective Blight exclaimed as she couldn't believe what she was hearing from Englewood at the crime lab. "You found lethal levels of arsenic in the wine bottle? Are you sure…I mean…"

Joan Englewood cut her off, "Look, Susan, arsenic is actually in a lot of foods, and it's commonly found in slightly increased levels in wine… but this is a significant toxic quantity. The amount of arsenic we isolated in the wine from that bottle was *not* created by nature. From what I can tell, this wine was intentionally used as a poison. You no longer just have a death in a bathtub, Susan…you have a murder here."

Blight took a moment to consider what she just heard. As she was about to continue, Englewood added, "The interesting question I have is how did the perpetrator get the arsenic into the bottle in the first place? Anyone opening a wine bottle would notice a small hole in the aluminum foil or the wax that is placed over the cork. I guess, maybe…someone could peel the foil off and then insert…"

Blight jumped in excitedly, "No, Joan…the bottle didn't have any aluminum foil over the cork! I visited the wine shop that sold the wine to the perp. Now I understand why he chose that particular bottle… there isn't any foil over the cork. Somehow, he managed to get the arsenic through the cork…maybe through a small needle…"

Englewood blurted in, “No…he wouldn’t need a needle…well, he would…but not *through* the cork. That would still leave an obvious hole that the victim would see…especially if there was no covering on the cork. No…I think what he did was very clever. All our perp needed to do was to pop the cork off, put in the poison and then re-cork the bottle. Yes, that’s it. He just needed to increase the pressure within the bottle…the cork would come off intact. Give me a moment, Susan. I want to go look at the cork you brought in…I’ll call you back in just a few minutes.” Englewood quickly disconnected.

The crime lab technician went to her workstation and retrieved the bottle cork from the evidence box. It had previously been neglected for any testing. Using her gloved hand, Englewood inspected the cork. It looked like a common cork from a wine bottle…about two inches in length with a slightly bowed appearance from years of being squeezed by the bottle’s neck. There was a slightly darkened, almost purplish color to the part of the cork that was exposed to the wine. Nothing extraordinary about the cork was apparent to Englewood’s sharp eye. She rolled the cork over a few times in her hand, and then had an idea. Englewood took the cork over to her microscope and put the cork on one of its flat surfaces. On low power, she inspected the surface noting nothing unusual. No holes or puncture sites were evident. She then inspected the edges of the coin-sized top of the cork. Englewood quickly pulled her head back away from the scope as she wasn’t sure of what she just saw. She then inspected the opposite, slightly purplish surface of the cork. And there it was again! There was an indentation on the edge of the cork. Englewood took the cork and rotated it so she could now visualize its side that aligned with the indentations. There was a consistent small groove on the edge of the cork from the top to the bottom. Englewood engaged the scope’s attached camera and took magnified images of the indentations and the groove. Satisfied with her findings, Englewood added her findings to the digitalized lab record and then quickly dialed the number to Blight’s cell phone.

“I found it,” Englewood started without saying hello.

“What? What did you find, Joan?” Blight asked hurriedly.

“Well, you can’t see it with your eyes…but under magnification, there is a groove along the cork’s edge that extends from top to bottom.

Remember you mentioned a needle…well, I think the perp did use one. Except he didn't puncture the cork with it, and he didn't draw any fluid through it…that would require too big of a needle. No…I think he placed a needle *alongside* the cork—between the cork and the inside of the bottle neck. And then he injected…air." Englewood was now thinking about the scenario as she was speaking. "He injected a bolus of air…that would increase the internal pressure within the bottle. Consequently, the cork would then slide out. Yes…that's what our perp did! He would then need to pour out some of the wine to allow for the added arsenic. Then he would have to re-cork the bottle. All the perp would need to do then was simply give it to the victim. I suspect the note you brought in was enough of an incentive for her to drink it. I think we're just lucky Sunnis didn't decide to share the wine with anybody else."

Blight responded, "Yes…very lucky…shit. Hey…any updates on the video playback from the wine store?"

Englewood stated, "Well, nothing that is determinative. We only got a partial view of the perp's face. He had gray hair and a beard, medium height. He wore a white, short-sleeve shirt…oh yes, he wore glasses. But nothing really stood out. He never looked up at the camera. But if we can isolate anything useful, I'll let you know." With that, the phones disconnected.

Blight was both excited and disturbed by the news. She felt there was foul play after her discussion with Doctor Cortes. This was now confirmed by the finding of arsenic in the wine and the devious method used by the perp to achieve his goal. The question that now bothered Blight was that which she wrote down in her tablet previously: *Why? To what end did this murder make any sense?* Having reviewed much of Sunnis's work, family, and social life, Blight could think of no reason anyone would gain by her death. There was also no effort by anyone to claim any credit for this heinous act—no ransoms, no threats, no contact to the police. Blight was both confused and frustrated. But that didn't last long. As Blight was mulling events over, her phone vibrated.

Blight recognized the deep voice on the other end of the line. "Detective Blight?"

"Yes, this is she," Blight responded.

"This is Doctor Contrell at the ME's office. I have that toxicology screen back..."

Blight cut him off, "Let me guess, Doctor...you identified arsenic in her system?"

"Why, yes...yes we did. How did you..." Contrell asked.

"I just got a call from the crime lab and the wine bottle was laced with it. Apparently, our perp managed to inject it into the wine and then re-cork the bottle. You were right, Doctor." Blight explained.

"About what, exactly?" Contrell asked.

Blight explained, "You were right...she didn't drown. Your autopsy findings didn't show any evidence of water being in her lungs. She didn't drown at all...she was poisoned."

"Yes, well, I'm pleased to know I was correct in my preliminary assessment, but...*why* is now the question." Contrell added solemnly.

Blight responded, "Yes, Doctor...we will understand the *why*... once we know the answer to the question now facing us...*who*." Blight thanked Doctor Contrell and hung up the phone. She opened her tablet and put down the information received. Blight then considered her only lead, that being the wine store. It would be unlikely the perp used his real name, *Tom*, but he did make two blunders. First, he went to a small store probably thinking any purchase would be difficult to trace. He found a bottle without a cork which seemed to be his prime directive—but foolishly he bought an expensive wine that was easy to track. Secondly, and stupidly, he paid for the wine with large bills, making the purchase memorable for Stephen, the wine salesman. The elderly Stephen certainly didn't have the best recollection, but it was tweaked by a few simple suggestions. Blight knew the time and day of the purchase by the bar-scan data at the counter. She made a notation for her office to check with Chicago police for any closed-circuit cameras that may have caught anything in front of the wine shop. Blight also wanted to check with Chicago police regarding their database of digital parking enforcement activity. If the perp parked his car on the street at that time, there might be a chance they could run down the tag numbers of his vehicle. Blight made a note to follow up on cars, say, within a two-block radius of the store.

After making her notes, Blight slowly closed her tablet. She knew it was going to be a long-shot to catch the unknown, gray-bearded man who bought the wine. She would await the parking information, and then begin the process of matching driver's licenses with the plate numbers—assuming the perp drove, and if he drove his own car. Blight knew what she needed to catch him: patience.

CHAPTER 31

Wheaton, IL

The news of the death of Rebecca Sunnis spread quickly within Gene Cortes's lab, and within twenty-four hours the entire staff at *Harris Therapeutics* was aware. It was a tight family at the company, and the shocking news of a promising young scientist lost to a drowning—let alone in her own bathtub—wasn't something that could stay contained. The funeral was attended by nearly all of the employees at *Harris,* and it was a difficult experience for everyone. In the absence of detailed information, rumors were formed and spread. At the time of the burial, only Cortes was aware of arsenic in a forged, wine bottle-gift, allegedly from him. Although he was not a suspect, he was advised by the police and his own attorney that this information should remain confidential until additional details were defined. He was understandably distraught, but also confused as to how and why one of his lab associates was murdered. Cortes was aware that most of the research and drug investigation at *Harris* was proprietary, and the company took extraordinary measures to assure its security. But there was nothing going on in their current lab experimentation related to a Department of Defense contract or any other highly valued investigation. Cortes surmised that perhaps Sunnis's death was related to someone or something in her personal life leading to this horrendous event. Consistent with his discussions with the police, Cortes suspected he was used as a decoy—as a tool to get Sunnis to accept the wine. Cortes knew the work in the lab would continue, and he would seek a replacement associate as soon as things settled down.

Bob Margolis was similarly quite shaken by the course of events. He felt Rebecca Sunnis was not only a colleague, but also a friend with whom he had discussed and shared many personal events in his life. Following the funeral, he knew he had to rethink his goals and accomplishments and re-prioritize his values. Margolis would not let Rebecca's tragic death be in vain. About a week after the funeral, Margolis reinvigorated himself about what he was doing with his life and had a clearer vision of his future. He was looking forward to his upcoming golf with Yamp. Margolis decided he needed to spend more time playing golf and doing the things that brought him enjoyment. He understood the work would always be there, and there was really no limit to the in-box. It was time to experience the opportunities for which he worked so hard to achieve. While driving home from *Harris*, Margolis instructed his voice-activated car infotainment system to dial Jay Yamp.

"Hey Jay, its Bob. I know we're supposed to play next weekend, but I have a free evening tonight and wanted to know if you would like to get together for a bite?"

Yamp responded, "Hey Bob…it's good to hear from you. I get so tired of always communicating with a short text or email. Sure… tonight would be fine. I should be home around six-ish. What did you have in mind?"

"Well…I know it's not fancy…but there's a new barbecue place that I wanted to try. It's only a few blocks from me, but…are you at University Hospital right now?" Margolis asked.

"I am," Yamp responded. "But that's only a few miles from you. Sounds like it would hit the spot…I love barbecue. How about we make it 6:30 p.m.? Just text me the address and I'll meet you there. I can't imagine on a Thursday it will be overly packed."

"Perfect," Margolis replied. "I'll take a quick shower and I'll see you there. We have a lot to talk about…we had a real tragic event at work…"

Yamp interrupted, "—my pager just went off. Let me get this and then we can talk tonight…I want to hear what's going on…I'll see you tonight, Bob." Yamp stated quickly, and then disconnected the call.

Margolis got home with plenty of time to shower and get ready for dinner. Upon reaching his apartment, he went into his refrigerator and grabbed a beer. He sat down on his couch, turned on the news and kicked his feet up. He was pleased with his recent introspection about what he was doing and why. Margolis was excited about where he was headed professionally, and what may lie ahead. He was also looking forward to developing a friendship and professional allegiance with Jay Yamp. Having a friend who also happened to be the director of a solid medical research program at one of the leading hospitals in the country was an enviable relationship for any biotech scientist. Thinking about the potential for real progress in pharmaceutical oncologic applications was exhilarating for Margolis. He was feeling good about where things were going, despite the recent loss of his friend, Rebecca. Margolis finished the last of his beer and decided it was time to get ready for the evening barbecue dinner.

Margolis took a hot shower and got dressed. Opening his medicine cabinet for a hairbrush, his eye caught the small cologne box in the corner. Margolis smiled as he recalled he received this at the golf event he chaired. His colleague's funeral was over now, and Margolis wanted to turn over a new leaf in his own life. Now that he was going to have dinner out, he thought it would be fun to use the new cologne for the first time. Margolis took the black box off the shelf and admired the elegant packaging. He tossed the box into the trash, removed the cap, and sprayed a small amount of the cologne in the air in front of his nose. The smell was truly great—it had a subtle citrus odor, yet was also very masculine. Margolis smiled, and then thought about the scientists who worked in the fragrance industry and how much testing they must do to get the scent just right. He liked it and proceeded to spray more onto his neck and chest. Margolis finished his dressing routine and turned off the bathroom lights. He then grabbed his keys and wallet and left his apartment and entered the hallway. Margolis heard the click of the door lock as he exited. The twenty-yard walk to the bank of elevators felt suddenly very long. He had lived on the thirtieth floor of the modern apartment building for five years... *Why did the distance to the elevators now feel so far?* he wondered.

The hallway became narrow and very dark—as if the lights had just been turned down. Margolis finally reached the elevator controls and pushed the *Down* button. Just as he pushed the button, Margolis realized he had forgotten his cell phone in the apartment. He was trying to remember where he left it and he debated about going back for it. Within seconds the car arrived, and Margolis felt himself almost lunge into it as he suddenly had a bout of nausea overwhelm him. Margolis slid down the side of the elevator car as he felt a wave of intense dizziness. He tried desperately to get up, but he couldn't. Margolis could see the *Call* button on the elevator control panel, but despite all his efforts, he just couldn't get himself to press it. He was sweating profusely. Suddenly, Margolis panicked as getting air into his lungs was difficult. *What the hell was happening?* he thought. As he was fighting to get air, Margolis suddenly fell onto his back and started to seize. His back arched as he experienced repeated uncontrolled muscle spasms. Margolis then vomited, and a steady flow of drool now poured out of the corners of his mouth. Another, and then another body contortion occurred. And then Margolis had a momentary reprieve before the next wave of spasms. He lay on the floor of the elevator trying to comprehend what was happening. Margolis looked up at the railings on the elevator wall and tried to reach them in an effort to get up, but he had no energy left. As he started to accept his fate, tears formed in the corner of his eyes. Suddenly, another wave of spasms occurred as the seizure activity started again. Within a minute Margolis passed out from the excessive activity—his rapidly beating heart unable to pump oxygenated blood fast enough to meet his body's sudden metabolic demands. The spasms then stopped. Margolis fell flat onto the elevator floor, his legs twisted behind him in a grotesque, contorted configuration. Margolis's muscles twitched periodically as his dying brain was starved for oxygen. Moments later he lay motionless on the floor of the elevator, his eyes were wide open. A *ding* rang out in the car as another tenant must have pushed the *Call* button. Bob Margolis never heard it.

As usual, Jay Yamp arrived at the restaurant early. It was a compulsive habit he just couldn't break. He walked into the darkened venue through heavy wooden doors. Upon entering, he could smell the rich aroma of barbecue—a sweet tangy scent with just the right amount of charcoal and smoke. It was all he needed to get his stomach growling; it had been a long day and having a beer and some slow-cooked BBQ ribs sounded like the right prescription for the doctor. Yamp looked around at the new establishment. It was packed, appearing to satisfy the large crowd already seated. Yamp checked in at the hostess desk. The friendly young woman informed him his wait would be about a half-an-hour. He took the table notification device from her and decided to start his first beer now. Yamp didn't know if Margolis was the type to show up on time or habitually late, but it really didn't matter right now—he was happy just to sit down at the bar and catch his breath with a draft *Guinness*.

At 6:50 p.m., Yamp finished his beer and looked around the bar area. There wasn't an empty seat available. The noise of the restaurant was louder than when he arrived. Yamp pulled out his cell phone and texted Margolis. After waiting for several minutes, he decided to call him—the call went to voicemail, so he just hung up. *Perhaps Bob was having trouble finding a parking spot.* Yamp decided to just relax and order a second beer. Shortly after 7:15 p.m., Yamp felt something was definitely out of order. A researcher such as Margolis would not be that tardy and would certainly call or text if running late. Yamp called again, but this time, he left a message.

"Hey Bob, Its Jay. It's a bit after seven…I know we planned to meet tonight…just calling to see if something came up…uhh…I'll hang out here at the bar a little while longer, then I need to pack it in as I have a full day tomorrow. Ok…well, let me know what's up." Yamp disconnected the call. He finished his second beer just as the table notification device started vibrating and blinking. Yamp picked up the device and returned it to the hostess. He informed her of his need to cancel the table, thanked her, and walked out.

As Yamp got into his car to go home, he went over the previous conversation with Margolis in his head. *It was tonight, right?* He thought about it again and realized he was correct. Something was definitely amiss. *Well, I'm sure there's a good reason for it*, he considered, and decided he would call Margolis in the morning. Yamp drove home, now upset that he didn't order ribs to go.

CHAPTER 32

Chicago, IL

The EMTs who first arrived at the apartment building of Bob Margolis were baffled. The elevator car in which Margolis was sprawled out had been placed on hold at the first floor and there was a crowd of observers surrounding his body. They needed to push through. Upon recognizing there was no pulse or signs of life, the police were notified. CPD soon arrived and quickly wardened off the area. Onlookers were pushed back, and other apartment dwellers were directed to use the service elevators located on the opposite side of the building's lobby.

Detective Melvin Rose was the first to arrive from the homicide division. He saw the lead EMT and questioned him on what the confusion was about.

"What doesn't make sense, here, John?" Rose stated while reading the EMT's name off his name tag.

"Well, sir," the EMT started, "from the contorted position of the body and noted foam at his mouth…well…it looks as though he had some type of seizure or convulsion…but that doesn't usually cause death. I mean…yeah, it can…just not that often. I think we need to wait for the medical examiner to see what he thinks."

Given the resources of the Chicago Police Department, as soon as a death is reported—particularly one with unclear or suspicious findings—the ME is notified. Rose walked towards the elevator car and observed the body of Bob Margolis. There was little question the body was contorted in an unusual manner. But he didn't want to speculate until after the ME had a chance to give his opinion. Rose directed the entire car be photographed from multiple angles, and fingerprinting be performed. Nobody touched or moved the body.

When the ME did arrive, he initiated his evaluation by looking for any evidence of external injury or trauma. There was none. He scoured the elevator car for any clues, but there was none to find. Being a luxury apartment building, the car was immaculate—there wasn't a single piece of discarded paper or visible dirt on the floor. No pills or needles were evident, and nothing to suggest any foul play was seen. The only thing inside the elevator car was the twisted body of Bob Margolis. Body temperature was taken, samples of the drool at the corners of Margolis's mouth were obtained, and additional close-up photographs of the body were also taken. With gloved hands, the ME unbuttoned Margolis's shirt; he did not visualize any evidence of injury. He did not feel any large fluid masses, or appreciate any bruising or subcutaneous emphysema (air) under the skin. The deceased's neck appeared to be normal. The ME found no evidence of bruising around the neck or throat area. He could not feel a broken hyoid bone or other stigmata of a possible strangulation. The deceased's back was also perfectly normal.

What the ME did find was an apparently well developed, healthy-appearing individual who died a very odd, and perhaps painful death in his apartment elevator. There was no evidence of foul play, but he was certainly unsettled to find the body in such an odd, twisted manner. The ME made a note to find out if there was any record of epilepsy when he pursued the deceased's medical history. After the ME was satisfied with his preliminary exam, he gave the okay for the body to be removed. Detective Rose asked the building manager for access into Margolis's apartment, and he took the service elevator up to the floor.

Rose opened the apartment door and turned on the light using a gloved hand. The first impression Rose had as he entered the unit was how tidy and clean Margolis kept his apartment. As he learned, the deceased was a scientist; it made sense that everything would be orderly. Rose started in the kitchen and was impressed by how immaculately clean it appeared. Rose thought about his own bachelor days and the disaster his kitchen area was. The cupboards were filled with neatly stacked dishes and glassware, and the pantry was well stocked with healthy foods. All of the opened boxes of cereal and pasta had been placed in plastic containers. Rose went through all of the kitchen cabinets, and was again struck by the organization of everything. The living and dining rooms were designed with a contemporary look. The glass shelves displaying pieces of art and souvenirs were evidence of someone with an active, interesting life. This was not the home of someone in distress or depressed. It had a vitality about it.

Rose walked into the bedroom. It too was immaculate—even the bed was made. Rose had entered many bachelor apartments and homes during his career. A well-made bed was the exception. The bathroom was clean and organized. The vanity was empty, with the exception of a bottle of cologne. Rose picked up the bottle with his gloved hand and noted the bottle looked full, as if it were brand new. His suspicion of the bottle being new was confirmed when he looked into the trash basket next to the vanity and noted a small black cologne box. He returned the cologne bottle onto the vanity. Rose then opened the medicine cabinet. As he expected, everything was in order and had a designated spot. Even the toothbrush had a defined location—he could tell by the small amount of white toothpaste residue on the shelf. It must have been where Margolis placed it after each use. A small drinking cup was next to it. This was odd, Rose thought. *Everything was apparently kept in the medicine cabinet... except the cologne? Perhaps it was recently purchased and hadn't secured a spot in the cabinet?* Rose made a mental note of this. Continuing his inspection of the cabinet contents, Rose was also struck by something else. Other than a container of *Tylenol*, a pink plastic bottle of *Pepto Bismol,* and a half-empty prescription bottle of *Ambien,* there were no other medications. Rose recalled the ME mentioning the need to find out if the deceased had any history of seizures or epilepsy. There was certainly nothing in here to suggest this. In fact, there was nothing to suggest any medical disorders at all.

Rose continued his evaluation of the apartment, turning up nothing unusual—until he did. Looking at Margolis's office chair next to his desk, he spotted the black edge of...yes...in the wedge between the seat and the back of the chair was a cell phone.

Rose quizzically looked at it for a moment. *How does someone this organized leave their cell phone on their chair? Perhaps it fell out while he was sitting there? Was he in a hurry, and it dropped out?* Rose took out an evidence bag from his pocket and carefully placed the phone into it with his gloved hand. Looking at the man's orderly desk, Rose noted a few opened letters. Two were bills, and a third appeared to be from the Human Resources Department at *Harris Therapeutics.* The letter was informing him of his need for an upcoming appointment to review his payroll deductions. Rose took note of the address of *Harris.*

Noting nothing else of importance at this time, Rose turned off the lights and closed the door. He now needed to find Margolis's next of kin to inform them of his death—a call he dreaded to make.

So why would an otherwise healthy man suddenly be found dead in his elevator? There was something missing in this matter that Rose couldn't identify, as he found the situation quite odd. Rose would await the medical examiner's findings and, in the meantime, would need to find out more about Robert Margolis. He put into his cellphone calendar the need to visit *Harris Therapeutics* tomorrow morning.

CHAPTER 33

Wheaton, IL

As an early riser, Detective Rose went to his office, filed his initial report of his investigation of Robert Margolis, handed off the evidence bag containing the cell phone, and was on his way to the western suburbs before 8 a.m. He reached the driveway of *Harris Therapeutics* at 9 a.m. sharp. Once inside the impressive facility, Rose went through the litany of security steps and was awaiting an escort to take him to where Margolis worked: the lab of Gene Cortes. After a few minutes, a young lab technician wearing a long, white coat appeared and led Rose towards the lab.

"So…welcome to *Harris*…may I ask what brings you here?" The inquisitive tech asked as they walked.

"I'd rather not discuss anything right now." Rose responded rather sharply. "I'm sure you will be informed of things in good time," he said, trying to take the edge off his initial response. The technician decided it best to remain quiet, and they continued their walk in silence towards Doctor Cortes's office. Once there, the tech asked him to take a seat, and someone else would assist. The tech scampered off looking intimidated as the detective thanked him and sat down. A young woman wearing jeans and a tee-shirt next approached Rose and invited him into Doctor Cortes's private office. As Rose sat there waiting, he looked around the room. The walls were covered with diplomas, certificates of accomplishment, and photographs taken with individuals Rose suspected were prominent in Cortes's field. The desk looked like a tornado just hit—it was covered with papers, journals, and books. A double-monitored computer sat on Cortes's desk. Next to one of the monitors, there was also a framed photograph. Rose looked at it carefully and recognized Bob Margolis next to Cortes, and assumed the others were lab members as well. The other framed images on the desk appeared to be family poses, perhaps his wife and children. As Rose was looking at the photos, the door opened quickly and a tall, handsome man with a trimmed beard entered. Rose saw the same face in the photographs, except this time, it wasn't smiling.

Rose stood from his seat. "Good morning, Doctor Cortes. My name is Detective Melvin Rose from the Chicago Police Department. I'm investigating…"

"Yes…I know…" Cortes quipped. He looked annoyed. "Another colleague of yours was here about two weeks ago. I told her everything I could. I appreciate your efforts, but I really don't know anything more I can tell you."

Rose looked confused and stated slowly, "I'm sorry, Doctor…I don't know what you're referring to…can you please explain? I don't have any colleagues who would have spoken to you yet."

Cortes stared at Rose for a confused moment. "I thought you were here to discuss Rebecca Sunnis. I was told a detective was here that wanted to talk to me. Isn't that why you're here?"

"Who is Rebecca Sunnis?" Rose asked.

Cortes pulled himself from behind his desk and sat down in a large chair directly across from Rose. He took a deep breath and began. "You really don't know? Rebecca was one of my lab associates. About two weeks ago she didn't come to work which was most unlike her. Rebecca was as dependable as they come—and one of the brightest researchers I've ever hired. Anyway, after a couple of days of unexplained absences, we learned she was found dead in her own bathtub. At first, everyone thought…" Cortes lowered his voice, "actually, many still believe, she died of an accidental drowning from too much wine while bathing. But another detective...give me a moment..." Cortes rifled through the papers on his desk and found her business card. "Ahh...yes... Detective Susan Blight from the Naperville Police Department." Cortes handed the card over to Rose. Rose pulled out his cellphone and took a photograph of the card before handing it back. He then pulled out his notepad to write down the details of what he was hearing. "Well, she came by and informed me confidentially, that Rebecca was found by autopsy to have been murdered. Apparently, they found arsenic in lethal quantities in her."

Rose could feel his pulse increasing as he listened intently to Cortes. His mind started to race thinking about the possibility Margolis's death could be related. Rose interrupted, "So, it was confirmed that..." Rose looked down to check his notes on the name. "Rebecca...was in fact, poisoned to death at her home?"

"Yes," Cortes said quietly. "But like I said, apparently, it's still being investigated. Nobody here at *Harris* knows these details. So, when I heard a detective was here, I assumed that was what you wanted to discuss. So, this is news to you? I mean, you really aren't here to discuss Rebecca's investigation?" Cortes's face turned white as he fell back in his chair. "Oh...for Christ's sake...why are you here then?" Cortes asked as he looked pleadingly at Rose.

Rose looked down at his notes as he tried to compose his thoughts. He said quietly, "Doctor Cortes, I have some very sad news for you... last night Robert Margolis was found dead in his apartment elevator."

Cortes looked like he was going to throw up. He started hyperventilating at the stinging news. His friend and colleague—*another* colleague, was found dead. "What the hell is going on!" Cortes slammed his fist on his desk. "These are good people...they are the best people!" It was obvious to both men these deaths were related. Rose now knew that whatever happened to Margolis was no accident. His death was not due to some medical condition, but had to be induced. Knowing the first victim was poisoned gave him more solid footing to suspect that a similar fate occurred to Margolis.

Rose looked at Cortes and noted his bloodshot eyes. Cortes was visibly shaking. Rose then asked, "Doctor Cortes...what type of work does your lab do here at *Harris*?"

Cortes stared at Rose as though the wind had been knocked out of him. He slumped in his chair, looked up to the ceiling, and seemed to be somewhere else for a moment. Cortes stated quietly, "We are working on developing drugs for treating cancer." Cortes regained some of his composure and sat upright. "We are developing next-generation, pharmacologic cancer therapies. There is nothing here other than that. We have no defense contracts, no special relationships with any countries…nothing. We develop new cancer drugs, that's all."

Rose wrote down a few notes and then stood up. "Doctor, I understand how hard this must be, but I'm going to ask that you keep our discussion private. Obviously, I think it's highly likely there must be a connection between these two deaths. At this time, we can't assume anything, or exclude anyone as a suspect—the perp…the perpetrator could potentially even be someone in the company. Obviously, I don't know if there was something that Margolis and Sunnis were working on together, or if they had been contacted by someone who might want to harm them. Has anyone in your lab complained to you, or have you noted anything unusual in anyone's daily routine?"

Cortes looked up at Rose and responded, "I haven't heard of anything unusual, but I'm sure when everyone at *Harris* hears of Bob's death, there will be pandemonium. This is a very tight company… everyone knows everyone. People will be scared."

Rose stated, "Nobody has determined that Margolis's death was a homicide yet. We still need to prove that. I want to talk to your CEO…I assume he's on the premises today?" Cortes nodded in the affirmative.

"I will have one of my staff take you to his office…it's upstairs. The CEO's office is always upstairs, right?" Cortes stated with a slight grin. Given the circumstances, that was all he could muster up.

Rose started to leave and then turned around and felt it necessary to repeat himself, "Please be careful what you say to others about this visit. At this time, we don't yet know who could be behind this. I must assume the perpetrator could also be an employee. Perhaps there was underlying anger or jealousy… perhaps something else. Please keep your eyes and ears open and let me know if you suspect anything. In the meantime, also be mindful of your own safety. I am going to talk to your CEO about additional security measures as we proceed. I'll stay in touch." With that, Detective Rose placed his card on the desk, shook Cortes's hand, and left. As soon as he was away from others, he made a call on his cell phone to the CPD crime lab. He informed the lab of his suspicion of a poisoning...and then he quickly hung up as a thought occurred to him. Rose ran out of the office waiting area and headed for the parking lot. The young lady in jeans ran after Rose reminding him to wait so she could escort him up to the main administrative offices.

"Tell the CEO I'll call him and set up a meeting...I need to run." Rose shouted, as he made his way out. The security personnel were running towards him as well, as they did not want any non-employees unaccompanied in their hallways.

Detective Rose finally reached his car on the enormous campus. He was gasping after the long sprint. He called on his cell phone for CPD to have a squad car in front of Margolis's apartment building and an officer stand outside Margolis's apartment door.

Detective Rose now understood this was most likely a murder case involving a poisoning. As he was talking to the crime lab, he thought about what he had seen in Margolis's apartment. There were no unlabeled or suspicious drug containers, and everything in the medicine cabinet seemed to have an allocated spot. Only one thing he recalled in the bathroom *was* out of place. The one thing that appeared new and possibly had never been used before Margolis's death—he wanted to secure the small bottle of cologne sitting on Bob Margolis's bathroom vanity.

CHAPTER 34

Wheaton, IL

Cortes was beside himself. Having weathered the loss of Rebecca Sunnis was hard enough, but to now deal with the death of another colleague and friend in Bob Margolis was just unbearable. Cortes called William Waters's office and asked the secretary if he could come up. As was typical in this small company, everyone had everyone else's back. He was, of course, welcome to meet with the CEO.

Gene Cortes took the short elevator ride up to the top floor of the building and walked the beautifully appointed hallway towards the head office. He was warmly greeted by the administrative staff, offered coffee, and then waited until Waters's completed his *Zoom* conference call. About ten minutes later, he was given the okay to see the boss.

The CEO's office could have doubled as an art gallery. The large rectangular room had a beautiful straw-colored bamboo, hardwood floor. The floor complemented burgundy, leather-covered walls. Because Waters did not want any nails or punctures to the smooth leather, all of the many contemporary paintings were suspended from the ceiling by fine wire. With the halogen lighting beaming down, the office looked like features in any architectural design magazine. Waters quickly stood up when Cortes entered. He too, was shaken by the loss of Rebecca and concerned about the rumors surrounding her death. He stepped out from behind his large, brushed-aluminum desk to shake Cortes's hand. The last time they saw each other was at the funeral for Rebecca.

"Bill, we've got trouble." Cortes started out.

Before he could get out another sentence, Waters stated, "I know Gene, I know. But we have to move on…"

"No, Bill…you don't understand…there has been another death!" Cortes shouted. "Bob Margolis died last night. He was found dead in his own apartment elevator! Two weeks ago, Rebecca, and now this!" Cortes had tears in his eyes as he thought about his relationship with these two colleagues he had worked so closely with. "What the hell is going on Bill? Have you heard anything…from anyone?"

Waters was visibly stunned by this news. Similar to Cortes's reaction with Detective Rose, he too, was expecting another discussion about Rebecca's death. After standing to greet Cortes, Waters slumped back down into his desk chair trying to absorb what he just heard. "This can't be…" Waters was mumbling quietly to himself. He then addressed Cortes, "What have we done…what's responsible…who's responsible for this, Gene?"

Cortes looked back with reddened eyes. "Bill, we're doing nothing different today then we were doing a year ago or even two years ago. This can't be coincidental. A detective came into my office this morning from Chicago. He said they didn't yet know the cause of Bob's death, but it isn't a stretch to imagine it was no accident. Has anyone contacted you? Any explanations or ransoms?"

Waters looked down at his desk and then he looked up to gaze at the beautiful artwork hanging. "Gene, I haven't heard a thing… nothing. I don't even know what we're supposed to do…I mean… what…what are we to do at this point if nobody is telling us what they want?" Waters was almost pleading with Cortes for answers. "Do we shut down *Harris*? What did the detective tell us to do?"

"He told me he was going to talk to you, but then I heard he quickly ran out of the building…he must have heard something." Cortes responded.

Waters was gaining his strength back. He looked at Cortes and stated, "How do we protect ourselves? I mean, is this happening to us from outside? Could it be from inside? I just don't know where to turn for help…" Waters trailed off as he looked up at the bare, cement ceiling. "Do you have the detective's card, or number? I need to talk to him…we need a plan to protect ourselves…and the company!"

Cortes replied, "Yes…I have the detective's card and number on my desk. I also have the card from the Naperville detective. What the hell is going on, Bill? Okay, well, let me go get the contact information and I'll text it to you. I'm also going home. I need to get my head around all of this." Cortes stood and looked at Waters directly. "I'm sorry all of this is happening, Bill. I just don't know what to say."

Waters stood up, shook Cortes's hand, and shrugged his shoulders. "I don't even know where to begin."

Cortes got up and went down the elevator to his office. He located the two detective's cards and texted the information to William Waters. He then turned off the lights to his office, closed the door, and informed his administrative assistant that he was going home for the rest of the day. She looked at him curiously, but didn't dare ask for any details.

Cortes got into his car and left the *Harris* campus. The twenty-minute commute went quickly as he was preoccupied with the recent events and discussions. As Cortes ruminated about possible links between the recent deaths and the work being done at *Harris Therapeutics,* he tried to think of any enemies. He then reminded himself he's a damn biological scientist—trying to find treatments for cancer! *What could he be doing to cause two workers in his lab to die?* Cortes's racing thoughts were disrupted as he drove up to his small suburban home in Bolingbrook, Illinois. He noted an unfamiliar car in his driveway. *Perhaps it was the detective? But why would he be in the house?* His wife was out of the country with the kids, and it was the housekeeper's day off. Cortes noted the license plate was not a municipal plate number, which would have begun with an *M. Something was not right!* Whoever it is, they certainly weren't hiding their presence. Cortes calmed down as he considered how unlikely it was that someone coming to do him harm would park in front of his home in broad daylight. He reminded himself that he had to get a grip, as he was completely consumed with work events.

Cortes gathered himself and approached the front door. It was 2 p.m. on a Tuesday; he considered if anybody wanted to find him, they certainly wouldn't be at his home at this hour. *Wouldn't they just try to see him at work? So, what could this be about?* Cortes took out his front door key and opened the door slowly. Nothing appeared out of the ordinary. As expected, all the lights were out, and there was no sound. *Perhaps the visiting owner of the car was in the backyard?* Cortes went into his small kitchen, which had a backdoor leading to the yard. Just as he entered the room, Cortes let out a gasp as he noted a stranger sitting at his breakfast table reading a small book.

"Who the hell are you…and what are you doing in my house?" Cortes shouted. Given all that had gone in in recent weeks, his first thought was that he was in imminent danger. Cortes tried to estimate his distance from the butcher block of knives on the counter near the sink.

"Relax, Doctor Cortes, I'm not here to hurt you. On the contrary, I'm here to ask for your help. I've been here waiting for you to come home, and I thought you would show up later. I'm delighted we can meet now." The voice from the stranger had a calmness and cadence that lulled Cortes out of his adrenaline-induced posture. The man stood and extended his hand for Cortes to shake.

"I asked, who you are?" Cortes again stated, with less fear and more curiosity in his voice this time.

The calm voice started, "I am a doctor, like you. Well, not exactly such as yourself. I'm not a research scientist, rather, my degree is in medicine." The stranger accepted that Cortes was not going to shake his hand. He continued talking with his calm demeanor and sat back down, facing Cortes. "Please, won't you sit? I think you'll find what I'm here to say is most interesting." The stranger pointed to the empty chair across the table. "I promise you—I'm not here to harm you in any way…please." The man again gestured to Cortes to sit.

Cortes sat down as requested. He felt like a stranger in his own home. Cortes put his briefcase down and sat across the unidentified man. Cortes asked, "Okay, so you're an MD, or so you say. What right does that give you to be in my home without my permission?"

The man smiled. "Actually, none. I promise you; I will leave shortly. But, before you send me on my way, don't you want to know why I'm here?"

Cortes acquiesced. "Fine, tell me why you are here, and then you can leave, or I will call the police."

"Fair enough, Doctor Cortes." The stranger began speaking very slowly and quietly. "I'm sure you noticed some of your co-workers are no longer with us. A tragedy I know, but a necessary predicate for what I'm going to ask of you. You see, Doctor Cortes, I work for someone who very much wants to have something you possess. I'm quite sure if I came here several weeks ago, you would have sent me on my way. But as we now sit, I believe you have witnessed what I am capable of. What I want from you is actually quite simple. I suspect you could, perhaps, give it to me now and we would never see each other again. I would be out of your life forever, and the unfortunate events that occurred to your friends and colleagues would be ancient history."

Cortes readjusted his position in his chair and said, "Go on."

"Well," the stranger continued as he stared directly at Cortes, "what I want from you is the synthesis protocol for the mRNA molecule used to create a specific cytotoxic T cell. You know which one—you developed this in your lab. The individual I work for doesn't want any of the mRNA itself. He wants the formula, the recipe, if you will, so he can make it himself."

"And why would I give this to you..." Cortes asked, anticipating the response.

"Well, that's easy to answer. If you refuse to give me what I am requesting, I'm afraid someone else dear to you will experience the same fate as your deceased friends. I think we've established I'm quite capable of slipping into and out of anyone's life quite easily. Should you fail to deliver what I'm requesting or attempt to notify anyone of this... *request*...well, I think you understand the consequences."

Cortes stared back at the stranger with absolute disdain. He asked, "And what guarantee do I have that you will honor what you say…that you will be out of my life forever?"

"Oh…none whatsoever, Doctor." The stranger replied as he smiled and crossed his legs. "But what I can guarantee is the corollary. If you *don't* comply, there will be hell to pay. And the number of individuals who will pay for your stubbornness will potentially be…unlimited. My suggestion, Doctor—and it's just that—is that you simply retrieve the synthesis protocol and hand it over to me. Easy. Just like that, and this nightmare for you will be over."

Cortes sat quietly for a moment as his eyes darted about the small room. He stated, "Certainly, with your medical background, you understand that simply having the protocol does not allow anyone to just walk into a lab and start making the mRNA. Even a sophisticated lab can take months, perhaps even years, to get up and running. Equipment requisites, obtaining the proper chemicals and biologicals from vendors—assuming there aren't any shortages or delivery delays—takes time. Setting up and assigning work-flows for associates in the lab requires more time and logistical planning. Acquiring the protocol is just the beginning of being able to actually synthesize it. Then the product must go through rigorous analyses to assure that what you made is exactly what is required. And despite the detailed algorithm for synthesis, each lab has its own variability. Accommodations and potential alterations must be made to produce exactly what is expected. This isn't like making a damn cake. But you already know all this, right? Because you're a doctor—or so you say. I don't think you have a fucking clue how difficult it is to produce a pharmaceutical grade product."

With an eerie calmness the stranger replied, "I think you underestimate my understanding, Doctor Cortes,"

Cortes was gaining his strength, and replied, "No, I don't. What… because you know how to mix…what was it…arsenic in wine? Jesus, a third grader could mix that together. All you need to know is how much…not too difficult to figure out. No. I don't think I underestimate your lack of understanding. I think you're some medical wash-out who gets paid a shitload more money than any of those devoted researchers you killed. And I'm supposed to believe you're some chemical expert? Well, I got news…you're not." The man was now losing his patience with the situation. It was obvious Cortes was not as soft as he first appeared.

Just then, Cortes decided a different tack. "Fine. What you've done can't be changed. Those whom you've killed won't come back. Whatever it is that you want, well, you can have it. My suspicion is that, at the end of the day, it's all about money and greed, and my life is more valuable than that. So yes, I will get you the precious synthesis protocol. That is what you asked me for. What you do with it, how long it takes you to get it up and running, well, that's not my concern. And no, I don't have it memorized and I don't have it here in my home. I will go to my lab and copy it. How do you want it?"

The stranger stood. Although he wanted to counter Cortes's comments about his knowledge and capabilities, he accomplished what he wanted, and knew it was time to leave. He also knew Cortes was correct about the time factors and potential complications of producing such a complex molecule. That was not his problem—he was hired to get the protocol.

The stranger stated quietly, "You will go to your lab. You will copy the synthesis protocol on this flash drive." He reached into his pocket and placed on the kitchen table the small thumb drive. "I will contact you and tell you where and when to leave it. You will inform no one of this meeting—ever. If you are compliant, then we will never meet again, and you can rest assured I will not harm you. It there is any deviation from what I just stated, your world will soon become extraordinarily painful. Am I clear, Doctor?"

Cortes responded dejectedly, "Yes, we are clear."

The stranger walked towards the entrance into the kitchen. Just before he pushed apart the cheap wooden, swinging doors, he turned around and faced Cortes. "Just one more thing I need to add to our conditions, Doctor. The synthesis protocol you are handing over had better work. I don't care if it takes two weeks or two years to test what you are delivering to me. If it fails to produce what my employer wants, I will find you. You had better hope they succeed in producing what they want." He then walked out. Cortes could hear the front door open and close as the stranger exited the home.

Cortes sat very still for a few minutes as he replayed the conversation he just had with the stranger. Cortes understood that whoever this person is, he was capable of doing what he threatened. And no doubt, the molecular synthesis protocol was going to be used for a new drug as it had no other purpose. Christ, it's an mRNA molecule designed to stimulate antibody production. Part of Cortes was of the mindset to simply hand the protocol over and move on. After all, this is not his fight. Another part was angry at how his work was being stolen, and precious lives had been taken by this monster. Cortes conceded that he just couldn't give this formula away. He knew he could make a slight modification to the formula that would prevent the synthesis protocol from ever working. Maybe it would take whoever is taking this protocol months to discover this alteration. Hopefully the detectives could solve this crime before that time is ever reached. Cortes realized he could only hope so.

CHAPTER 35

Chicago, IL

Prior to going into his first procedure of the day, Yamp called Margolis. Again, he listened to the voicemail monologue. Yamp left a message asking for Margolis to return it when able. It was odd, he thought, but well, who knows? Yamp had a four-hour, robotic-assisted, surgical procedure on the table, so his inability to reach Margolis would have to take a back seat. The day was long and full for Yamp, and he never gave a second thought about Margolis's absence. Although disturbing, Yamp decided to forget about the failed return call. It wasn't until the beginning of the following week when Yamp was sitting in his office and decided to reach out again. After all, the two of them still had a golf day approaching. When he dialed Margolis's cell phone this time, he no longer heard the now-familiar voicemail message. Instead, Yamp listened to an automated recording informing him that the number he dialed was no longer in service. *This is certainly odd*, Yamp considered, and he then asked his office assistant to contact *Harris Therapeutics* directly. Once connected, the call was forwarded to Yamp at his desk.

"Good afternoon, this is Doctor Jay Yamp at University Hospital. Can you connect me to Doctor Robert Margolis, please?"

"I'm sorry, your name again, sir?" the telephone operator at *Harris* responded.

"Yamp, Doctor Jay Yamp," he answered with less charm. Yamp could feel himself getting slightly annoyed with all of this effort. *After all, I have left him several messages,* he reminded himself while waiting. Yamp could hear telephone clicks as it sounded as though his call was going through. *Finally*, he thought.

"Ahh, Doctor Yamp…" the unknown voice stated.

"Yes, this is Jay Yamp. May I speak with Bob Margolis," Yamp stated clearly.

"Well, sir…my name is Edwin Robinson…I am the lab coordinator for Gene Cortes's lab here at *Harris…* "

"Yes…well, thank you Mr. Robinson, perhaps the operator misdirected this call. I'm trying to reach Bob Margolis." Yamp stated.

"Are you a friend of Bob's or a professional acquaintance?" Mr. Robinson inquired.

Yamp pulled the phone away from his ear and looked at it while trying to understand why Margolis is suddenly so hard to reach. He returned the phone to his ear, "I'm not quite sure I understand the relevance, sir. I'm simply trying to reach Bob…uhh…we are friends… and well, yes…I'm also a colleague. I'm The Chair of Urology at University Hospital. May I please speak with him?" There was a long pause on the other end of the line. "Hello…Mr. Robinson…are you there?" Yamp asked.

"Ahh…yes sir…I'm sorry, Doctor…but…ahh…Doctor Margolis passed away a few days ago. I'm sorry you are now finding out about this." Robinson said solemnly.

"What!" Yamp shouted into the telephone. "I was supposed to have dinner with him…what…last Thursday…let's see…that's four days ago!" Yamp stated in disbelief.

"Well, I'm sorry Doctor…wait…did you say Thursday?" Robinson asked.

"Yes…yes…we were supposed to meet for dinner at 6:30 p.m. last Thursday at this new barbecue restaurant. I don't recall the name of the place, but he never showed up. I've been leaving him messages without any return, so that's why I decided to try him at work. What the hell happened?" Yamp asked while shaking his head.

"Well, sir…we really don't know all the answers at this time. From what we've been told, he was found dead in his apartment building elevator…actually…last Thursday night…could it be he was on his way to see you?" Mr. Robinson asked.

"Are you kidding me!" Yamp replied. "I'm sorry…ahh, yes…that could be. I mean, I spoke to him maybe a few hours before we were to meet. That's when we made the arrangements to have dinner together. He sounded perfectly fine on the phone…I mean, he was happy and excited to get together. He did mention…well, something else he wanted to talk about…but I don't recall. My God…this is not the conversation I was anticipating when I called…I mean…is there any investigation…I mean…is there a funeral scheduled?"

"Yes, Doctor…I do know the police have been here…actually… there was a detective here a couple of weeks ago…" Robinson stated.

Yamp cut in, "A couple of weeks ago? I thought you just said Bob died four days ago…what is going on over there?"

Mr. Robinson replied sounding rattled. "Yes, sir…I know…it's been rather chaotic here…but I'm not sure I have the liberty to discuss all of this. I'll find out about the funeral and send you the information. Can you give me your email address?"

Yamp held the phone in silence for a few moments as he tried to process what he was hearing. It was obvious there was very unusual and highly suspicious activity going on at *Harris.* Yamp understood he would not be getting the information he wanted from Mr. Robinson. He gave Robinson his email address, thanked him for his time, and disconnected the call. Yamp decided he would try to find out what he could, but wasn't really sure where he should start.

CHAPTER 36

Chicago, IL

The cologne bottle was retrieved and analyzed carefully at the crime lab. Knowing the details of Rebecca Sunnis's death helped direct the investigation in the right direction. Rose discussed the case with the pathologist assigned to perform the autopsy. The toxicology evaluation of the cologne revealed highly toxic levels of what the pathologist called a *V-series* nerve agent. The pathologist explained, "Certain cholinesterase levels may be decreased after exposure to certain agents, and exposed individuals may demonstrate lab abnormalities consistent with metabolic acidosis and the breakdown of skeletal muscles." The pathologist continued, "The *V-series* agents are organophosphate esters. They are extremely potent acetylcholinesterase inhibitors, and their biological effects include seizures, salivation, diaphoresis, vomiting, and muscle spasms. These effects appear to be consistent with what was reported from the crime scene." After ruling out other potential causes, the pathologist concluded that the autopsy and chemical analyses of the cologne bottle in his home were consistent with *V-series,* or Novichok agent poisoning.

The case was now officially classified as a homicide, which gave Detective Rose additional resources to assist in the investigation. Rose received a detailed listing of Margolis's cell phone text messages, contact list, and recent calls. He was most interested in the last voicemail recording made on the night Margolis was found in the elevator. The time stamp of the message and associated texts were all from someone named, Jay Yamp.

Rose noted the name and number of Yamp, and he decided to find out more about this person before he contacted him. It would be highly unlikely that anyone involved in a plot to murder someone would be stupid enough to leave their traceable number on a victim's phone, but Rose had seen it all. He knew better than to ever confuse the degree of intent with the intelligence of the perpetrator.

Back in his office, Detective Rose was intrigued to find out Yamp was really *Doctor* Yamp, a urological surgeon and professor with an outstanding reputation. Rose contacted Yamp's office and made an appointment to visit with him that afternoon. In the interim, Rose went through additional calls and texts lifted from Margolis's phone. None appeared to have urgency or threat—there was no evidence of any malfeasance. Rose went through Margolis's last month of credit card charges. Again, nothing stood out as out of place or unusual. No charges were placed for any type of personal hygiene products; in particular, no cologne was purchased. Perhaps the barely used, tainted bottle Rose found in the bathroom was a gift. Finally, Rose reviewed Margolis's bank statements. There were no unusual deposits or withdrawals over the past six months. Margolis's life appeared squeaky clean—not even a damn parking ticket.

Rose completed his tedious background work, and then drove to University Hospital to meet Doctor Yamp. He wasn't quite sure what to expect; from the doctor's curriculum vitae and multiple reviews, Rose understood Yamp was well respected in the medical field. He suspected Yamp would be a stodgy, unapproachable academic.

As soon as Rose walked the distance from his car to the hospital lobby, and then to the attached professional building, he felt he had achieved his daily 10,000 steps. The hospital facility and campus were enormous. It had been awhile since he visited a hospital, but they now looked like fancy hotels, with atriums and lobbies the size of football fields. The buildings were packed with people walking in every direction. It felt like a small city—a well-financed city at that, Rose mumbled to himself.

Upon reaching Yamp's private office, Rose was greeted by Yamp's office assistant. "Hello, Detective Rose. My name is Arnold Jackson. I work for Professor Yamp. Please take a seat, and I'll let him know you are here." Rose sat down in the small anteroom as the large man disappeared through an attached door. He returned momentarily and told the detective to go on in, pointing towards the room he just came from.

Upon entering, Yamp was finishing up a call. He stood up with the desk phone still in his hand, extended his free hand to shake Rose's, and then motioned for Rose to take a seat. Rose did as instructed. As Yamp was doing his best to end the call, Rose looked around the office. Again, a wall of accolades and certificates seemed to be the designer theme for these academics. Another wall was covered with photographs, apparently taken by the doctor himself. Rose could make out the doctor's signed name on the matting beneath each image. He also noted a small collection of trophies under the window. They looked like they each had a small metallic golfer on top—not at all what he was expecting.

Yamp completed his call, loosened, and then removed his tie, and looked directly at detective Rose. He began, "Detective, I am so glad you are here. What the hell is going on?"

Rose was a bit taken aback by Yamp's directness. He liked him immediately. "You're absolutely right, Doctor. What the…hell…is going on? Well, why don't we begin by you telling me how you know… err…knew, Robert Margolis."

"Of course," Yamp began. He sat upright in his office chair. "I heard of Bob's work at *Harris Therapeutics*. He was a major investigator on work coming out of there…he worked quite closely with Gene Cortes, a big name in oncologic pharmaceutical research. Anyway, I have an interest in cancer research and was invited to play in a golf event sponsored by *Harris*, oh…maybe three weeks ago or so. I was fortunate to be paired up with Bob, and we had a wonderful time playing golf and getting to know one another. We both wanted to get together again to play more golf and also see if we could develop a partnership with *Harris* and my own lab's work here at University Hospital. We talked… or maybe texted…I'm not sure…a couple of weeks ago. We set up a golf date…actually for this coming weekend. Anyway, last week…I believe…yes, it was Thursday, we spoke and decided we would meet for dinner…sort of a last-minute thing. We were supposed to meet at 6:30 p.m. at this new restaurant he wanted to try. So, I got there a little early and ordered a couple of beers while waiting for him. But Bob never showed up. I texted him and even called. I left a message."

"I know," stated Rose.

Yamp continued, "Yes...well, anyway, I guess I must have left about forty-five minutes later. I think I may have called him the following morning...thinking something must have come up. Again, I never heard from him. I again tried earlier this week...Monday, I believe...I called, but his number was disconnected. So, I decided to call him at work." Rose listened carefully. Everything Yamp said checked out exactly as it happened. "So, when I called *Harris Therapeutics,* I was connected with someone...someone named Robinson...that's it. Robinson told me there was some chaos or something to that effect at *Harris*, and Bob had died a few days before I called. I also recall..." Yamp now looked up at the ceiling as he was trying to remember something.

"Go ahead, Doctor..." Rose stated while carefully listening.

"Yes...Bob told me during our phone conversation while we were planning to meet for dinner that he was upset about something at work. I think it was the chaos that Robinson was referring to, but he never explained it. Do you know what he was talking about?"

Rose stared directly at Yamp. He was considering his possible responses to Yamp's question.

Rose knew Yamp had been completely honest and forthright with him. More importantly, Rose knew, legally, none of what had recently transpired was privileged, as others knew of it as well. "I may need your help downstream with this case, Doctor. What I'm going to tell you is not classified, but I also do not want it discussed with anyone. I want you to keep it to yourself for now. Are we clear?"

Yamp leaned forward in his chair and nodded.

Rose stated quietly, "What killed Doctor Margolis was poison."

Yamp asked incredulously, "Bob was poisoned? By whom...for what reason? I mean, I know you don't know the answers...I mean..."

Yamp trailed off without completing his sentence. He looked around the room as he was obviously thinking through what he just heard. "Is this what Robinson meant when he said there was chaos at *Harris?* Was Bob being threatened by someone at work?"

"No, Doctor...its worse than that." Rose said flatly.

"Okay...well...go on." Yamp said impatiently, with his hand extended waiting for an answer.

"There was another death a couple of weeks earlier...another employee...a researcher at *Harris*. She also worked with Doctor Margolis."

"This is unbelievable," Yamp said quietly. He looked down at his desk taking in what he just heard, and then he suddenly looked up at Rose. "No...don't tell me..."

Rose read his mind and responded, "Yes...it was also a poisoning."

"What the hell! Was it the same one...I mean, the same poison?" Yamp asked quickly.

"No. The woman who was murdered a few weeks ago died from arsenic poisoning. Doctor Margolis died of what appeared to be a Novichok nerve agent." Rose said quietly.

Yamp asked, "Novichok? Isn't that what the Russians have used? Have there been any demands or ransom...any threats?"

"Nope. None. It's odd." Rose stated. "I'm trying to figure out how the perp...the perpetrator got the Novichok in Doctor Margolis's apartment."

"You mean to tell me you found the poison...you identified the source in his apartment?" Yamp asked, skeptically.

"Yes...it was in a small bottle of cologne in his bathroom. It looked as though he had never used any of it before as the bottle was still full." Rose answered.

Yamp looked out of the window as he was thinking about what he just heard. He stated slowly, "That's odd…I…"

Rose interrupted him, "What's odd? What are you thinking about, Doctor?"

Yamp looked at Rose and said, "It's probably nothing."

Rose stared at Yamp and said, "No, please, tell me what you think might be nothing."

Yamp replied, "Well, I was just thinking about when I first met Bob…at this golf outing…we each got a small bottle of a cologne in our gift bags…I don't see…"

"Please describe the cologne, Doctor Yamp," Rose stated, as he readied his pen ready to write.

Yamp again looked up at the ceiling while thinking. He stated, "Well, it was in this small black box…and I think…"

"My God," Rose blurted. That's it!" "It's a small black box that contains the bottle. By all means, Doctor, do not open that box! I'll send someone to your home to retrieve it."

Yamp looked at Rose. "Actually, I put it in my surgical locker here at the hospital. But sure, I'll get it to you." Yamp then looked painfully at Rose, "Detective, as I recall, *everyone* at that golf event received a bottle of that cologne in their gift bag."

Rose looked stunned. He quickly asked Yamp, "You stated *Harris Therapeutics* sponsored that golf outing, right?"

"Why yes…it was their effort to bring in clients and showcase their work…" Yamp stated and was then cut off as Rose put his hand up in the air signaling Yamp to stop.

Rose pulled his cellphone out of his jacket breast pocket and dialed his office. "John, its Mel…listen, we may have more bottles of that Novichok cologne out in the open. I need you to contact *Harris Therapeutics*…I don't know...call them...perhaps the media department...no, try public relations...and get the listing of all the guests at a golf outing they had about three weeks ago. We need to contact everyone who received a black box containing a cologne. Apparently, it was in a gift bag all the participants received. Find out their numbers and tell them...I don't know...that there has been a recall of that cologne and under no circumstances is anyone to use it...that its dangerous...well, think of something...we don't need a panic situation...but we need to get those bottles! Yes...okay...thank you." Rose disconnected the call.

A few minutes passed as Yamp and Rose were contemplating the situation. Rose's phone vibrated, and recognizing the number, he answered it quickly and spoke into the phone, "Yes, John...what have you got? No way! I'm sitting with someone who was at the event... he said he got it in the gift bag they gave away! Okay...okay. Go do some detective work...find out how that cologne found its way into the damn bags!" Rose clicked the phone off.

Yamp looked at Rose and asked, "What was that all about?"

Rose looked dejected. He stated, "My associate located the department at *Harris* that set up the golf event. They had a list of all the names of the participants, and a listing of all the sponsors who contributed tee-gifts for the players. A gift of a bottle of cologne was not on the list."

Yamp stated emphatically, "That is where I got the cologne! Either they are wrong, or someone unknown to the *Harris* organizers put that cologne in...*each* bag!" After that statement both men were suddenly very quiet as they considered what Yamp just implied.

Rose looked directly at Yamp and stated very solemnly, "We've got a problem. No. That is an understatement. We have a much *bigger* problem than I was aware of when I walked in here." Rose looked slightly pale. "This is obviously a multi-jurisdictional case that could affect everyone who played golf in that event. We may have a disaster on our hands. We need the assistance of the FBI on this."

Yamp looked at Rose and stated, "I think I may be able to help with this." Yamp went to his phone and called his assistant who was busy in the anteroom. "Arnold, can you look through my contact list and get me the phone number of FBI Deputy Director Robert Jacoby. I need to speak with him."

Rose looked quizzically at Yamp. He stated, "How in the hell do you know the Deputy Director of the FBI?" Rose then happened to glance over at the many framed photographs near the windowsill and noted one with Yamp and the deputy director together.

Yamp said smiling, "I met Robert about 7 years ago when he was investigating…" Yamp stopped speaking for a moment as the details came back to him. Then he started again. "That's interesting…"

"What…what's interesting?" Rose asked.

Yamp began, "Well, I met Robert Jacoby as he…well, really, *we* were investigating a series of deaths here at University Hospital. It turned out behind everything was a pharmaceutical company… *Yonie*…that's it…it was *Yonie Pharmaceuticals.* Actually, they are headquartered up in Glenview…about 45 minutes north of here. Anyway, *Yonie* was involved in some scheme trying to illegally promote their sale of opioids—or at least someone at the company was. But because the deaths occurred here at University Hospital, I spent a fair amount of time with Robert. It was a remarkable series of events that should be written about one day; it would make a great story. Anyway, a couple years after that—actually sometime after the COVID outbreak—there was another company selling online drugs. Give me a moment…yes…the company was called, *Alive.* They were based out of Slovenia. Anyway, it was a complex case where people who purchased the drugs were being blackmailed. Because multiple deaths occurred, the FBI was brought in. I saw Robert in the cafeteria one day as he was working the case, and well, we just started meeting after that. Over the course of his investigation, we became friends."

"Yes, that's interesting, but it sounded as though something else struck you as you were thinking about this." Rose stated.

Yamp continued, "Yes, well, what I was just thinking, in these cases where I interacted with Robert Jacoby, drugs were also involved. I mean, *Yonie Pharmaceuticals* makes drugs, *Alive* sold drugs, and now… *Harris Therapeutics* develops them."

Rose looked at Yamp. "That is odd, isn't it? Well, whatever the reasons are you befriended him is alright by me. I think we could use whatever help we can get. This case just grew exponentially." Rose stood to leave. "Doctor Yamp, I'm glad we met. I'm sorry it's under these circumstances, as you lost a friend." He extended his hand to shake. "As you can understand, we have to go through proper channels to get FBI involvement, but a call to Jacoby couldn't hurt."

Yamp shook Rose's outstretched hand and stated, "Yes, I'll get on it. If I can be of any further assistance, please call. I'll let you know if I can think of anything else that might be useful to you, and I won't open that bottle of cologne. I don't know the woman who died, but Bob Margolis was not only a nice guy, but he was also a rising star in the field of cancer therapeutics. Whoever did this must be caught."

The two men said goodbye. As Rose walked back to his car, he considered how all of these lives and events he was investigating seemed to intersect together. He also could not believe that Jay Yamp had a direct line to the Deputy Director of the FBI. Rose had a slightly more upbeat pace to his walk on the way out of the colossal hospital. He reminded himself they are going to catch the son-of-a-bitch who is responsible for all of this.

CHAPTER 37

Chicago, IL

"Hey Jay…it's great to hear your voice!" Robert Jacoby stated with authentic enthusiasm.

"So, how are things in our nation's capital, Robert?" Yamp replied. "Are you helping to keep us all safe?"

"Well, Jay, to be honest, I feel all I do is shuffle papers around on my desk. I really do miss being out in the field and getting my hands dirty. I spend most of my day in one meeting after another, as we make plans to plan our next meeting. I mean, it's like being caught inside of a circle you can't get out of. It's odd, but the Director has a very defined role of what it is he does and how he goes about his business. But as the *Deputy Director,* my job description is a bit more vague. I mostly fill in the gaps for engagements and various committees. Nothing really seems dependent upon my presence or actions. But…I like to think I have some influence on the direction of policy within the bureau. So, tell me, what's going on? What trouble are you finding yourself in these days?" Jacoby asked jokingly.

Yamp changed his disposition. "Well, to be honest there is something going on that will probably require the bureau's intervention." Yamp explained in detail the poisoning deaths of his friend and the woman at *Harris Therapeutics*. He went on to describe the concern about the possibility of additional poisonings occurring from the cologne bottles that were distributed at the golf outing. "To make matters even worse, the organizers of the event have no record of the cologne bottles even being part of the gift bags that were handed out!"

"Jay…you're right. This is a true threat. And you said no ransom or notice of responsibility has occurred?" Jacoby made sure he heard correctly.

"Not that I'm aware of, Robert. But given these series of deaths and knowing the manner with which they were killed, wouldn't that be cause for the FBI to assist the investigation?" Yamp asked.

"Well, technically, deaths are not considered a series unless three or more have occurred. However, your Chicago detective is correct… these murders occurred in multiple jurisdictions, and for that reason, the FBI can come in. I'm quite concerned about the potential for more to come…but not necessarily from the cologne bottles." Jacoby stated.

"How do you reach that conclusion, Robert?" Yamp asked, wondering how the Deputy Director could reach that decision so quickly.

Jacoby explained his point. "Well, both deaths occurred to specific individuals who not only worked at the same company, but who worked in the same lab at the company. These murders were not random by any means. I don't see why a perpetrator who obviously made detailed study of his victims lives—to know both how and when to get the poison to them in such a surgical manner—would then distribute a poison at a large event like the golf outing. The deaths from the outing would then be random. Whoever sent these poisons knew his victims well and was doing this for a specific purpose. Poisoning a mass of people does not fit the modus operandi of the perp."

Yamp listened carefully to the expert. "You're making sense Robert…but…"

Jacoby then cut in, "My bigger concern is the risk to other employees at *Harris*, and in particular, those that work in that lab. If your detective has the manpower and resources to retrieve the cologne bottles, well, okay. I'm not saying it's wrong, but I just don't think the effort will bear results. I'll call the Chicago office to get an agent over to *Harris* and see what's going on. I'm sure it's a shit show over there right now. I'll keep you posted, Jay."

"Thank you, Robert. I appreciate your help." Yamp stated. "I was telling the detective that every time you and I have been part of an investigation, it always seems to revolve around the drug business." There was a pause in the conversation as Jacoby was processing what Yamp just stated.

"Yes, you're right Jay…it was *Yonie Pharmaceuticals* and then *Alive*…sure…I remember. And now *Harris Therapeutics* is the target of something nefarious. Well, I'll see what I can do to help figure this out. Anyway…I'm sorry to hear from you under these circumstances. If and when I get back to Chicago, we have to go out for beer and some deep-dish pizza."

Yamp replied, "Its on me, Robert. Many thanks." The phone call was disconnected. Yamp slowly put the phone back into its cradle and sat back in his chair. He thought about *Yonie Pharmaceuticals* and how that catastrophe of events was initiated by his old colleague Max Conit. They had worked together on a terrific hydrogel project for kidney stones. It, too, was insidiously used as a poison, of sorts, Yamp reconciled.

Thinking about that project peeked Yamp's curiosity to learn what was going on in the pharmaceutical world. *Did the lab where Bob and the other woman work discover something of significant value? Was that value medicinal or financial? Is there a difference today?* Yamp suspected a new drug development project was going on at *Harris Therapeutics,* and it was responsible for the recent tragic events. Yamp had no resources at *Harris* that could fill him in. As *Yonie Pharmaceuticals* certainly had its problems in the past, it was a juggernaut in the industry and had ties to many pharmacologic investigations going on in the world. Despite the debacle that occurred years ago in their Pain Management Division, *Yonie's* Oncologic Pharmaceutical Division was well respected. Yamp picked up his cell phone and searched for the mobile number of someone he knew at *Yonie* in oncology. His friend there *might* know something about what was going on at *Harris*—or know of someone who does.

"You've reached the mobile phone of Jason Kogan. I'm not available to take your call at the moment, but please leave a message and I'll return your call as soon as possible." The message was followed by an automated tone.

"Hi Jason, long time, no hear. Its Jay Yamp. Can you kindly give me a call? Thank you." Yamp left the brief message and hung up. Satisfied that his curiosity would soon be addressed, Yamp tried to go back to the bottomless *inbox* on his desk, but too much had transpired that day. After a full day of surgery, meeting with detective Rose, talking to Robert Jacoby, and now trying to understand what was evolving at *Harris*, Yamp couldn't focus on the work in front of him. He looked at his watch and saw it was now around 5:30 p.m. There was probably at least another two hours of good sunlight. Yamp grabbed his keys, shut off the lights, and closed the door to his office. Everyone else in the department had already left for the day. It was time to get all of this off his mind and go to the driving range and hit a bucket of golf balls.

CHAPTER 38

Chicago, IL

It wasn't until the next day that Jason Kogan returned Yamp's call. "Jay, it's Jason…how have you been?"

Yamp began, "Thanks Jason…all is fine…work is work…you know. The reason I called, Jason, is because a friend of mine was…well…he worked at *Harris Therapeutics*, and he was recently found murdered." Yamp just remembered that Detective Rose asked him to keep this quiet.

"Oh, man…I'm sorry to hear…murdered?" Kogan responded.

Yamp began, "Yes, well…it's actually a bit worse than that…please keep this whole conversation just between us…please. Anyway, one of his co-workers at *Harris* also…ahh…died. Obviously, something is going on over there. The police, and now the FBI are going to get involved. I know you have eyes and ears at *Yonie* that might have some knowledge as to what's going on over there at *Harris*. Have you heard anything?"

After a brief hesitation, Kogan responded, "Well, actually, Jay, I was let go from Yonie…they didn't like that I was opposed to their efforts to move away from chemotherapeutics and throw everything into immunology and biologicals for cancer therapy. I mean, I certainly understand where things are moving…but you just can't throw away fifty years of work…" Kogan trailed off.

"No, of course not," Yamp stated quickly. "Of course, the biologicals are looking promising, but we've had great success with some chemo agents…look at *Platinum*-based treatments for testicular cancer…I can't believe *Yonie* wants to pull out of that area of drug development."

Kogan continued, "I agree, it's really a shame. Well, you know how it is…they are going where the money is—its business. Anyway, I was rather outspoken in my disagreement with the Board, and they decided to replace me with an idiot who knows nothing but will be a terrific *yes* man. I think it's a mistake, but what can I say? Maybe they're right, and I'm just a dinosaur."

Yamp got on his pedestal. "No…there is ample evidence both types of treatments can co-exist. They will work synergistically for some diseases. But to change over a complete line of known, effective treatments purely for profitability is an abomination. Well, I suspect other companies will now capitalize on *Yonie's* decision. They will find a way to fill in the gaps and start making the chemotherapy line that Yonie is dropping—probably at a higher cost. It really is a drug war among these Goliath's—a race to the top…and for what? How much profit is enough?"

Kogan replied, "I get it Jay…believe me, I just lost my job because of it. Anyway, between you and me, I may not have too many friends left at *Yonie,* but I have something much more valuable. When they abruptly *escorted* me out of my office, I managed to keep a small token of *Yonie* with me. As you know, I had access to every ounce of research going on in the Oncologic Pharmaceutical Division I headed for so many years. Let me go through the files I have and see if I can find any work that was similar to *Harris's. Harris* is really a newcomer to the pharmaceutical industry, but it has some interesting work going on—at least from what it was reporting and publishing. I know it has some big names heading-up some of its labs. Let me see what I can find out and I'll get back to you. Sounds like we both disclosed things to each other we probably shouldn't have…but I know we're doing it for all the right reasons…I'll let you know."

Yamp thanked Kogan for his willingness to help, and realized how clever his friend was. Kogan was perceptive in understanding what Yamp said was off the record. It also appears he had taken privileged information with him at his departure from *Yonie.* Yamp knew all too well, that *information* was power.

CHAPTER 39

Chicago, IL

James Knight was the Chicago-based FBI Special Agent hand-picked by Deputy Director Jacoby to investigate the deaths of Bob Margolis and Rebecca Sunnis. Knight was a veteran in the bureau and was well-known and respected among his colleagues. He had had multiple opportunities to move up the food chain, but he was grounded in Chicago, and wanted to remain there. Advancing in the bureau would require moving to Washington, DC, which was not on his, nor his wife's, radar. Knight's wife had been diagnosed with multiple sclerosis ten-years ago, and with her noted progression, he wanted her to remain with her doctors and have the comfort of her family nearby. His career progression was secondary to his devotion to her and her increasing medical needs. When he received the call from the deputy, he was more than happy to assist with an investigation regarding possible malfeasance at a local biotech company developing new drugs and therapies.

After first reviewing the police files of the victims, Knight contacted Detective Blight and Detective Rose for an update on their investigations. Unlike many cases where the local police prefer to keep the feds out of their jurisdictions, Knight was pleased to know both detectives welcomed his presence. They were both at an impasse in their ability to move forward and needed the assistance and the resources afforded by the FBI. A meeting was scheduled at the Chicago field office for the three of them to sit down and share information. In addition to what existed in the files, they all understood open communication and discussion was the best tool they had to solve this investigation.

Although Detective Rose had worked with the feds in the past, it was a new experience for Blight. She had visited the federal building in downtown Chicago for a variety of meetings and conferences, but going there as an investigator on an active crime was exhilarating. She was excited to work with arguably the finest crime investigative agency in the world. She entered the old limestone structure after climbing the twenty or so well-worn steps. After displaying her badge to the guards and removing her service weapon, Blight felt proud of what she was doing. She knew she was part of a team that would find justice for *her* victim, Rebecca Sunnis. She was pleased to find Detective Rose and Special Agent Knight to be both professional and considerate. As a female detective in a small suburban police force, those attributes were often overlooked by her colleagues. The meeting was almost three hours in length. Blight was impressed by the thoroughness of Agent Knight as he asked insightful questions. It was obvious he was an expert crime investigator.

Knight asked, "Detective Blight, you mentioned in one of your reports that you were going to investigate the tag numbers of the cars parked in front of the wine shop. Also, did any CCTV systems catch the perp's face or activity?"

Blight responded, "We were able to use the bar code scan data at the wine shop to pinpoint the exact time the purchase was made. We were also able to identify a gray bearded man leave the shop less than a minute from that time. The footage was captured from across the street by a small dime-store camera. We could trace him turning to his left upon exiting the shop. By stitching the video feeds from multiple CCTV cameras along the street, we tracked his walk just over two blocks away from the store. We then lose him as there is a blind spot along the route he took. Initially, we performed a plate check on all parked cars located within a two-block distance from the wine shop. Once we noted he was parked just outside of that perimeter we extended that search another two blocks. Unfortunately, most of those parking spots are unmetered, so no car data is available."

Knight then asked, "Is the street one-way or two-way?"

Blight responded, "Broadway is a main street for business in that neighborhood. It's a two-way street."

"Well," responded Knight. "Perhaps we might get lucky. You know what time he left the wine shop, and given he walked on the same side of the street as the shop, it's possible he was parked on the same side as the shop as well. That would mean if you took into consideration the time it took to walk—call it three blocks—there should be a car passing in front of the wine shop by our perp at the estimated time. I know it might be a long shot, but if you were to review images of passing cars at the known time, one of them could be our boy. There could be a few cars or maybe a few dozen, but any information could turn out to be useful. Certainly, the perp could have turned the corner after getting into his car or even be parked in the opposite direction. Obtaining footage from all the cameras down the street would not only be extremely time consuming, but it would probably be a waste of time. But we do know—within say a minute or so—that he could be driving right in front of the shop. See if you can find anything out on that." Blight nodded her head and agreed to follow up as instructed.

Detective Rose then joined the conversation. "When we determined that a black-boxed cologne was part of the gift bag at the golf outing, we were concerned that a potential mass distribution of poison could have occurred. I spoke with Doctor Yamp about this, who later informed me he discussed this possibility with Deputy Director Jacoby. After thinking about Jacoby's reasoning, I believe he is correct…it wouldn't fit the MO of our perp. But, when The Public Relations Office at *Harris Therapeutics* told us that no cologne was ever on the gift list, it got me wondering how the cologne got in the bags. I interviewed the volunteers who distributed the bags that morning to the golfers. None of them reported anything unusual. However, the woman who was the event coordinator informed me that earlier, some guy did come around and stated he had some additional items to add to the bags. She remembered the guy showing up dressed in khakis and he had a name tag with the logo from the golf course. It was about 8 a.m. when he appeared. She said the morning was quite hectic, and she lost sight of him. She recalled directing him to where the players' gift bags were being stored before the registration was to begin at 10 a.m. Apparently, the bags were in an unlocked, large, white minivan the company used for various tasks."

Knight nodded his head. He then asked, "Is there any camera footage of that van?"

"No such luck," Rose answered. The only video camera of the parking lot is at the entrance and exit. The parking lot itself is unmonitored."

"Okay," said Knight. "The event coordinator said the unknown guy was there around 8 a.m." Knight stopped for a moment to do some math. "Let's assume he got permission to enter the van and then proceeded to unload the cologne into each bag…how many players were at the event?"

Rose said, "One-hundred-and-twenty were registered to play."

Knight stood up and began talking, "Okay…so assume it takes him…what maybe fifteen minutes to drop a cologne box into each bag…give or take…then what? I bet he leaves. There isn't any reason to stick around. He must have known which bag was going to each player as they were pre-labeled. He did his thing and left. How many people are *leaving* a golf club at…oh…maybe 8:30 a.m. in the morning?"

Rose smiled at the obvious reasoning Knight used to give them another potential piece of information about their perp. "I'll get right on it," Rose said while taking some notes.

Knight stated, "Excellent. I would like to see if you can fill in the blanks in those areas…say within the next 72 hours. That would give us Friday to get together again. But I also want us to interview Cortes and Waters at *Harris Therapeutics* as well…so, I'll have my office set that up for Friday afternoon. Perhaps after we meet with those two, we can go over these details as well. I think it would be wasteful for Detective Blight to drive into Chicago for our meeting and then have to go back to the western suburbs to meet at *Harris*. I'll have my office let you know what time we can get that meeting." With that, Knight stood up and shook both of their hands. "Detectives, there are clues out there…we just have to continue to use every resource to find them."

Blight and Rose were then escorted out of the office. They were both impressed with Knight's thorough knowledge of their case's details. He also demonstrated how he used every reasonable bit of available information to try to piece things together. As Blight got into her car, she was excited to get to work on the video footage outside of the wine shop.

CHAPTER 40

Aurora, IL

Detective Rose drove out to *The Richie Country Club* and was met by the director of security as pre-arranged. The images from the video camera located at the parking lot exit gate were saved offsite at a company whose sole function is to keep whatever video, audio, or digital records their various clients require. The requested files were sent over the day before and were made available for Rose to review. Before doing so, he surveyed the club's entranceway, lobby, ballroom, and locker facilities. Having previously interviewed the event coordinator, he knew exactly where the white van with the gift bags was parked on the day of the outing. Rose walked out to the half-empty parking lot and took notes regarding various distances. He timed how long it took to walk from the clubhouse entrance to the van's previous location. He then drove to the middle of the massive parking lot and noted the time it took to reach the exit gate.

The video footage taken on the morning of the golf outing was precisely as Special Agent Knight had anticipated—there was very little traffic leaving the facility. No vehicular traffic exited the facility until 8:44 a.m. when a gray Dodge Charger was recorded exiting the gate. The license plate was clearly visible, and Rose recorded the number. Only three other vehicles left before 10:00 a.m. Rose took down those tag numbers as well, but given the time when the perp was first encountered by the reception staff, the Dodge seemed to be the most likely vehicle of interest.

As Rose was collecting this information, Detective Blight was doing the same—although her task was far more difficult. She, too, timed the walk from the doorway of the wine shop to approximately 2-1/2 blocks down the street. She then proceeded to the various businesses to retrieve video footage from their cameras of street traffic that passed in front of the *Barducci Bros. Wine Shop.* She limited her search to coincide with the estimated time it would take the perp to leave, walk to his car, and then drive in front of the shop. There were nearly 90 cars that she identified in front of the wine shop within the selected time frame. No license plate information was available from the side view of the street traffic, but with slow-speed review, a good image of each passing car could be obtained and printed.

On Friday at 1 p.m., Special Agent Knight and Detectives Blight and Rose were escorted into a conference room at *Harris Therapeutics.* Their scheduled interviews were first with William Waters, and then secondly, to meet with Gene Cortes. After being served coffee and fancy European crackers, Waters walked into the room. Cordial introductions were made, and the meeting began. Knight led the meeting and was aware Waters was knowledgeable of many of the details previously identified by the police. But as a seasoned veteran, he never assumed anything—nobody was ever excluded as a possible suspect or accomplice until proven otherwise. The discussion was initially a review of where *Harris's* mission and goals were focused. Waters went into exquisite details of why and how the company was founded, and the direction the company was headed. He went into a granular discussion of the various research projects that were ongoing as well as a breakdown of each lab—who headed it, who worked where, and each lab's expected outcomes at various work-flow intervals. It was obvious that Waters had the pulse of the company and knew exactly what was occurring under his roof. It was also clear to Knight, as much as Waters understood his company and employees, he was in the dark as to why two valued employees would be murdered. Waters denied receiving any ransom, threats, or other information shedding light on what happened, or what may yet still occur. Knight felt Waters was truly distraught about recent events and was shaken by the deaths of his employees. Both detectives sat quietly as the interview proceeded. They, too, observed someone who was deeply troubled by recent events, and at a loss for an explanation of what was happening to his company and vision.

Doctor Cortes was then invited into the conference room. Agent Knight performed his pre-interview background work, and was well aware of Cortes's reputation and previous accomplishments. He felt Cortes had absolutely nothing to benefit by the loss of his associates, and indeed, suffered a significant loss to his lab's continuity and ability to proceed with its goals effectively. Cortes described how his lab group was focused on developing next-generation advances in human antibody capabilities through the use of mRNA-directed therapies. However, when asked about knowledge of any ransom or threats, it was clear to Knight and the detectives that something was off with him. Cortes answered all of Knight's questions, but he appeared uncomfortable and unsure of himself. Knight made a note of Cortes's behavior and planned to ask the detectives of their impressions of his responses. When the interview concluded, Knight and the detectives acknowledged their appreciation to Cortes for his help. He appeared anxious to leave and did so promptly.

Although it would have been convenient and comfortable to remain in the room to continue their debrief and compare findings, Knight insisted they leave. He pointed to the conference room's built-in microphones and stated, "You never know who's listening when you're out of your own den. As much as I hate to do so, lets continue this discussion in the van." The three investigators were met at the conference doorway by a security guard and were politely escorted out of the building.

"I've never seen a civilian company with such security in my life," Knight began. It was obvious to him that whatever research they were performing had to have either a role in national defense, or a significant monetary value to mandate such protection. "It's like a fortress in there," he continued. "I think we need to understand more about...what was it..." Knight trailed off and looked at his notes. "We need to have a clearer understanding of what mRNA is and what it does. From what I can tell, that's the only thing that makes Cortes's lab have a particular value. Could he be working on something others want? And if so, why would killing lab associates be useful? If somebody wants what they are doing, killing the workers won't help... unless a competitor wants their work to be delayed? Thoughts anyone?"

Detective Blight nodded her head in agreement and stated, "I agree. Somebody wants to stop or delay whatever is being developed in that lab. Did you notice how jittery he got when you asked him about ransoms or threats?"

Knight nodded his head. "Yes, he was definitely hiding something, but I can't put my finger on it." Knight looked back down at his notes, and stated, "There is a definite disconnect here. Cortes has no significant wealth...the money, if that is what is being demanded, would have to come from Waters—he controls the company's purse strings. But Waters appears to be in the dark as to why these murders happened. Cortes, I suspect, does have some understanding of what's going on, but isn't able, or isn't willing to discuss it." The three investigators sat quietly in the van as they thought about what was just stated.

"Perhaps Cortes is being used," Detective Rose stated. "Maybe he's being threatened in some way...maybe he's afraid to tell us anything for fear of repercussion?"

Knight replied, "So are you saying that Cortes was threatened... that he's been directed not to talk to us about slowing down work in his lab? If he wanted to slow, or shut down the project, he could just do so as its under his direction. This just doesn't make sense." Knight shook his head, "But there is no question he knows something, but just can't or won't say. Well, we need to tread lightly here. I don't want him to know we suspect anything peculiar in his behavior...at least not yet. Let's put a pin in that for now." Knight looked at Detective Rose, "Tell me what you found out regarding the car."

Detective Rose opened his file and produced a print of a gray Dodge Charger. "This is a photograph taken at the exit gate at the golf club. It was taken at 8:44 a.m. on the day of the charity event. No other vehicles left the property to coincide within the time frame of when the perp approached the reception desk and was directed to a van loaded with the gift bags. Given that nobody has any record of cologne being distributed, it's our conjecture the perp put the cologne boxes into the bags while they were still in the van and then left. Agent Knight was correct there would be limited outgoing cars from the golf club at that hour. But here is where it gets sticky. I ran the license plate number on the car…and as would be expected, the tag and the car were a mismatch. That plate was reported stolen…nearly 6 months ago. So, either the perp has been planning this for a very long time…"

"Or he has a pile of stolen plates to choose from." Knight interrupted. Detective Rose nodded his head in agreement.

Detective Blight opened her briefcase and stated, "Here are the photographs of all of the vehicles that passed in front of the wine shop shortly after our perp bought the wine." She passed around the ninety or so images. Rose and Knight each grabbed a handful and sifted through them.

After several minutes of looking through the photographs, Rose stated excitedly, "Here he is!" Knight grabbed the image from Rose.

"Yep…that's our boy," Knight said as he then gave the image to Detective Blight. "A gray Dodge Charger. Excellent. I'm going to take this image to our field office and see what our lab boys can determine. For sure, they will know the year. With surface recognition algorithms, the computer will match the car body characteristics to known specifications given to us by the various manufacturers. But what amazes me is how the lab guys will correctly guess it ninety-nine percent of the time—without needing the computer. Some of those guys can tell you the year, make, and model of practically any car by simply showing them a photo of any quadrant of a car. Those guys are unbelievable… anyway, we'll know the year of the car by the end of the day. I'll then do an Illinois…no, make it Illinois, Indiana, and Wisconsin search for registration data. Our perp may have exchangeable license plates, but I'll bet the car is his. We'll find out how many gray Dodge Chargers there are in those three states, and then match that information to registration data. We'll then cross-reference that information with driver's license photographs. I'm sure some of those Charger owners have gray hair and beards—or at least gray hair. We may not be able to isolate him just yet, but we'll narrow down our search."

Detective Rose was nodding his head as Knight was rattling off how the FBI investigation would proceed. He then asked, "How do you know it's his car?"

"Honestly, I don't," Knight replied. "But something tells me our boy has an ego. He has the ability to walk into a victim's life, learn about him or her, and then plot his or her demise from a distance. A person who plants a poison can tell himself he didn't do it…the victim did. The perp tells himself the victim is the one who drank it or inhaled it. Somehow, I get the feeling our perp thinks he's smarter than everyone else. I think somewhere along the line, his ego got in the way, and he made a make a mistake. We need to find that mistake. I bet the idea of parking blocks away to get the wine from some obscure wine shop in a large city, and then using stolen tags on the car was all he thought he needed. Well, maybe so. But not this time."

CHAPTER 41

Chicago, IL

"So, tell me what you've got so far," FBI Deputy Director Jacoby asked Special Agent Knight on the late afternoon telephone call.

"Well, sir, it's certainly an unusual case," Knight began. He brought Jacoby up-to-speed on the investigation. "My suspicion is there is one perpetrator involved in both murders. We have the same car being identified at the purchase of the wine used for the arsenic poisoning, and also being recorded leaving the scene where the Novichok tainted cologne was left at the golf outing. We are doing our best to track down the owner of the car."

Jacoby stated, "Sounds like you're making progress, Knight. Any thoughts about the company where the victims worked?"

"I believe the company is clean. Their work has definitely been hampered by the loss of those researchers, but something is off..." Knight stated. "The director of the lab where the victims worked is holding back information. I don't believe he has anything to do with the murders, but he isn't telling us all he knows."

"Perhaps he's been given a directive not to." Jacoby interjected.

Knight continued, "Yes, we reached the same conclusion. The question is by whom...maybe the perp? Oh...before we conclude this call, I'm wondering if you have a good resource for me. I need to understand more about something called mRNA…it's a molecule… or something like that, involved in antibody production. I need to understand if this could be the reason *Harris Therapeutics* is the target. I could go to the lab boys, but…"

"Yamp. Jay Yamp is who you want to talk to," Jacoby stated without hesitation.

"The doctor who called you in on this?" Knight asked.

"Yep, Jay will tell you what you need to know…and if he doesn't, he'll direct you. You can count on that. I'll text you his cell number," Jacoby answered.

"I know you two go back, but he won't mind an unexpected call from an unknown FBI agent?" Knight asked.

"Mind? Yamp? Are you kidding me…the guy will want to join you on the investigation. I mean literally *join* you! No, you don't have to worry about bothering Jay. He'll do everything he can to help out. Let's see…its 5:00 p.m. here in Washington…as I recall, he usually gets out of his clinic around 3 p.m. Knowing how predictable he is, he's probably in his office now. Give him a call and see what he can do for you. Oh, and remember something, Knight—Jay Yamp won't hold back…you can trust what he says."

"Great…I'll get on it now," Knight answered enthusiastically and disconnected the call. Knight waited for the text message containing Yamp's number to arrive. As soon as it appeared on his phone, he touched his cellphone screen to make the call. After two rings, the phone was answered.

"This is Jay Yamp," Yamp stated quickly.

"Good afternoon, Doctor. This is FBI Special Agent Knight…I was given your cell number from Deputy Director Jacoby."

"Oh…good afternoon, Agent Knight. Feel free to call me Jay…I'm not your doctor." Yamp said easily.

"Well, thank you…but I'll stick with *doctor* for now," Knight said awkwardly, as he wasn't used to altering protocol. Knight wondered to himself, *Was Yamp the deputy director's friend, or is he an asset to assist on the case? Perhaps he is both.* "Do you have a free minute or two? I have a question about the case you brought to the deputy director's attention…well, actually, I have several…"

Yamp cut in, "Sure…I'm just doing some paperwork that I detest. What can I help you with, Agent Knight?"

Knight was surprised how smoothly the conversation proceeded. Most of the time people were reserved when speaking to the FBI. He felt he should be having a beer with Yamp right now. Knight began, "Well, for starters…I'm a bit confused understanding what an mRNA is, and how that relates to what *Harris Therapeutics* is doing at its facility. I understand its involved in antibody production…or something like that…but, well, understanding biology was never my strongest subject."

"Sure…no problem." Yamp began, "It's a confusing subject. Let me do my best to break this down for you. By the way, I'm glad to hear you're looking into this. The scientist who was poisoned was really a good guy, and someone I feel could have made significant contributions to medicine. Let me see if I can help you…" Yamp kicked his feet up on his desk before continuing the discussion. He spoke to Knight as the professor he was. "The immune system is the body's defense system. Let's imagine something foreign invades the body…say a bacterium or a virus. The invading entity will have specific proteins on its surface we call antigens. The immune system will be stimulated by the presence of the antigens, and through an extraordinarily complex sequence of events, one of the responses of the immune systems to produce what are called immunoglobulins, also called antibodies. Antibodies will attach themselves to the antigens, and through another sequence of events, they allow the body to destroy the invader. So far so good?"

Knight nodded his head and responded into the phone, "Yes…so far so good."

"Okay, great," Yamp continued. "Now, mRNA—and we really don't need to discuss what the letters stand for—carries genetic information used to produce proteins necessary for cellular function. Basically, they are messengers to carry information from the DNA in the nucleus of a cell to the outer parts of a cell where proteins are made. Now, as far as their role in antibody production is concerned, let's insert a specific mRNA into a cell. That cell will be instructed to make a particular protein. If that protein is say, a viral protein, then as part of a normal immune response the immune system recognizes the protein is foreign, and now the body will produce specialized antibodies. Once produced, antibodies remain in the body so the immune system can quickly respond to the invader if exposed again. So, for instance, if a person is exposed to a virus after receiving an mRNA vaccination, antibodies can recognize it and mark it for destruction before it can cause serious illness. Does this make sense?"

"Yes…thank you," Knight responded. "So, it sounds like *Harris Therapeutics,* or more accurately, Doctor Cortes's lab within the company, was involved in making a certain type of mRNA. I guess now the question is why that *particular mRNA* was so valuable that two scientists involved in its production were killed?"

"That's a good question, Agent Knight," Yamp responded. "All I can tell you right now is that the science of understanding mRNA sequencing—how different mRNAs can instruct the immune system to behave a certain way—is exploding. This is particularly true in the field of vaccine production. From my end, we are interested in understanding the role of vaccine production as it relates to possible cancer treatments, or more precisely, cancer prevention. Perhaps, Agent Knight, you want to investigate who was using or buying the products that *Harris* was producing." Yamp hesitated, and then continued, "But to kill the investigators making the mRNA would slow down development and subsequently, production. So, maybe begin by looking into competitors producing the same products as *Harris* would make more sense. What do you think?"

Knight responded, "Yes, I think you're right. It's not that someone wants what they have…perhaps they want to knock them out of the marketplace. I'll start poking around and see what I can come up with. I really appreciate your time, Doctor."

"Anytime. I'm happy to help out. Give my best to your boss," Yamp replied and hung up.

Knight now felt he had a better handle on what this investigation was about. He considered what had transpired. *Perhaps, what it came down to was just a simple crime of someone trying to block a competitor in a very complicated and lucrative aspect of scientific discovery. But if that were the case, why was Doctor Cortes behaving so oddly when questioned? As the lab's director, he had the authority to slow down the lab's productivity—nobody would need to be murdered. And why was he evasive when questioned about threats? No, there was more to this.* Knight made his notes of what he learned and what needed to be done.

CHAPTER 42

Chicago, IL

After hearing the news of Jay Yamp's friend being killed in such a brutal manner, Kogan, too, was curious about what was happening at *Harris*. And, to then learn of a second murder in the same lab, the event was obviously not coincidental. Kogan was able to find out that both individuals killed had worked in the lab of Gene Cortes, the distinguished researcher highly recruited by *Harris*. It was a big deal in the biotech world to learn that Cortes had left his cushy academic position at Harvard to throw his efforts into the *war zone* of the private sector. He must have asked for a fortune...and received it. Kogan always admired Cortes's work in immunology and antibiotic drug development, and he knew that Cortes would one day be at the epicenter of innovative research in the field. With his newly assigned task of grasping what was happening at *Harris*, Kogan spent the next week reviewing Cortes's recent publications and presentations. Cortes's work and ability to envision where the field was moving before others even caught up to the present was beyond impressive. What Kogan previously did not know was actually how close Cortes was to engineering the next generation of vaccines.

With his oncologic research background, Kogan was able to read and decipher the myriad of data Cortes and his team had accumulated in the field of viral immunology. Kogan could understand why other companies would be envious of the breakthroughs *Harris* had the potential to evolve. Kogan also knew that *Yonie*, with its desire to lead the pack, would have considerable interest in what was being developed in that lab.

After performing his extensive review of what Cortes and *Harris Therapeutics* had been investing its well-funded resources into, Kogan was convinced there was the significant potential for huge profits to be made. Kogan also knew that *Yonie Pharmaceutical's* business model was predicated on its ability to overtake another company's successful drug developments and make it its own. As one of the bigger players in the pharmaceutical industry, *Yonie* success relied more on its financial size and ability to intimidate than with its own internal scientific innovation. Knowing *Yonie* as intimately as he did, Kogan felt there could be a link between the two companies—a link that was not based on mutual interest in research and development. Kogan felt there was no way *Yonie* would allow a competitor—let alone one less than forty-miles away—to have the edge in new drug development. Kogan now understood what started as a request by Yamp to find out information about *Harris* was going to turn into a study of what *Yonie* was up to. Looking at the full picture, Kogan suspected something nefarious was occurring at *Yonie,* and given his distrust and disdain for his previous employer, he relished the opportunity to investigate.

Kogan went into his study and unlocked the small safe he kept behind some rather large and boring molecular biology books on his credenza. He always felt nobody in their right mind would want to move, let alone read, those boring texts. And as the months passed since his dismissal from *Yonie*, he now felt fortunate that the days of having to read those books were now over for him. In the corner of the safe, Kogan found the small flash drive he had taken on his last day of work at *Yonie*. He knew the data on it would be several months old—revealing research activities performed up until the day he was dismissed. Kogan suspected that would be current enough for his needs. Nothing in research was accomplished quickly, and simply trying to gain an understanding of where certain labs were headed would suffice.

The flash drive contained a massive amount of information. Kogan had managed to download it shortly before he was escorted out of his office. It was a compilation of laboratory communications and detailed workflow plans for drug development in the Oncologic Pharmaceutical Division. All fourteen active labs working in that division were mandated to keep their data and research findings current with each day's work. In short, it meant literally hundreds of thousands of pages of research protocol, initiatives, and collated data were on that drive. Kogan realized it could take him many hours to sift through everything he had in his possession. But he also knew the majority of what was on the flash drive would not be pertinent in his search. To narrow his research down, Kogan used the embedded filters to limit any query of data from the past three months only. Given his last day of work was approximately three months ago, this would give him the task of reviewing information now six months old. Consequently, he would have to risk foregoing review of any data older than six months—good enough, he thought. That move alone eliminated a significant amount of data he would have to study. Next, Kogan decided to review all fourteen individual lab's records of objectives and areas of development. As the previous director of the division, he was aware of what each lab was doing in a broad sense, but he now needed to take a deeper look into each of their protocols and methods. Kogan wanted to see budgets, equipment acquisitions, and review the personnel working in each lab. He wanted both the *30,000-foot view* as well as a granular perspective of what was going on. In his previous employment at *Yonie,* Kogan was tasked with the administrative duties of running the division. The details of the day-to-day aspects of each lab was charged to each of the individual lab directors.

As the previous division head, Kogan knew some, but not all of the details of each laboratory's work. The labs working on the same drug development project for over five years, he decided to discard in his search. This narrowed his work down to five labs to review. Knowing *Harris* was trying to advance itself in anti-neoplastic, vaccine drug development, Kogan again adjusted the embedded filters on the flash drive and removed those labs at *Yonie* not engaged in that direction of drug development. He was left with only three labs that would potentially have email communications or have made reference in some manner to *Harris Therapeutics.* Kogan transferred the data from his desktop computer to his laptop, and settled into his recliner as he understood the size of the review he was about to undertake.

Being an expert in drug development research, Kogan was quite adept at gleaning over the massive amount of information in front of him. With his knowledge base, he was able to ignore the great majority of what was on his laptop. Data analyses and trial results were dismissed quickly. His main focus was on intra-laboratory communications and tracking references sited in the research being conducted. He wanted to know not only how each lab was progressing, but *why* researchers were proceeding down particular investigative pathways. In any laboratory investigation, there were always options to perform specific experiments, and not others. Kogan was trying to determine if any influences from *Harris's* published work were making their way into the work and direction of these labs. After nearly five hours of continuous work, nothing was apparent. By midnight, Kogan had had enough. He shut down his laptop, plugged it into its charger, and went to retire. He would return in the morning and continue his assessment. As Kogan lay in bed, what troubled him the most wasn't that he would find something. Kogan was more worried that he wouldn't find anything. That would prompt his concern that he may have missed something.

The morning came too quickly for Kogan. Having reviewed thousands of documents of lab data, email communications, as well as the personal impressions and plans of the lab investigators, sleep did not come easily. He got up, prepared a pot of coffee, and went right back at it. Two hours after he started, he took a brief break. It was nearly six hours later when Kogan came across a personal communication he thought could potentially lead to something. A lab technician named Amy Kelly made an interesting notation in one of her lab reports. She highlighted that it was a verbatim statement she made to Shamus O'Donnell during a private discussion she had had with Dr. O'Donnell in his office. Why she would take the time and effort to record a specific statement she made was unusual.

"I believe the difference in outcomes between those trials would be nullified if we had an effective cytotoxic T cell. If we were to try to build our own utilizing a synthetic mRNA vector…"

Kogan read and re-read this passage in her lab notes. He knew Shamus's lab was working on efforts to develop a new prostate cancer vaccine. Kogan thought about the possible situation prompting her to record her statement. *Did she write this down because Shamus told her to? Unlikely. Perhaps she wrote it down because it elicited a reaction from him? Maybe.*

Kogan went back to previously written lab details both Amy Kelly and Shamus had recorded weeks prior to this entry. Kogan was trying to understand the need for "an effective cytotoxic T cell" in the context of Shamus's lab objectives—to produce a cancer vaccine. Shamus was looking for a means to synthetically create a cytotoxic T cell, and he needed an mRNA molecule to do so! Kogan felt he was onto something, but he couldn't quite isolate it yet. He could see where the lab was headed and understood the mechanism for the mRNA to sequence the T cell production. Kogan thought about the situation Shamus's lab was facing: *to make an mRNA molecule specifically for...could take...* Kogan started writing down what would be needed, and then slowly put down his pen and took a long breath. He looked out of the window while reaching a conclusion. He said out-loud, "It could take years!"

Kogan went back to his online review of publications and presentations by Cortes at *Harris*. He researched as far back as three years. He found what he was looking for: Cortes had synthesized that precise mRNA molecule! The very thing that Shamus needed, *Harris* already had! Kogan was so focused, he was oblivious to time; he had worked through lunch and dinner. He had ignored his wife's calls and was completely entrenched in his review. Kogan was trying to understand what was inhibiting Shamus's work. *What was preventing Shamus from trying to develop the mRNA at Yonie?* Kogan understood setting up a new lab would take time—okay, he accepted that. He also knew that *Yonie* had the financial resources to set up the lab. So, having the money wasn't the issue either. Kogan understood putting those two variables together—time and money—wasn't the problem *Yonie* was facing. And then he changed the priorities of those issues and made a realization.

Kogan came up with a plausible explanation: Time *costs* Money.

He knew the direction *Yonie* was headed in its Oncologic Pharmaceutical Division—it wanted to jump into the cancer vaccine race. Kogan postulated Shamus had apparently advanced his work on the prostate cancer vaccine to the point where he could actually produce it if he had this critical molecule. A molecule that a competitor had, and he wanted. A competitor that was just an hour's drive away. So, if *Harris* had already developed the protocol to synthesize the molecule that Shamus wanted, *why didn't Yonie just offer to buy it?*

Kogan knew it was late, but he didn't care. At 11:00 p.m., he called Jay Yamp.

Kogan started, "Jay, I'm sorry…but…"

"No, no…its ok, Jason…what's going on?" Yamp replied after shaking off sleep.

"I know you asked me to find out what *Harris* was up to…and I did. But I think I found out even more." Kogan described in detail his workflow and findings.

Yamp was now sitting upright in bed with his complete attention focused on the conversation. He reiterated the situation as he understood it to Kogan. "So, *Harris* has a protocol to synthesize the mRNA…which is necessary to then produce the specific T cell this investigator…err… Shamus O'Donnell at *Yonie* needs for the production of his prostate cancer vaccine…correct?"

Kogan replied, "Yes, exactly." He continued, "For *Yonie* to build out a lab to synthesize the mRNA could take years. It would also be expensive, but they have the financial resources for that. My concern, or rather…what I'm now wondering, is if *Yonie Pharmaceuticals* might have something to do with the recent events at *Harris."* Kogan continued, "Hear me out, *Yonie* wants to lead the industry in cancer vaccine development. Shamus is one molecule away from being able to do it–or so I think. If *Yonie* had this mRNA, it could potentially own the market…it could make…literally *billons* before anyone else."

There was silence on the phone. Yamp then stated, "Well, if that's the case, why wouldn't *Yonie*—with all its cash—just make an offer to buy the synthesis protocol, or make an offer to buy *Harris Therapeutics* and then own the process outright?"

"I know…that's what I'm stuck on, Jay." Kogan replied, as he was slowly thinking the situation through out loud. "They have the money…but if *Yonie* bought the protocol, then the purchase would eventually be exposed, and everyone would put it together. They would lose their jump on the market! But, if *Yonie* got the synthesis protocol cryptically, it could begin production under the radar. *Yonie* knows if it were then caught, it would take years—maybe even a decade—in litigation with *Harris*. Within that time, it would be the first to market—maybe even own the market—and *Yonie* would have made its billions. *Yonie* might *then* offer to buy *Harris* as part of a deal."

Yamp was putting it all together. "Then what we need to do, Jason, is see if we can link those deaths at *Harris* to *Yonie*. If this hypothesis is correct, somebody knows something—and might want to talk. My gut tells me the decision to somehow *take* the protocol from *Harris* was not from a scientist or investigator. It most likely came from an administrator, or someone involved in the financial sector at *Yonie*. I'm going to talk to my friend at the FBI and see what he thinks. He might be able to squeeze the right person to lead us to the right answer... assuming this is what happened."

"Yes, Jay," Kogan responded. "I think we need to leave the rest of this up to those who do this professionally. If the folks at *Yonie* were really behind this...and that's still a big *if*, and they have demonstrated their willingness to take lives, we don't need to be anywhere near this."

Yamp replied, "Agreed...I'll let you know what happens. Thank you for all your effort in analyzing this, Jason. I know it was a lot of work."

Kogan replied, "Thanks, Jay. But...what if we're right? This is all very unsettling...well, good night."

The phones disconnected. Yamp was wide awake and thinking through the series of events that were just described. He would talk to Agent Knight in the morning—after his first case of the day. *How the hell does this shit find me*? Yamp wondered as he tried to go back to sleep.

CHAPTER 43

Wheaton, IL

Cortes was always punctual in getting to the lab at 8 a.m. sharp. His habits were so predictable that the security guards could set their watches by when he would walk into the building. Today was an exception—he arrived at 7 a.m., and it was noticed by the guards.

"Early start today, doc?" One of the guards inquired.

"Yes, John. I need to get a head start on some paperwork," Cortes replied. He was impressed they even paid attention to him, but realized they probably knew the work habits of all the employees at *Harris*. He collected his briefcase after it passed through the scanner and wished the guards a good day. Cortes got to his office and activated his computer from sleep mode. He inputted his user ID and twenty-digit passcode. Cortes then opened the file containing the protocol for manufacturing the mRNA molecule the stranger had requested. The entire production methodology was contained in this encrypted file. The file also contained the necessary information to adjust scalability, assess purity, and allow monitoring of production.

To understand the synthesis of mRNA first requires a basic explanation of DNA. DNA, or deoxyribonucleic acid, is the molecule inside a cell that contains the genetic information responsible for the development and function of an organism. Essentially, DNA contains the instructions for an organism to survive and reproduce. To carry out these functions, the DNA template (sequences), must be transcribed (copied) into messages (mRNA) that can be used to produce the necessary proteins for the cell or organism to live. To manufacture mRNA in a laboratory setting is an immense undertaking. The necessary equipment, materials, personnel, and knowledge base required to create and store molecules of such immense complexity with absolute purity is extraordinarily difficult. It is also an extremely time-consuming, technologically advanced, and expensive process. The target sequence must be determined, optimized, synthesized, and then inserted into a DNA plasmid (a DNA molecule that is physically separate from chromosomal DNA and replicates independently) to use as a template for mRNA synthesis using in vitro (outside of a living organism) transcription (copying a segment of DNA into RNA).

Cortes reviewed the nearly six-hundred-page scientific file. Having been the primary author of most of it, he was intimately knowledgeable of its details. He understood that handing over the *recipe* would mandate that a sophisticated lab and personnel would be required to produce what the file instructed. Years of painstaking research went into creating this protocol that resulted in a highly reproducible and pure mRNA molecule. It would be highly unlikely that someone could create the molecule without error at first. But given enough time and effort, as well as having the necessary knowledge, it could be accomplished.

For Cortes, this was his baby. This was his creation, and to simply hand it over—to have it taken from him with threat—was against everything in his being. He understood the risk he was taking, but Cortes was searching for one subtle change in the protocol he could make that would be difficult for the thieves to identify. He wanted to make a modification in the protocol that would give the receiving scientist sleepless nights and infinite aggravation: inconsistent results. Cortes knew it was in front of him. It was somewhere contained within the hundreds of pages and tens-of-thousands of words and diagrams. But he just couldn't see it. Certainly not under these circumstances. After staring at his computer monitor, Cortes understood he would need to visualize in his *minds-eye* the precise diagrammatic explanations and abstract chemical reactions in order to pinpoint what to modify in the protocol. He simply couldn't do it on demand by looking at the file. Cortes would have to put this review aside and come back to it—not when the time was convenient, but rather, when he could *see* the problem clearly from all angles. Cortes recalled his chemistry professor in college telling him once to stop looking for answers, but rather, focus on understanding the problem and then the answer will likely present itself. Cortes closed the file and turned off the computer. He placed the blank flash drive he was given into his desk drawer and locked it. When he is ready, he will download the information. Cortes then did his best to proceed with his directorship tasks—reviewing yesterday's data collection, and then assessing and assigning workflow schedules for the remaining lab associates. While doing so, Cortes thought about how challenging it has been to fill the void by losing two lab associates. External searches and job offerings had been placed in the scientific community expressing opportunities for scientists to work with him at *Harris.* News travels quickly in the small biotech world, and there hadn't been much in the way of applicants as of yet. Cortes hoped that, with time, people would seek jobs and forget some of the details and rumors that were undoubtedly circulating.

The day went slowly, but 5 p.m. did come eventually. Cortes locked his office and returned home after some brief grocery shopping. Fortunately, the kids would be spending the rest of the week with his wife, visiting his in-laws. He prepared and ate dinner, watched the night's baseball game—not really caring if the Cubs won or not—and went to bed. Cortes slept restlessly as he ignored his old professor's advice and tried to force a solution. The answer simply wouldn't come to mind. The rest of the week was essentially a rinse and repeat cycle for Cortes. He would go to work, perform his necessary tasks, come home, and eat alone. The nights were long, but eventually he focused less on the synthesis protocol and more on himself. By the end of the week, Cortes was so engaged in getting the lab running smoothly again that the need to modify his mRNA protocol before loading it onto the flash drive was no longer top of mind—until he received a note from his secretary. She entered his office and informed him that someone called and wanted her to deliver a message. He retrieved the message from her and read it to himself:

Dear Doctor Cortes, I believe you are in possession of something for me. I expect delivery in 48 hours. Additional details to follow.

Cortes felt a chill run down his spine. He quickly looked at his secretary who obviously did not understand what this was about.

Almost pleading, Cortes asked her with a dry mouth, "Did the caller… leave a return number?"

"No…no he didn't," She replied matter-of-factly. "It was an odd call…usually the phone number shows up on the caller ID screen. This one didn't. It just said *caller unknown*. Well, I suppose if you don't call back, he'll call again." She then smiled and said, "Maybe he used a *burner*. Anything else you need from me?"

Cortes shook his head quickly to inform her, "No." He hesitated a moment, and then asked, "What's a burner?" His secretary looked at Cortes as though he was from Mars.

His secretary was no longer smiling. She said apologetically, "I was just kidding, Doctor. A burner phone is one of those pre-paid phones you can buy practically anywhere. You can probably buy them on a street corner in downtown Chicago. They only last for a certain number of minutes…and then you throw them away. But they never show the caller ID. I think their reputation is they are used a lot by criminals and gang members. I was just kidding…I know you wouldn't have someone call you on one of those. If he calls back, I'll let you know." She then retreated to her desk.

Cortes was left sitting at his desk holding the note. He could see his hand and the note shaking. Cortes felt completely out of control. The strength he felt just a few days ago as he contemplated a means to alter the synthesis protocol was gone. He opened the mRNA file again on his computer. As Cortes looked at the massive file, he was immobilized and couldn't identify what he wanted or needed to do. It was as though the detailed information in front of him was foreign, even though he wrote nearly every word. Cortes scanned though page after page without being able to locate a section to modify. It all looked like a blur. Cortes started to wonder…maybe he should just give the stranger the damn thing and be done with it.

Cortes looked out the window. He'd been reviewing the file nonstop for more than three hours, and it was now dusk. He shut down the computer and left his office. Cortes needed some fresh air and to get out of the building. He reached his car and mindlessly drove home. The radio was on, but Cortes didn't hear a thing. As he approached his driveway, he suddenly felt the symptoms of a panic attack. He hadn't had one in years, but he recognized the signs and symptoms. Perhaps, it was the consequence of coming home with the expectation to see an unknown car again in his driveway. Maybe it was just the cumulative stress of the week that Cortes did his best to suppress. He tried to think of what was causing him to sweat so profusely...*did it really matter what the reason was?* Cortes tried to calm his rapid breathing, but the oncoming anxiety was overwhelming. Cortes had the presence of mind to quickly put the car in park once he was on his own property. He was able to unbuckle himself from his car seat. Cortes grabbed the door handle with his shaking hand and then allowed himself to just slide out of the car onto his driveway. He sat there for a solid minute just trying to focus on his breathing. *In and out...in and out...slowly...in through the nose and out through the mouth.* Cortes gained control and could slowly feel the anxiety dissipate. He sat on the ground in the dark for another couple of minutes and soon felt tears well in his eyes. He let them flow as he could feel another wave of panic begin to take over. But, he was able to inhibit it and gain control this time. Cortes turned his fear into anger and could now feel his fists involuntarily clench. He was once again determined not to let this stranger manage his world. Cortes pulled himself off the asphalt, opened his car door, and retrieved his briefcase. He then entered his home, flicked on the lights, and walked straight to the living room. The room was small, perhaps eighteen feet by twenty. It had an old sofa and two chairs surrounding a small glass table. The walls were bare. The light from the hallway was all he wanted.

Cortes poured himself a scotch from his small bar and sat down on his well-worn, pale blue sofa. He picked up his remote control off the glass table and turned on his stereo. He then turned up the volume and listened to Luciano Pavarotti sing *Nessun dorma* from *Turandot.* After a few minutes of listening, Cortes was now calm, clear-headed, and felt a purposeful direction—he now knew he would find a way. He reheated his take-out Chinese dinner from two days ago and caught the last few innings of the Cubs loss to St. Louis—again. It was nearing 10:30 p.m. and he suddenly felt exhausted from all the emotional fluctuations, the scotch, and the food. It was time to retire. Cortes was without a plan, but now having renewed confidence, he was determined to shed his fear and focus tomorrow on the problem—*not* the solution.

At about 3 a.m., the problem appeared in focus. As if a bell went off in his head, Cortes suddenly sat upright. His mind never stopped analyzing the situation, but his need for an answer kept getting in the way. Once he let go of the pressure, it all clicked into place for Cortes. Just as he realized previously, creating the mRNA molecule—while placing limits on manufacturing reproducibility—would be the key. If the synthesis protocol he is being forced to give up could make the product, Cortes would then be off the hook. He could hand over to the stranger the proper production sequence of the requested mRNA molecule, but Cortes now understood a vulnerable aspect of this project was the ability to preserve the molecule. The mRNA as designed *decays* in approximately one minute. That potentially gives whoever is synthesizing it an opportunity to realize they created what they intended. But, without proper preservation, the new mRNA molecule has an inherently weak structure. It is chemically labile and prone to heat degradation. Cortes understood that following *in vitro* transcription, during which the DNA template is transcribed (copied) to mRNA, the final mRNA structure requires an additional process to create a stable and mature mRNA. This process is known as 5' capping. Capping is performed after mRNA purification and requires a specific capping enzyme. Modifying this step *could* produce a vulnerable mRNA molecule the user would be able to identity. But due to its structural instability, the molecule would be rendered useless in the production of whatever it is that necessitates the mRNA. *Yes, that's it!* Cortes thought to himself. He turned on the bedside light and wrote down some notes. He would get to the office early again, make the noted modification in the protocol file, and then copy the edited file onto the provided flash drive. Cortes turned off the light and fell fast asleep. It was the best sleep he had all week.

CHAPTER 44

Wheaton, IL

As if on cue, 48 hours after Cortes's secretary received the first call from the stranger, he called again. This time, he wanted to speak directly to Doctor Cortes. The secretary tried to explain that he was in a meeting, but the incessant man wouldn't take *no* for an answer. "Okay, sir…just give me a few minutes. I need to get him out of a conference," she stated as politely as possible, wanting to hang up on the *asshole*. The secretary placed the call on hold, and walked quickly into the small conference room where the lab personnel were engaged in their weekly group discussion.

"Doctor Cortes, can you come outside for a moment?" the secretary whispered to Cortes. "There is a rather insistent man on the phone for you. He wouldn't introduce himself, but I think it's the same guy that I said used the burner phone a couple of days ago."

"Excuse me…it will just be a couple of minutes," Cortes stated apologetically to the group. "John, continue to lead the discussion in my absence. I'll be back shortly." Cortes quickly got up from his chair and went into his office. The call was then transferred to his phone.

"Good morning, Doctor Cortes. How are you today?" the cheerful voice began.

"Cut the crap. You don't really give a shit how I feel," Cortes stated defiantly. He was amazed at how non-emotionally he responded. "I have what you want. Tell me how to get it to you and then we are done."

Even the stranger on the phone was impressed by Cortes's coolness. He decided to ignore Cortes's glib response and not engage in any extraneous conversation. Burksdale too, had an objective to fulfill his obligation to Ashwood and ultimately to his employer, and getting sidetracked would not help him accomplish it. "I'm glad to hear it. Any problems with the upload?"

"Other than the fact I'm trying to keep a lab functioning that is down two of its important associates…what could possibly be a problem?" Cortes responded.

"Yes, well, collateral damage to achieving an objective," Burksdale continued. He wanted to remain on point. "Are you familiar with Chicago's Lakefront Trail?"

"I am," Cortes replied.

"Excellent. On the northern trail just past Foster Avenue, there is basketball court on the east side of the trail. There is a fence around the court. Behind the fence, next to the northern basket, is a bench. Unless there is full court game, the bench is usually empty. I want you to put the flash drive into a small manila envelope and tape it to the underside of the bench tomorrow morning exactly at 9 a.m." Burksdale replied.

"Tomorrow is Saturday. Won't the court be busy?" Cortes inquired.

Burksdale then spoke slowly and calmly. "Not at 9 a.m. I am in that area frequently, and the basketball players don't show up until late morning or noon. Now, the flash drive I gave you has a GPS tracking mechanism in it. I will know when it's in place. You will not need to look or wait for me. Just go to the bench, sit down, use duct tape to secure the envelope to the underside of the bench. I recommend you do it quickly and without drawing any attention to yourself. There should be no excessive activity. You will then leave the area. I am a man of my word, Doctor. As I told you before, if you deliver what I request, you will never hear from me again. If there are any observers that I detect at the drop site, if the data you supply doesn't meet expectations, or if I feel there is something you have done to compromise our arrangement, I will become your worst nightmare. Are we clear?"

Cortes was doing his best to remain calm. The strength he had just a few minutes ago was slipping away. He responded, "Yes, I understand," and then he swallowed hard. He could feel his mouth become dry. The phone call then disconnected. Cortes continued to hold the phone next to his ear until the long beeping tone of the phone became irritating. He slowly returned the phone to its cradle. Cortes then unlocked his desk drawer and retrieved the flash drive and placed it into his shirt pocket. As he stood up to return to the meeting, he thought for a moment, and then retrieved the flash drive out of his pocket. Cortes sat back down at his desk and placed the flash drive into his computer.

A digital watermark is a piece of code embedded in a digital file. An invisible digital watermark (IDW) is a type of steganography that conceals information in a medium to prove ownership or provide additional information. It can be used to cryptically, digitally mark intellectual property or copyrighted documents.

Cortes created the IDW on the modified file, removed the flash drive, and replaced it into his pocket. He then went to his secretary and obtained a small manila envelope from her. He placed it into his briefcase and then returned to the meeting. Cortes knew what he had to do, and reassured himself that his editing of the protocol file performed earlier in the morning would be secure, unlikely traceable, and highly effective in preventing the protocol from working. It took Cortes several minutes to clear his head and get back into the logistical planning that was ongoing in the meeting. He was able to then re-engage in the discussion, knowing that after tomorrow, all would be normal again.

CHAPTER 45

Chicago, IL

Cortes was up at 6 a.m. He quickly showered and ate—he did not want to be late to the bicycle trail bench. Although traffic would be light, Cortes knew the parking situation along the lakefront could be challenging. He wanted to arrive no later than 8 a.m. Not being completely familiar with the area, he wanted this process to be over and done without any glitches. Cortes was surprised he found parking easily and had to walk only one block to the trail. He assured the envelop was secure in his pocket, and the roll of duct tape was in his backpack. Just as the stranger had stated, despite it being a Saturday, the bike trail and basketball court were nearly empty. A few joggers and bicyclists went by, but the area surrounding the court was quiet. By 8:30 a.m., Cortes was sitting by himself on the assigned bench. It was a warm, calm morning. He looked out at the lake, which was smooth as glass. Wanting to do everything as instructed, he took out his newspaper and did his best to read while waiting for the time to pass. Cortes's ability to focus on the news articles was nonexistent, but he went through the motions of trying to read to help with his anxiety. At exactly 9:00 a.m., he opened his backpack, tore off a few strips of the gray-silver tape, and attached them to the manila envelope. He then looked around, assuring nobody was in his vicinity. Cortes then bent over and attached the envelope to the underside of the middle of the bench. He pressed the tape firmly onto the undersurface of the wooden bench. Cortes continued to sit there for a few moments, again checking for any observers. As none were seen, he got up, returned to his car, and felt a massive sense of relief. Cortes then drove home. His work was now done.

Burksdale observed everything through his binoculars from nearly 200 yards away. Despite his previous bravado, he wanted to make sure Cortes performed as instructed. Burksdale needed the flash drive and was dependent upon Cortes to comply. He didn't observe anyone in the vicinity who appeared to be keeping tabs on the bench. As he observed the activity, Burksdale reflected that he actually respected Cortes for his intellect and scientific endeavors. But he also reminded himself that he wouldn't hesitate to eliminate Cortes when necessary. First, he needed affirmation that the protocol Cortes supplied worked—then Cortes would be a simple target.

Once he knew the flash drive was in place, Burksdale waited patiently until he spotted what he needed: a young boy riding a bicycle by himself. Burksdale approached the boy and offered him $100 to retrieve the envelope. The child complied, and within minutes, Burksdale had his flash drive. As he opened the envelope to assure the device was there, Burksdale thought about all the steps he had taken, the background research, the tailing, and the planning and effort he exerted to get to this point. Burksdale justified his actions as necessary, and believed others would have had the same collateral casualties to achieve the same endpoint. He felt he *earned* his payment on this job, and this would be reflected by his higher than usual fee before turning the flash drive over. Ashwood may have brought him in, but only because of his incompetence and over-confidence in his computer skills. Burksdale knew Ashwood was the link to the payroll, but Burksdale held the prize. He put the flash drive into his pocket and made his customary two-block walk back to his car. It was time to contact Ashwood and make the exchange for payment.

CHAPTER 46

Chicago, IL

Yamp finished his last surgical procedure of the day around 4 p.m. By the time he finished discussing his findings with the patient's family, changed into street clothes, and completed the three-block walk back to his office, it was nearly 5 p.m. He considered waiting another day to contact Special Agent Knight, but tomorrow looked like a disaster on his calendar. Yamp located Knight's contact information and dialed his cell.

"Agent Knight, this is Jay Yamp."

"Good evening, Doctor. To what do I owe this call?" Knight responded.

Yamp began, "Well…I had a long discussion last night with a friend of mine who was the director of a division at *Yonie Pharmaceuticals*, one of the largest pharmaceutical companies in the world. I should preface this by telling you I previously asked him to look into the research that *Harris Therapeutics* performs. In doing so, he uncovered some unusual activity going on at *Yonie* that may be pertinent to the recent murders. I guess I should disclose that years ago, I was doing my own clinical trials with a chemical…more precisely…a *hydrogel,* that I helped develop to treat kidney stones more effectively. That hydrogel was later identified to be used in some horrific murders instigated by some administrators at *Yonie.* They were engaged in corrupt marketing of their opioids, and *Yonie* ended up paying a huge penalty along with the guilty administrators going to jail. Obviously, not everyone at *Yonie* is corrupt…in fact, one of the people they were trying to murder was an honest whistleblower in their own company! Their Oncologic Pharmaceutical Division, however, is outstanding…or…well, I know it was when my friend was its director. Anyway… are you still with me?"

"Yes…I'm just listening…and trying to take notes when I can," Knight answered.

Yamp continued, "okay, well, let me get straight to the point. My friend, Jason Kogan had some data files that he…ahh…took with him when he left…or rather, when he was let go from *Yonie.* As the previous director of the division, he had access to all the research going on. Jason was able to pick through it and eventually identify one of the labs in the oncologic division that was currently working on developing a new type of cancer vaccine. This is a huge new area of cancer therapeutics that is expanding worldwide. These vaccines may turn out to be the future of cancer treatment and possibly its prevention. Everyone wants in on it, but few companies have the resources to enter that arena. What Jason was able to determine, or at least what he thinks he found, is that a lab at *Yonie* is close to developing the cancer vaccine. But it needs a particular lymphocyte called a T cell. The means to make that T cell is via the mRNA molecule we talked about the other day."

Knight cut in, "Yes…I recall."

Yamp continued, "The lab at *Yonie* needs the mRNA molecule to make the required T cell. This T cell is part of the immunological response that interacts with the cancer the body is attacking. But *Yonie* doesn't have that particular mRNA…which means it needs to acquire it somehow. Guess who happens to have the capability and methodology to make that mRNA?"

Knight listened carefully. He then responded, "Let me guess… *Harris Therapeutics*?"

Yamp enthusiastically answered, "Exactly! *Harris* has the capability to manufacture the mRNA. But…more important than that…its Doctor Cortes's lab that makes it!"

"You've got to be kidding me!" Knight replied. "But if *Yonie* is as big and powerful as you say, why don't they just buy *Harris* out? Then they would own the mRNA as well."

Yamp replied, "I agree…they could…and they probably should. But to do so would bring about regulatory investigations, disclosures, and it would require a significant amount of time. If *Yonie* had the mRNA molecule they needed before anybody else knew what they were creating with it, they would be months to years ahead of everyone else developing and marketing a new cancer vaccine. The profits could be in the *billions!*"

There was a long silence on the other end of the phone. Knight was writing both what he heard and what he was thinking. "So, if I'm hearing you correctly, Doctor Yamp, you believe someone at *Yonie* is behind all of this. If this is true, then it's also ironic that in a pharmaceutical company battle, the murder technique would also be pharmacologic…using poisons. But this doesn't explain why two scientists would be killed? What did they have to do with any of this? Could they have been selling out to someone at *Yonie*…meaning they were being paid to give proprietary information to *Yonie,* and once they complied, they were eliminated?"

Yamp replied quickly, "No way. Bob Margolis was honorable. I can't speak about the other victim…err…Rebecca Sunnis…but Bob wouldn't jeopardize his reputation or his career for this. It would go against…well, I didn't really know him *that* well, but this was not consistent with what I knew about him."

Knight responded, "I'll do a check on the victims' bank accounts… see if there were any unusual deposits made over…perhaps the last year or so. But I would agree, knowing what I do about them, this wouldn't be a plausible explanation."

Yamp asked, "Could their deaths have been meant as a threat to someone else?"

"Explain," Knight stated.

Yamp began, "Well, let's assume *Yonie* didn't want to buy the mRNA molecule from *Harris*—that would give other competitors a leg up on what they were doing. I also suspect *Harris* could have then charged *Yonie* an astronomical fee…whatever it wanted. Maybe *Yonie* felt it didn't want to run that risk either. Intra-pharmaceutical company espionage is certainly not new. *Yonie* knew what *Harris* had, and they wanted it. So, I guess *Yonie,* or someone who worked at *Yonie,* could have decided to steal the mRNA."

Knight interjected, "I was at *Harris Therapeutics,* and let me tell you, that place is like a fortress. If their cybersecurity is anything like their physical plant, nobody is stealing anything from them. I've never seen anything that secure outside of a national defense installation. I doubt stealing would be easy, or even possible."

Yamp thought for a moment and then answered, "Well, if you can't steal something you want, perhaps you need to somehow *encourage* someone to give it to you."

Knight suddenly perked up. "Repeat that again, Doctor…I was just thinking about something else."

Yamp said again, "I was just saying that maybe encouraging someone to give you something might be the next alternative, if you can't take it."

Knight was suddenly aware of what he was distracted by. "It's interesting you are saying that…a little while ago, Detectives Blight and Rose were with me at *Harris* interviewing Doctor Cortes and Waters…the CEO. We all felt that Cortes was behaving a bit peculiar… particularly when we asked him if there had been any threats to his lab. He denied any. Maybe the threats were…"

Yamp cut in, "Maybe the threats were directed to him. Maybe the deaths of his associates were intended as an incentive for Cortes to comply with certain demands?"

Knight considered what he just heard, and then replied, "That's an interesting thought…if it's true, it would be a pathetic waste of life. But most people would still find a way to reach out to us for help when threatened."

Yamp added, “Not unless the person is absolutely petrified…maybe the killer didn’t threaten Cortes directly…perhaps he threatened Cortes’s family members—people he knew he couldn’t protect or help. I can’t think of any other reason he would hold back. Wait a minute. I have another thought. Cortes controlled the lab…if someone threatened him for something he oversaw, wouldn’t it be possible Cortes could have planned a countermeasure of his own?”

Knight responded, “Meaning?”

Yamp continued his thought, “I mean, if someone wanted to know how to do something, or create something…sort of like someone asking you for a recipe, and you willingly give it—but you leave something out…you leave out a certain ingredient. Maybe Cortes knew he was trapped, but by somehow camouflaging what he was giving up would allow him to escape the threat.”

Knight cut in, “Or maybe it would just delay things until the absence of that ingredient is identified.”

“Maybe,” Yamp acknowledged. “But Cortes is a brilliant scientist… he also knows his own lab inside and out…maybe he could have changed something that is so subtle it wouldn’t be found out until…”

“Maybe until we come in?” Knight added. “It’s a good thought, Doctor. I think it’s time I had another chat with Doctor Cortes.”

“Yes,” Yamp agreed. “I’d be interested to hear if that’s what happened. Well, please let me know what evolves…and if you have other questions, don’t hesitate to call.”

“Yes, thank you, Doctor Yamp. I appreciate your call today. I think this discussion may have put us in the right direction. We’ll talk again.” The phones disconnected.

CHAPTER 47

Chicago, IL

Detectives Rose and Blight notified Knight to set up a meeting immediately. They put together their discoveries and wanted to discuss them with the FBI before proceeding any further with their investigations. Coincidentally, Knight felt a meeting was similarly necessary after his discussion with Yamp the night before. They arranged to meet in the Chicago field office of the FBI. When the three were assembled, Knight began the discussion.

"Doctor Yamp called and informed me of some incredible findings," Knight began. "It appears that another company called *Yonie Pharmaceuticals* in the northern suburbs has been developing a new cancer drug that...well, from what Yamp's sources have informed him, their prospective drug development requires the specific molecule that Doctor Cortes's lab created. For what could be solely financial reasons, *Yonie Pharmaceuticals,* or some nefarious individuals at that company, could be behind the murders of the scientists at *Harris Therapeutics.*" Knight continued to discuss the reasoning behind this assertion.

"That's incredible...if, of course, it's true," Blight stated. "But it sounds like we now need to begin an investigation of *Yonie.*"

Knight interrupted, "Well, perhaps...but I don't think it will be as daunting as it may sound. Although *Yonie* has something like 50,000 employees worldwide, we would just have to focus on the specific lab that is...ahh...*hoping* to use the mRNA molecule. Predicated on that investigation, we would then branch out from there. I sincerely doubt any of this was initiated by the lab scientists. I guess it's possible, but my suspicion is there are upper-level individuals at the company that conjured up this scheme—again, assuming this is the case. Nobody is going to hire an assassin and financially support such an operation without a significant bankroll behind it. And, if this is the situation we are facing, someone who is able to control and hide money transfers within the financial sector of the company would more likely be the culprit. There is no way this would come out of the mind-set of a scientist. Remember, it's still just a hypothesis based on putting some disjointed pieces of information together. We haven't proven they are doing anything wrong...yet. Also, I checked on the financials of the victims—Sunnis and Margolis. Yamp and I wanted to make sure they weren't being bought off for assisting in any transfer of intellectual property from *Harris*. We were considering that their deaths could have come from some type of participation with our perp. Neither one had any significant or unusual deposits in their bank accounts prior to their deaths. So, I think it's safe to assume they were not part of some scheme by *Yonie* or anyone else to try to buy them off."

Rose interjected, "Well, before we go over to investigate *Yonie,* we had better be ready for all possibilities. If we go there and sniff around, and individuals at *Yonie are* the instigators, word will travel fast, and our perp or perps will be gone in a hurry. At this point, Blight and I may have what we need to take down who we believe is the assassin."

Knight added, "Terrific. Tell me what you turned up."

Rose pulled out his notes. "As it turns out, we were able to identify the car leaving the golf course right after the cologne bottles were dropped off. It was a 2016 gray Dodge Charger. Given the owner could have changed the original paint on the car, we ignored its color in our search. In 2016, just over 73,000 of those cars were sold in the US—most were sold in Texas and Wyoming. We cross-referenced those vehicles with registration data stored at the DMV in the tri-state area, and were able to isolate a little over three thousand still registered in our search area. We then started with Illinois registrations, and this state currently uses a designated PIN and registration ID for plate renewal. Recall we didn't have the actual tag number on the car—the plates on the car were stolen. But at one point, the perp had to register the vehicle. By cross-referencing registration information with digital driver's license photographs, we narrowed our search considerably. We ignored owners younger than 40, and women. That alone eliminated nearly 85% of the owners."

Knight cut in, "Why eliminate those less than 40?"

Rose replied, "Recall our perp was reported to have gray hair and a beard by the wine shop clerk. I know it's not scientific, but I started turning gray around 45 or so, so we decided to use 40 as a cutoff."

Knight smiled, and responded, "Well…fine. I don't know if there is a scientific way to include everyone who could be gray…and of course, our perp could have dyed his hair…or the car could be registered with say, his wife or girlfriend for all we know. But I'm okay with your methodology… go on."

Blight jumped into the conversation, saying, "I went back and got a more detailed description of the man who purchased the wine bottle used on Sunnis at the wine shop. As you remember, Stephen, the wine store attendant, said initially the perp had gray hair and a beard. He was of average height. But after tweaking his memory, Stephen also recalled our guy wore glasses. Stephen also remembered specifically that our perp wore *horn-rimmed* glasses. A little weird, as they are certainly not fashionable, but okay. Anyway…I'm sorry, go on detective."

Detective Rose smiled at Blight. He appreciated her enthusiasm. "Yes, as I was saying…we were now able to narrow our driver's license images to about fifty owners in Illinois who had gray hair and beards…we had the lab time-adjust the photographic images for those taken three years ago. And…when we add in those who require optical correction, the search is now down to only fifteen individuals who fit our description."

Knight jumped into the conversation. "You are assuming the glasses and beard were not part of a disguise?"

Blight stated, "No, of course that is a possibility, but two other things...I was able to identify the same car in front of the wine shop after the perp made his purchase. The driver was slightly darkened in the videos, but with image sharpening tools, we could see he had glasses on while driving. I think it would be unlikely when not required, the perp would keep glasses on."

"Unless the lenses were without prescription," Knight added. "Or he's very good at maintaining a disguise even when alone. Okay...let's assume the glasses were real...go on."

Blight glanced at Rose. She continued with obvious frustration. "Listen, I took the images of the fifteen faces we lifted from the DMV. The wine shop clerk was able to point out two guys he thought could be our perp. I also asked the woman cashier about the images...she also picked out two photographs she felt could be him. Independently, they both pointed to the same images!"

Knight was pleased. Despite trying to punch holes in their work, he realized they had narrowed the available data down carefully, and had eyewitnesses verify their findings. "Excellent work, detectives. I want to go back to *Harris* and have another meeting with Doctor Cortes. I think he is holding back. It's also possible he's met our perp as well—so Blight, bring those images of possible suspects when we go there. I think we're close. But if what Yamp said is accurate, and the perp is working for someone at *Yonie,* we don't want whoever set this whole thing up to run. We can't grab the perp just yet.

Burksdale contacted Ashwood via a rather cryptic text message to inform him that he had retrieved the information that was requested:

From: Jonathan Burksdale
To: Lucifer Ashwood
The job is complete. How would you like to proceed?

Ashwood was pleased to hear this good news and responded:

From: Lucifer Ashwood
To: Jonathan Burksdale
Excellent. Let's meet at the same spot as previously.

Burksdale replied:

From: Jonathan Burksdale
To: Lucifer Ashwood
Will do after balance is wired to my account. Use the same account number as before. Fee expected is 1.0. Inform me when transfer is complete and then set up time and date to meet.

Ashwood acknowledged his understanding. As in the past, they used either fractional or digital denominations to represent the expected payment amount. No actual dollar sign of the payment amount was ever communicated. '1.0' represented one million dollars. Ashwood felt Burksdale was charging a higher than usual fee, but he also understood the greater than usual amount of effort expended. Ashwood would also submit a significant, albeit lower fee to Neil Goodall as well. All told, he would communicate to Goodall that 1.25 million dollars was expected for the retrieval of the mRNA synthesis protocol. Once payment was received from Goodall, Ashwood would make the transfer to Burksdale and then set up their meeting.

Goodall received the message from Ashwood. He was expecting a large fee and knew he had little recourse to negotiate once the job was assigned. As per his reputation, Ashwood was never cheap, but he always delivered. Goodall wired the requested amount to Ashwood's Cayman Island account using a series of intermediary banks that had laundered money for him in the past. By the time the money was in Ashwood's account, the 1.25 million dollars wired out would now *appear* on the *Yonie* books as money that was spent on a new, but unfortunately failed, investigative means to use algae for a new drug program. Goodall was a master at manipulating the *Yonie* financial documentation, and he knew where the company bones were buried. After all, he buried most of them.

Goodall received confirmation that Ashwood would deliver the information on a flash drive, and they arranged a meet in 72 hours. Goodall was pleased to know that Shamus O'Donnell's lab would soon have the protocol and could begin its work. He knew it would take time…perhaps even months for the lab to be able to begin manufacturing the necessary molecule. Goodall would need to assess how things were progressing before considering any intervention on Shamus. He would have to see how the scientist behaved himself. Goodall would keep Shamus on a very short leash.

CHAPTER 48

Wheaton, IL

Having completed his obligation to Burksdale and successfully rearranged the workflow in his lab to accommodate the loss of his associates, Cortes finally got his lab back into a functional routine. And although it had only been 48 hours since he gave Burksdale the flash drive, it seemed like a lifetime ago. He was feeling relaxed and able to concentrate on his work. When Cortes was informed by his secretary three law enforcement officers were back in the conference room and desired to speak with him, all those good feelings vanished. Cortes knew he had to oblige them but was quite uncomfortable regarding their presence. In the past, the officers made appointments to see him; this time they appeared unannounced. Cortes also understood that if he wanted to move on with his life, he shouldn't open any doors that could lead to trouble. He reminded himself of his last discussion with the stranger and knew he needed to remain quiet.

Cortes opened the conference room door, and smiled as he acknowledged the investigators. "I really didn't expect to see you again," he stated while looking at Agent Knight. He noted none of the investigators smiled back. Knight motioned for him to sit down, and Cortes complied.

"Well, we have a way of showing up when people least expect us, Doctor." Knight made an effort to keep the meeting positive...

at least initially. He continued, "We just have a few more questions for you, Doctor Cortes. In a case that involves double homicides, the number of facts and findings that need to be tied together will increase exponentially. Nothing by itself makes sense sometimes in these investigations. But when we start putting elements of each murder together, we start to see patterns that need to be explored. I'm sure you understand what I'm saying."

Cortes responded, "No question about it. More variables lead to more issues to account for. Well, what can I help you with today?"

Knight, Rose, and Blight previously rehearsed their intended discussion. Blight thought it might be effective to display the images of the possible perpetrator to see if they elicited a reaction from Cortes. If so, they would exploit that. None of them knew if he was a poker player and could hide his emotions. They would just have to use their experience and intuition to make that assessment at the time. Given the concern that he might not be forthright in answering questions up front, this was the plan they eventually agreed upon.

Blight joined the conversation, "Doctor Cortes, I have some pictures we're wondering if you could take a look at. Would you mind?"

Cortes looked at her curiously and then said, "Well…sure… what are they of?" As she moved closer to him, the others positioned themselves where they could have a clear view of his facial expressions. The movements around the table didn't arouse any suspicion from Cortes, as he assumed they, too, wanted to look at the images. Everyone bent over the conference table as Blight revealed the first image. It was intentionally an image of no suspect in this crime, but rather, of a simple shoplifting case from several years ago. The image had no resemblance to the suspected perp.

Blight asked, "Doctor, have you ever met this individual?"

Cortes looked carefully at the image and shook his head from side-to-side. "No, I have never seen this person," Cortes confidently responded. Blight then repeated this with three additional photographs, and they all elicited the same response. Blight then revealed the image they thought was the perp.

In the world of poker, there are many things that can give your hand away. Subtle movements, gestures, or behavior changes are what are referred to as tells. *To understand another player's tell, one typically needs to witness the same movement or behavior previously and associate it with a particular outcome.*

Both Blight and Knight had previously witnessed Cortes's behavior when uncomfortably questioned. Knight remembered his reaction when he initially questioned Cortes about being threatened. Knight recalled how Cortes's eyes darted about during the conversation, and he was unable to look straight at him. At that time, he felt Cortes was not being truthful. Blight, too, recalled that initial interview and his jittery behavior when asked that question. As Blight pulled out the next photograph, she again asked him if he recognized the face. Cortes said, "No."

And there was the tell. Blight and Knight picked it up immediately. She looked him straight in the eye and repeated, "Are you sure you don't recognize this face?"

Cortes looked down and away from her when he responded and repeated his answer, "No, just as I said before…I've never seen this face before."

Knight felt it was time to intervene and stated, "Doctor Cortes, are you aware that lying to a federal agent about an investigation is a crime? It's a felony, Doctor. Are you sure you want to go to prison for protecting someone?"

Cortes felt his throat become parched. He looked at Knight with pleading eyes and slumped back into his chair. Cortes whispered, "You don't understand."

Knight looked straight at Cortes. "Make me understand, Doctor. Is this the man who threatened you?"

Cortes looked at the photograph again, and then nodded his head. Again, in nearly a whisper he said, "Yes."

Knight asked in a kind voice, "What did this man tell you, Doctor?"

Cortes looked up with red eyes and his hands visibly shaking. He cried out, "You can't understand what it's like to have two of your closest friends…people you worked with…killed! And…then to be threatened yourself…yes…yes…I met this face before." Cortes now started crying. He took a moment to regain his composure before continuing. "He came to my house and threatened me…he told me in no uncertain terms that if I informed anyone of our meeting, I, or someone in my family, would meet the same fate as Rebecca and Bob. He used their murders as examples for me. How do you think that makes me feel, Agent Knight?"

Knight didn't respond. Cortes continued, "He was after *my* protocol to produce a specific molecule for someone…and he used my colleagues as mere pawns to influence me. And yes…it worked."

Knight glanced quickly at detective Rose and Blight and stated, "So you gave him the synthesis protocol?"

Cortes looked up…tears were rolling down his cheeks. "Yes." He lowered his voice to being barely audible as he looked down at the table. "Yes…I felt I had no choice." There was silence in the room for a few moments. Cortes then looked up and turned directly to Knight. This time, his expression had changed. Cortes had a sheepish grin on his face. "But I didn't give the fucker everything. I modified the protocol."

Blight looked at her fellow investigators. She then commented, "But won't they discover that? Won't he just come back again?"

Cortes felt himself gaining his strength. "Yes…maybe…but not for quite a while. You see, I gave him the proper instructions for creating the molecule…but it's quite fragile. Without supplying them the specific method necessary for what we call capping…that's a means to preserve the molecule…it will decay quite quickly…within only a minute or so. So, whoever gets this protocol will be able to make the damn mRNA molecule, but it won't survive very long. It will be degraded before they can put it to use. It's a very delicate molecule and quite finicky to work with. Perhaps that's why it's so valuable."

Detective Rose came into the conversation, "Doctor, how long before they would discover this modification?"

Cortes felt he was no longer a victim now...he was the hunter. His demeanor changed as he became professorial while considering the question. Cortes looked at all three of the inquisitive investigators. "My suspicion is that whoever now has the protocol must have the facilities and possesses the fundamental scientific knowledge to produce the mRNA. So, we would be dealing with an expert in molecular biology and laboratory technique." Cortes looked at the ceiling as he was trying to make some calculations. "Still, it would probably take them a few months to obtain some of the specific materials needed—assuming there is no back-order or delivery delays. They would then need to weed through the synthesis protocol and reprogram certain required computerized equipment. My best guess is it would be about three to four months until they would identify the problem they had. When I considered how to modify the protocol, I was hoping the time delay would be enough for somebody to stop whatever was going on." Cortes opened his arms in front of the three of them as he stated what he was hoping for. Cortes knew they were on his side, and he felt ashamed for trying to evade their questions.

Knight sat back in his chair as he considered what he just heard. He then stated, "Look, we know the name of perp who threatened Doctor Cortes. We have his address...and he doesn't know we know. He has the protocol information and must get it to someone, who will then get it, eventually, to a lab. So, there are several intermediaries involved. The question is when to nab him. If we jump too quickly, the others will disappear. If we allow time for the protocol to make its way into a lab, there are more potential opportunities to interrupt and catch those involved."

Blight added, "Agreed. Knowing we have a three-month window is helpful. So, let's assume for a minute the protocol is in the hands of a scientist at *Yonie*. Should we work backwards from the scientist...who might also be the weakest link?"

Rose stated, "Yes...we know which lab is working on the suspicious project at *Yonie*. I suspect the scientist will be like Doctor Cortes...and will want to stop this from progressing. Maybe he is also under some type of threat."

"Unless the scientist has a vested interest," Cortes added. "Greed has no limits to any particular profession."

Knight then rejoined the conversation. "I agree with Detective Blight. If we work backwards from the lab at *Yonie*, we will climb the food chain of this case more effectively. However, I fear if word got out that we were investigating the lab, even our presence there would create panic, and those involved would fly away."

Detective Rose asked, "What do you suggest?"

Knight looked at everyone in the room. "I suggest we eliminate any potential for flight. It could be risky, but one option would be to grab the perp at the same time we invade the lab. I think with the information we have, we could get a search warrant for *Yonie.* I'll run this by Deputy Director Jacoby and get his take on this. I also want to talk to Doctor Yamp as well as his source…I want to make damn sure we have this tight as a drum before we jump."

"Agreed," added Blight. Rose nodded his head.

Knight looked at Cortes, "Doctor Cortes…we appreciate your information and ultimately coming forward. We understand how difficult this has been for you. This conversation, however, shall remain confidential. Not a word of it is to be shared with anyone. Am I clear?"

Cortes shook his head in the affirmative. "Yes…I understand. Thank you all. This has been a nightmare for me. I appreciate your efforts and help."

The investigators walked out of the building. They accomplished what they intended.

As they each got into their cars, Knight turned to Rose and Blight. "Now the real work begins. I'll stay in touch."

CHAPTER 49

Glenview, IL

Goodall decided he would leave his ivory tower and go into the trenches—to the laboratories in the Research and Development Buildings at *Yonie Pharmaceuticals.* He wanted a face-to-face meeting with Shamus O'Donnell and make sure he was a team player. It was one thing to *talk the talk*, but Goodall needed to know that the one-and-a-quarter-million dollars he just spent would be put to use without delay. If Goodall sensed any doubts from O'Donnell, he wouldn't hesitate to take him out of the picture—literally.

As he entered the building where O'Donnell's lab was located, Goodall was immediately affronted by the smells of research. The odor of animals and their excrement, a variety of pungent chemicals, and the strong scent of disinfectants and sterilizing agents made him want to turn around and return to his comfortable confines. He couldn't imagine spending entire days in such a wretched environment. Goodall much preferred the comfort of his leather chair, the soothing quality of the music he listened to, and the aesthetic beauty of the artwork hanging on his office walls during his pampered, well-paying workday. He walked the pale green industrial hallways until he reached O'Donnell's lab and opened the metal door. There were five or six people working, all wearing long, white lab coats. Some were working through a glass box while their hands were inside of black rubberized gloves. Large metallic machines whirred as their robotic arms could be seen moving a variety of flasks and other containers around. There were a variety of types of hazard signs posted throughout the room.

There was also silence. No music, and very little discussion between workers. Unlike the carpeted, clean, freshly scented elegance of the administrative building, this was where the real work of science lived.

Goodall asked the closest lab worker where he might find Doctor O'Donnell.

The lab worker responded, "Oh…sure…Amy…do you know where Shamus went?"

Amy responded, "No…not really." She looked at Goodall. "Hi…is there anything I can help you with?"

"Are you Shamus O'Donnell?" Goodall asked sarcastically.

"Well, no…of course not…I'm Amy…his senior lab associate." She ignored his snide remark. "I'm sure he'll be back soon. Perhaps you want to sit in his office?" Amy's hands were full of glassware, so she pointed her head towards the door that led to O'Donnell's private office.

"Excellent idea, Amy. I'll do that," Goodall replied arrogantly and walked towards the office door.

Once he entered the office, all the lab workers looked at one another. It was obvious to them the unknown, obnoxious man was from administration—the ID badge color he was wearing delineated which department an employee worked in. He looked and behaved as though he was from the *better* side of town.

Inside the cramped office, Goodall tip-toed around the many papers strewn about the floor. Eventually, he reached the chair with the least number of books stacked on it. Goodall simply pushed the books onto the floor with absolute disdain and sat down. He was disgusted with the manner with which the office was kept. Yet, he understood O'Donnell had an international reputation and was revered in the scientific pharmaceutical world. He sat waiting for O'Donnell to return and passed the time checking emails on his cellphone. After fifteen minutes, a hurried O'Donnell entered.

"Oh…I didn't know we had a meeting scheduled today…my apologies," the flustered scientist said.

"No, we don't. I just wanted to stop down and see how you are doing. Everything okay with you?" Goodall inquired.

"Well, yes…yes…things are just fine…thank you for asking." O'Donnell answered, curiously. "Is there anything in particular you were wondering, Mr. Goodall?"

Goodall began, "Well, let's get right to the point, shall we?" You recall…may I call you Shamus?"

"Yes…of course…that's what I go by around here," O'Donnell replied.

"Good. Okay, Shamus. Remember awhile back you came to me with the great idea for our advancement into cancer vaccination therapies…prostate cancer, more specifically?" Goodall asked.

O'Donnell stated, "Why, yes…of course I do. But to do that, we needed a specific mRNA molecule…"

Goodall cut him off, "Well, we have it. Well, not exactly…" Goodall used his hands to gesture quotations around "it". "We have the formula, or whatever term you use, to make it now."

"That's terrific news!" O'Donnell exclaimed. Despite whatever Goodall thought of O'Donnell, that was precisely the response he was hoping for.

"I'm glad to hear you're still onboard, Shamus," Goodall stated, while still trying to assess if the scientist was gaming him.

"Absolutely…if you have the protocol, I'll get working on it ASAP," O'Donnell stated, enthusiastically.

Goodall stared at O'Donnell for an extended moment. He decided the man was being straight with him. Goodall really didn't know what else to ask. He reminded himself that sometimes things are exactly what they look like. Goodall reached into his pants pocket and produced the precious flash drive. "Here's your…protocol, Doctor."

Shamus walked up to Goodall and plucked it out of his hand. He immediately went to his computer and placed the flash drive into the USB port. As the computer's internal cooling fan started to whirr, Goodall moved next to O'Donnell so he could see the monitor as well. After a few moments, the file opened. Shamus started scrolling down through the text, images, and diagrams. He was impressed with how massive it was—hundreds of pages long.

Shamus stated, "This is incredible." He continued to scroll down, periodically stopping to read a line or two. "This is most impressive... Mr. Goodall." Shamus looked up from the monitor and looked at Goodall. "I don't want to know and I'm not going to ask how you obtained this. But this is an elegant piece of science." Shamus sat back in his chair and looked around his office. "I suspect, however, it may take several months at least, to go through this entire document, identify what supplies and equipment we need, have them delivered, and have the lab reconfigured for production. Even then...there are variables we can't predict right now...but we will get right on it."

Goodall appeared disappointed at hearing the anticipated time frame before they would have what he wanted, but he also understood he was in no position to debate what the scientist just stated. "Well, Doctor...do your best to produce it as quickly as you can. I don't think it bears repeating, but I will anyway. This information is confidential. What you are going to do with it is the same. I don't give a damn what you tell your laboratory *help,* but they mustn't be informed of me giving this to you. Is that clear?"

"Understood, Mr. Goodall," Shamus stated. "As far as they are concerned, the document was conceived and written right here at this desk. They'll give us no trouble."

"Good to know, Shamus. I'm counting on you. Make this happen," Goodall stated firmly.

"I'll keep you posted," Shamus replied. Goodall then slipped his way past the papers on the floor and exited the office. Despite several of the lab associates stating their goodbyes, Goodall ignored them and left the laboratory. Completing the several-block walk back to his office building, Goodall was pleased with what had just transpired. As he reached the comfort of his leather chair, he felt confident that Shamus would produce the molecule he needed. *He'd fucking better*, Goodall thought to himself, as he turned his attention to the quad-monitors adjacent to his desk and reviewed the stock market trends for the day.

In the lab, Shamus cleared his desk and prepared to dive into the mRNA protocol. Just as he was about to begin, Amy walked in.

"So, what's that guy's story, Shamus? What an asshole!" Amy stated.

"Yes...well, he's an administrator...what can I say," Shamus replied while avoiding eye contact with Amy. He wasn't yet prepared to deal with his associates asking questions. "He...ahh...wanted me to look into some QA issues...nothing to concern yourself with."

"That's weird," Amy stated, while shrugging her shoulders. "I've never seen the suited guys from the tower come over here for that."

Shamus cut her off. "Well, I think there is other stuff going on that we're not privy to...nothing for you to concern yourself with, Amy." Shamus wanted to change the conversation. "Is everything going okay out front?"

"Sure, why wouldn't it be?" Amy asked curiously. "By the way... are you going to the conference this weekend at McCormick Place?"

Shamus was relieved to know the conversation was moving on. "Absolutely...the meeting should be interesting, but more importantly, I always enjoy seeing some of my old pals. Us older guys like to reminisce about the good ole' days in the business."

As Shamus returned his attention to his computer monitor, Amy took this as her cue and left his office. Once Shamus heard the door close, he looked up at the door and exhaled a large sigh. He needed to figure out how he was going to move through this project. His lab associates were all bright and inquisitive—there was no way he could just drop this on them without serious questions or even some push-back. Shamus stood up and stretched. He still didn't know how Goodall got his hands on the synthesis protocol, and perhaps it's best he didn't. Shamus considered that he could tell his staff the project they were going to soon begin was part of a dual-company enterprise. He knew they would accept and work with that explanation if a reasonable—and inclusive—discussion about the project was made. In a way, it was, he reminded himself. Shamus decided he would think about how he would present the protocol to his staff, as there was still quite a bit of time before he could get through the lengthy file anyway.

CHAPTER 50

Glenview, IL

After three days of pouring over the details of the synthesis protocol, Shamus was physically and mentally spent. He had taken detailed notes of the impressive file and felt he understood what needed to be obtained. Would he be able to put it together as outlined, was his major concern. Shamus knew that every scientific laboratory is similar to a chef's kitchen—slight variations in equipment design can affect outcome. However, when you are talking about the production of *molecules,* entities that are measured in *nanometers,* there are essentially no allowances for variation—there are none. If the molecules are to react predictably and consistently after production, there can simply be no deviation in size, weight, or function. After reading the file, Shamus was similarly concerned if he would be able to produce the mRNA according to the time schedule he previously suggested to Goodall. Well, it wouldn't be the first time in his career that anticipated dates of experimental progress would need to be adjusted. He would just monitor how things went. Hopefully, Goodall would accept an explanation.

With that conclusion, Shamus shut off his computer. It was Friday evening, and he wanted to go home, relax, and then review the agenda for the upcoming Midwest Pharmaceutical Conference—the yearly meeting of scientists from both academia and industry, convening to compare notes and, well, show off. The meeting was always enjoyable for Shamus. Although he ran out of patience making it through the actual meeting presentations, Shamus liked to walk around the exhibits and catch up with old colleagues. The meeting was also a very strange get-together of friends and foes—everyone who registers for the conference is working on a proprietary project they are prohibited from discussing. Yet, everyone also knows what everyone else is working on. So, it's sort of a cat-and-mouse game of letting competitors know, *in-part*, what you are up to, but not telling the whole story. Perhaps, it's that very collegial gamesmanship that Shamus enjoys the most.

As anticipated, on the first morning of the meeting, the large plenary session was packed by 8:00 a.m. Shamus knew that by the third day of the three-day meeting, that same large room would be only one-quarter full. The meeting was divided into two daily segments—a morning plenary session, and a shorter one in the afternoon. The attendees were expected to visit with the exhibitors as well. Many of the vendors in attendance represented companies that made significant financial contributions to allow the meeting to occur. There was always a fine line between contributing and persuading, but everyone knew the rules of how the industry worked. For the most part, the attendees abided by unwritten standards of interaction with each other and the represented companies.

By the third hour of the morning's presentations, Shamus had had enough. He left the conference hall and made his way to the restroom. It was only after he was exiting that he looked over to an adjacent water fountain and thought he recognized an old colleague.

"Jason…is that you?" Shamus announced loud enough for people even outside the building to hear. Immediately, Jason Kogan lifted his head from the running water to see who was calling his name. Just as he lifted his head from the fountain and spun around, he identified Shamus walking towards him with a big grin. For reasons Kogan couldn't understand, Shamus was approaching him like a long-lost friend and Kogan was caught off guard. It had only been slightly more than a few months since he was dismissed from *Yonie Pharmaceuticals*, but the time obviously seemed longer for Shamus. As the Director of the Oncologic Pharmaceutical Division at *Yonie*, Kogan was Shamus's boss, but he always kept a social distance from the various lab directors in his division. Kogan never wanted to allow the potential for any perception of favoritism at *Yonie*. He would see Shamus at the monthly departmental meetings and would always keep interactions friendly, but professional. Both men worked at *Yonie* for well over two decades, but they were never close friends. After Kogan cryptically reviewed the work currently being investigated in Shamus's lab, he was the last person Kogan wanted to be speaking to or seen with.

Shamus stated, "Jason, how long has it been?" He extended his paw of a hand to Kogan.

Kogan shook Shamus's extended hand. "Actually, it's only been a little over three-months," Kogan responded while glancing around to assess the damage.

"Three-months? That's all? It seems like you've been gone at least a year. I guess time really does fly, right?" Shamus said with a broad smile. "So even though you're retired, you still like to come to these club meetings?" Shamus said jokingly.

Kogan responded in a more serious tone, "Well, yes…I like to stay relevant. I'm not so sure I'm ready to hang everything up just yet, so I want to see what's going on." Kogan really did not want to stay on the subject of his retirement. Given that it was more of a forced resignation, the wounds were still fresh. Perhaps it was this moment of insecurity regarding both his running into Shamus, and the topic of his retirement, that Kogan let another issue slip into the conversation. In his effort to change the topic off himself, he carelessly said to Shamus, "It's really a tragedy what happened at *Harris Therapeutics*, isn't it?"

"Oh…I didn't hear…what *happened* at *Harris*?" Shamus asked slowly. The jovial nature of bumping into his old director was now suddenly gone.

Kogan thought it was common knowledge, but perhaps Shamus doesn't get out of the bubble of his lab much, he thought. Maybe the news he heard from Yamp about the *Harris* related murders was still a case under investigation and wasn't to be broadcast. Kogan felt his face and neck get flush with anxiety. But it was too late to retract the statement. "What? You didn't hear?" Kogan asked as he was trying desperately to think of a plausible explanation…but none would come. He settled on telling the truth. "There were two murders of lab workers at *Harris*."

Shamus looked stunned. He stared directly at Kogan and then asked, "Whose lab?"

"Oh…that…I'm not sure of. I just heard it was at *Harris*. Maybe they weren't lab workers at all." Kogan did his best to get out of the discussion. He was now convinced he spoke out of line in mentioning anything. "Listen, Shamus…it was great to see you, but I have another commitment to keep right now. Enjoy the conference." With that, Kogan made a quick exit to the outside corridor of the conference area. He had to get out of the building. He also felt he had to inform Yamp of what just transpired.

Shamus stood for a moment by himself. The joyous nature he just had a few minutes ago was now replaced with an unsettled feeling of suspicion. He wondered if it was possible…a coincidence the flash drive he received just a few days ago was preceded by *murder?* Shamus needed to know. He asked himself, *That damn protocol just landed into Goodall's hands?* He berated himself for being so naive.

Hurriedly, Shamus walked into the exhibition area. He looked around the room for someone he knew…anyone. He walked down the brightly colored plush carpeting as he searched for a known face. He spotted one of the vendors who supplied customized scientific glassware to his lab. Shamus quickly approached him.

"Jack. Jack! Its Shamus…Its…Doctor O'Donnell." Jack McDowell looked startled as Shamus nearly accosted him.

"Oh…yes…Doctor O'Donnell. It's good to see you..." an uncomfortable Jack McDowell responded.

Shamus cut him off. "Jack…have you heard anything about what happened at *Harris Therapeutics* recently?"

Jack was still unsure what Doctor O'Donnell was asking about. "Recently…you mean like in the last couple of days or so?" he asked.

"Well, no…not that recent…I mean, well…I guess in the last month maybe?" Shamus was obviously anxious as his Irish brogue got thicker as he spoke faster with more emotion.

Jack looked at him incredulously, and said, "Well yeah…they had those scientists die. I'm not exactly sure of the details…but yeah…

they had some deaths over there. I don't think anybody actually *died* in the building...but rather they worked there. That's about all I know."

Shamus cringed as he listened to the vendor speak. Anticipating the answer, but knowing he had to ask, Shamus said slowly, "Lad, do you know whose lab those scientists worked in?"

Jack looked at directly at Shamus. He couldn't believe Doctor O'Donnell hadn't been aware of the news. He said quietly, "I heard they worked in Doctor Cortes's laboratory."

Shamus looked up at the ceiling. He felt as though he was going to lose his balance for a moment. Jack recognized this and immediately put his arm around Shamus to steady him. Jack asked, "Are you alright, Doctor?"

Shamus regained his composure. "Yes...yes, son, I'm fine...thank you. I'm sorry for jumping in on you like I did...my apologies, Jack." Shamus managed to slip away from Jack. He looked for the closest place to sit down, and after a desperate search, found an isolated vacant chair about twenty paces away just outside one of the curtains delineating the exhibit hall. Fortunately, no one else was around. Shamus dropped down into the black, folding chair and felt himself trembling. He didn't know if it was from anger or fear...perhaps a bit of both. *How could he have brought this upon these people?* Shamus recalled it was his idea to go to the administrative building. There he met Goodall and convinced him of the need to get the damn mRNA molecule for his own selfish needs. Shamus started weeping uncontrollably. From his perspective, this was all his doing. Good people died because of his greed, his selfish need for fame, for money—from Shamus's perspective, they died for all the wrong reasons he became a scientist.

After berating himself, Shamus sat very still for several minutes. His tears dried up as he processed and reviewed in his mind all that had transpired and what he just now learned. Shamus accepted the fact that he couldn't change what happened, but he may be able to influence the present. All he could do now was try to make corrections, and then he could focus on his atonement. Shamus also understood he must tread carefully. If Goodall had the capacity to kill innocent people—even those who worked at another company—then he could certainly take vengeance upon himself or others in his lab. The thought of any of his lab associates getting harmed by Goodall made him nauseous. Shamus now needed to get home. The conference he so very much looked forward to was now the place he desperately wanted to leave. He needed to be in his own quiet environment to think through his options and come up with a solution to this crisis.

Shamus understood Goodall's objective—no matter what, it was to obtain the synthesis protocol. Maybe Goodall didn't consider the consequences of what he had done to achieve that goal and perhaps Goodall didn't *care* about the consequences. But Shamus knew Goodall needed *his* lab and *his* expertise to create this drug—this damn gold mine of a drug. Shamus also knew he had the upper hand. As far as Goodall understood, Shamus appeared on-board and was a willing participant in this scheme. Shamus had to think though his next moves. He needed someone he could trust. When Shamus got home, he picked up his phone and made a call:

"Hello?" the receiver of the call answered.

"Hello Jason…this is Shamus. I need your help," Shamus said quietly into the phone.

Over the next hour, Shamus discussed with his old division director the circumstances he now found himself in. Kogan knew Shamus to be quirky, but he was a solid scientist and was driven by the right motives. Shamus pleaded his mea culpa to Kogan as he described his early motivations for the vaccine development. Kogan was well aware of the situation: a scientist who studies for years, is paid poorly, and is treated like a lab rat by the suits of the company becomes disillusioned and frustrated. Kogan had witnessed this throughout his tenure as the division director. But Shamus didn't ask for such atrocities to be committed, and he cannot be held responsible for what, apparently, Goodall put into motion. Kogan decided it best to come clean and inform Shamus of how he was able to learn of the connection between Shamus's cancer vaccine development project and *Harris Therapeutics*. The two old colleagues now had a mutual bond. For different reasons, they shared the same intent: to bring down *Yonie Pharmaceuticals*.

"Shamus, let me give you the name and contact information of my friend who might be able to direct you to people who could help. His name is Doctor Jay Yamp."

CHAPTER 51

Chicago, IL

After a series of calls, text messages, and emails, a meeting of Yamp, Knight, the detectives, Cortes, Kogan, and Shamus was finalized. The presence of the investigators was obvious. Yamp was needed given his ability to act as a liaison for the scientists since both Kogan and Shamus trusted him. Everyone understood what was at stake—they not only needed to catch and stop a murderer from possibly continuing his rampage, but they needed to prohibit *Yonie* from developing that which they stole. What was determined through the myriad of discussions was the Chief Financial Officer at *Yonie*, Neil Goodall, was at the heart of this situation.

Given the need for secrecy, and the unknown variable if Goodall was having Shamus or Cortes followed, they decided to meet at an FBI safe house in downtown Chicago. From the outside, it appeared to be just another bar—which it was. But once inside the darkened establishment, a series of back rooms which had restricted access and monitoring, were used for a variety of FBI meetings and interrogations. The meeting was set to take place at 6 p.m., when going to a bar after work would not be an outrageously unusual event, even for the suburban visitors.

No reports were made of anyone suspicious being observed by the team of agents posing as loitering customers both outside and inside the bar's entrance. Once inside, the attendees were instructed to proceed to the back of the bar, where another group of agents were assigned to observe and maintain privacy of the small group.

CHAPTER 51 – *To Cure Or Kill*

Blight was the first to arrive. Upon opening the establishment's heavy wooden door, her eyes took a few moments to adjust to the darkened atmosphere. Most of the lights were illuminated with small red or white bulbs that surrounded the mirrored wall behind the bar. Shelves located in front of the mirror were filled from floor to ceiling with bottles of all shapes and sizes. The place looked and felt like a real drinking establishment—customers could be seen sitting at a row of high bar stools next to a polished wooden surface for them to put their drinks on. The old red-brick floor had a certain stickiness to it that Blight could feel as she stepped. The talk was muted, but mostly jovial. Detective Blight was unable to ascertain if the people at the bar were true locals, undercover agents, or hired professionals. Perhaps it was a mixture of all of them. She immediately walked past the bar and towards the rear. There she was eyed by two men who nodded at her. Behind them she saw a doorway, and she made her way past the men and into a smaller hallway. She was greeted by an unshaven, bulked-up man, who pointed her towards a room that she entered.

This room was considerably different from the bar area. It was well-lit with clean, white walls. In the center of the room was a moderate-sized conference table, complete with modern swivel chairs. Microphones were hanging from the ceiling in strategic locations. On one of the walls was a 75-inch LCD television, and on the opposite end was an equally large white board. There were no windows, and there was no other entranceway into the room. A small buffet was present with soft drinks, coffee, and cookies. Blight put her purse on the table in front of one of the middle chairs and served herself a *Coca-Cola*. As she sat quietly, Blight pulled out her cellphone only to notice there was no service; there must have been a cell-jammer in place preventing calls and texts into or out of the dedicated conference area.

Over the course of the next 15 minutes, the other invitees showed up to the bar and were similarly led towards the back room. When the entire consortium was present, Agent Knight walked into the room and took his seat at the head of the table. Two additional suited agents followed and stood at the now closed door.

"Good evening, everyone, and thank you for coming," Agent Knight began. "I understand some of you had to deal with evening rush-hour traffic to get here. My apologies for that…but I feel at this stage of our investigation, it's critical we are all together and on the same page. Before we begin, I want everyone to clearly state their name. I don't believe everyone has been previously introduced to the group," at which time Knight looked at Kogan and Shamus, saying "and secondly, because this meeting is being recorded, and we need to have a sound-check of everyone's voice." Responding to Knight's request, everyone stated their name and their professional status. When Doctor Cortes announced himself, Shamus sheepishly looked at him apologetically.

Knight detailed what events led to the meeting and the investigative leads they had gathered. "We have accumulated incriminating evidence against one particular individual." On the television screen, the image of Jonathan Burksdale appeared. We have evidence linking him to the purchase of the arsenic-tainted wine bottle used in the Rebecca Sunnis murder, and we have evidence of a vehicle registered to him at the scene where the Novichok-laced cologne bottle was placed. Finally, and most definitive, we have Doctor Cortes's statement confirming Burksdale was the individual who threatened him and demanded he turn over the molecular sequencing protocol. Using those murders as an incentive, Cortes was faced with an imminent threat against himself or his family if he failed to comply with Burksdale's demands." At that moment, Knight looked directly at Cortes, who nodded in agreement.

Knight continued, "We also have a statement from Doctor Shamus O'Donnell, who as you all now know, is a senior scientist who's been working at *Yonie Pharmaceuticals* for the past 20 years. He's confirmed to us he had a meeting with the CFO at *Yonie,* named Neil Goodall." An image of Goodall was now projected on the conference room screen. "At that meeting, Doctor O'Donnell explained to Goodall he needed a particular molecule for experimentation and to create a new generation of cancer medications—drugs that are essentially anti-cancer vaccines. Apparently, Goodall decided to pull all stops and obtain the molecule he needed—one that was being made by Doctor Cortes's lab at *Harris Therapeutics*. Believing *Harris Therapeutics* would not release their molecule to *Yonie* without a significant cost and, more importantly, concerned that attempting to purchase the molecule would reveal to the scientific pharmacological community what *Yonie* was developing, Goodall decided to take action. Rather than even make an effort to buy the needed molecule, he decided it more appropriate to steal the protocol so the molecule could be manufactured at *Yonie*. Burksdale threatened Doctor Cortes to copy the molecular synthesis protocol onto a flash drive, which he subsequently handed back over to Burksdale. Goodall understood trying to make the molecule on their own could take a significant amount of time—time that could be used selling their product and making a fortune. From what we have estimated, *Yonie* could potentially make billions from their subsequent drug sales." Knight paused and took a drink of water.

"What we know currently, is that *Yonie* does have possession of the molecular synthesis protocol. They are in the process of reviewing the file that Cortes handed off to Burksdale. By Doctor O'Donnell's estimate, they will probably have the capability to produce the molecule in about three months."

Doctor Cortes cleared his throat and spoke up. "*Yonie* may be able to create the molecule, but it won't be sustainable." He looked directly at Shamus. "I modified the capping procedure on the file I gave to Burksdale. The mRNA molecule will decay in about a minute after it is created."

Shamus looked straight at Cortes but didn't say a word. Although Cortes previously revealed this information to the investigators, nobody in the conference room had the scientific background to truly appreciate how subtle and clever this modification by Cortes was—except, of course, Shamus. The room was silent with everyone looking back and forth between Shamus and Cortes. After Shamus considered what he previously read in the file and now, hearing this admission from Cortes for the first time, he suddenly broke out into a large grin and stated, "that is absolutely brilliant, doctor!" Cortes looked like he was about to break out into tears. After all the recent events, being appreciated for his work was something Cortes hadn't heard in a long time.

Cortes looked at Shamus and said, "I didn't know what else to do…I had to slow down whoever was going to get ahold of this file. I knew failure to create the structure would cause Burksdale to come back for me. But if the molecule was producible but not sustainable, perhaps he would think the failure was…well, yours…or rather whoever was trying to make it…and not mine."

Shamus again smiled broadly and nodded his head in the affirmative. "Doctor Cortes, that was truly an elegant modification to the protocol. And you are correct...I don't think I would have identified that as an issue until very later on. My hat is off to you, doctor."

Yamp joined the conversation. "That was brilliant, Doctor Cortes. I'm glad to hear *Yonie* won't be able to use the molecule...yet...but obviously over time they will resolve that issue." Both Cortes and Shamus nodded in agreement.

Knight interjected, "Well, doctors...I am pleased to see you each reaffirm each other's expertise." He looked at Doctor Cortes and stated, "Doctor...excellent...well done. But we are still faced with other issues. First of all, we don't yet understand the link between Goodall and Burksdale. If there is a direct relationship and we apprehend one or the other first, someone will run. If we take them at the same time, there is a better chance of an admission."

Detective Blight entered the conversation, "We can't just raid *Yonie Pharmaceuticals*. Goodall will claim ignorance of the whole thing and we have no proof the protocol they have was taken. They will take us to court and sue the FBI and probably our departments for millions," she stated while looking at Detective Rose." Rose nodded in agreement.

Rose added, "I think she's correct. What proof exists the file was taken from *Harris*?"

Cortes raised his hand and stated, "I think we can prove it is *Harris* property."

All the eyes in the room now turned to Doctor Cortes. Knight said, "Please explain, Doctor."

Cortes looked at Knight and said, "I digitally watermarked the document with the *Harris Therapeutics* logo."

Shamus looked at Cortes. "I didn't see any watermark on the file, and I looked carefully!"

Cortes now smiled, "I placed an IDW…an invisible digital watermark. By definition, you can't see it, but I know how to bring it out. The IDW will be proof it's *Harris* property."

Knight now smiled and stated, "Doctor Cortes…your skills are far more advanced than your average genius. Brilliant move…particularly given the stressful situation you found yourself in." Knight now turned to the table, "Okay people, we caught a break…I suspect we could now obtain a legitimate search warrant to assess that intellectual property from *Harris* is now on a *Yonie* computer. But…we still don't know if there are others at *Yonie* who could be in on this. Again, what is the link between Goodall and Burksdale? Is there another intermediary between them? We can't move until we know the answers to these questions."

Yamp now asked, "Jason, you and Shamus both know Goodall. If confronted, will he fold and volunteer information?"

Kogan thought about the question and then answered. "Goodall is basically a bully. He is greedy and conceited. He is also clever and manipulative, but I believe at his core, he is basically weak. I think his insecurities are matched by his need to surround himself with the appearance of wealth. My experience tells me he will consider consequences only as they directly affect him. He really doesn't give a damn about others. From his perspective, the world revolves around his needs. I think if it's made clear to Goodall that if he cooperates then any potential punishment for him will be reduced, then he'll sing."

Yamp replied, "If that's the case, perhaps we don't need to be concerned if we identify others. Goodall would likely give them up if he perceived doing so would be a benefit for himself. But from what I can assess, if Goodall and Burksdale are captured simultaneously, an intermediary has no direct means to know about their plight…correct?"

Knight listened intently, and responded, "True…but there is a risk if there are others involved, they could become suspicious in the interim and take off."

Yamp listened carefully to the discussion and tried to imagine all the possible scenarios that could play out. He stated, "It sounds as though we have identified the main players. Goodall probably conceived of this plot and Burksdale carried it out. If caught, why would either one of them not try to cut a plea?"

Knight nodded his head in agreement. "I agree. I see no significant benefit by holding off capturing these two. I think if others are involved, it will come out and we will track them down wherever they hide. From what I can gather, we should coordinate our teams to get them both. We know who our targets are, and we know where they are." Everyone in the room nodded in agreement. It was time to end this.

CHAPTER 52

Chicago, IL

Special Agent Knight reviewed his plans with Deputy Director Jacoby. The deputy was in complete agreement that Goodall and Burksdale should be apprehended sooner rather than later. If there was an intermediary between Goodall and Burksdale, that individual would have to be apprehended once those two were in custody. From what Knight could ascertain, stealing the molecular protocol was Goodall's initiative with Burksdale carrying out the murders. The first priority of Jacoby and Knight was to prevent additional harm to others. Knight suspected Cortes was still under threat even though the protocol was in *Yonie's* labs. Knight was also concerned that Goodall could potentially go after Shamus if he got the least bit suspicious of him or his efforts to produce the mRNA. Shamus may be a brilliant scientist, but his ability to camouflage thoughts and intentions may be stunningly obvious to a ruthless individual like Goodall. Knight ascertained Goodall was one who considered all potential scenarios and would not be one to leave a trail behind. Shamus may already be the next person on Goodall's list to wind up dead.

Knight coordinated with the Chicago Police Department. There would be a SWAT-led raid on Burksdale's home in the early morning hours once they were able to ascertain he was home. The plan would be to then grab Goodall at *Yonie*. Any leak or miscalculation of the FBI or police presence could lead to Goodall's disappearance. Having researched Goodall, Knight was convinced the man had both the financial means and the street knowledge to be difficult to locate if he escaped. Agent Knight also suspected Goodall was prepared for an emergent departure if he ever felt threatened. They would only get one shot at him. Knight and his team of agents devised a plan that would keep Goodall out of his routine, and more vulnerable to capture.

Burksdale lived in a single-family home in the Lincoln Park neighborhood in Chicago. This posed both advantages and disadvantages for the SWAT team. Most obvious was the fact they could surround his home with minimal disruption of his neighbors. In an apartment building, they would need to cordon off the floor, manage the elevators, and work in close proximity to the target's neighbors. On the other hand, a homeowner had the distinct advantage of having potentially multiple exit locations, as opposed to an apartment or condominium that typically only had a single point of entry. A home could have significant unknown architectural modifications—the potential for traps or unforeseen obstacles were numerous.

Having observed Burksdale enter his home on the preceding evening, the SWAT team huddled at 4 a.m. the following morning. Scanning equipment was directed towards his lawn, revealing no unseen monitors. Infrared cameras were able to determine a heat signal emanating from an upstairs bedroom. Detective Rose accompanied the group and was surprised at the lack of any sophisticated alarm or intruder detection equipment on the property. Perhaps this was simply consistent with Burksdale's over-confidence in himself. The same confidence allowed him to walk into the wine shop without any disguise in place. His arrogance would be his downfall.

At precisely 5:00 a.m., the silent SWAT team surrounded Burksdale's residence. Their professionalism was impressive to Rose, as their coordinated movements were well-rehearsed and expertly performed. About a block away from the target's home, a command vehicle was parked. Inside the unusually shaped vehicle, high ranking officers coordinated the team's movements and recorded all the network communication and high-definition video transmissions. There was no unnecessary chatter among the team members as they took their pre-planned positions around the perimeter of the house. At exactly 5:15 a.m., when all of the team was in place, the SWAT leader gave the order to enter. Using a forty-pound, all-steel battering ram, the wooden door of the home caved without much resistance. Immediately, six SWAT members wearing SWAT-G (super wide angle tactical goggles) for ultra-high situational awareness in low-light conditions, entered the home. Three members quickly climbed the staircase. The others remained on the first floor as back-up should the target manage to escape the upper-level team. Burksdale's bedroom was identified. The door was closed. Again, the battering ram was employed, and the cheap door crumpled open easily. The entire process, from entry on the first floor until reaching the confused Burksdale still in his bed, took less than 30 seconds.

"Are you Jonathan Burksdale?" The unit commander asked in a loud voice. His 9mm Glock was raised at Burksdale. The two other SWAT officers pointed ominous-looking FN P90 submachine guns at him as well.

Burksdale was in REM sleep when the intrusion occurred. With the bright light from the officers' flashlights aimed directly in his eyes, Burksdale mumbled in the affirmative. Within seconds, he was zip-tie cuffed and read his Miranda rights. It was only after the overly tight zip-tie was on his wrists that he was fully conscious of what had just happened. Burksdale initially struggled, but soon realized he was overpowered and would be unable to escape from his captors. He realized his only option was to be cooperative and compliant. He asked if he could put some acceptable clothes on. For reasons that were unclear and later scrutinized, the lead officer complied. He allowed the zip tie to be cut, allowing Burksdale to put on sweatpants and running shoes. Under their careful watch, he went to his dresser and slipped on a tee-shirt. What the officers did not see in the limited light was the small pea-sized object he quickly took out of his dresser drawer and slipped into his sweatpants pocket. Burksdale was then re-cuffed and led out of his home. He was placed into an awaiting squad car and taken away. The entire process of entering and exiting the target's home took less than 9 minutes.

As soon as Burksdale was off the premises, another team of officers and technicians entered and searched the home. It appeared to be a text-book capture of their *wanted* subject.

At approximately 5:30 a.m., Rose placed a call. "Agent Knight… we got him, sir."

Knight was wide awake as he was anticipating the call. He responded, "Glad to hear it, Detective. Were there any complications?"

Rose replied, "None, sir. Everything went down as smoothly as it could. Burksdale is in a squad car now and they are heading in."

"Excellent, work," Knight stated. "We won't enter *Yonie* until after 9 a.m. If we go in too early, it might tip-off security that something doesn't appear right…something we definitely do not want. We will enter casually and hopefully avoid attention. Let me know if Burksdale says or does anything noteworthy."

Detective Rose replied, "Will do sir." Rose had no idea how true that would soon be.

CHAPTER 53

Chicago, IL

Cyanide is a naturally occurring chemical and has been used for poisoning for two millennia. It is highly lethal regardless of whether it is inhaled as a gas, ingested, or absorbed through the skin. Cyanide inhibits the ability of cells of the body to use oxygen, and subsequently, these cells die. The heart, respiratory system, and central nervous system are the most susceptible organs to cyanide poisoning. Cyanide kills quickly, as death occurs within seconds of a lethal dose of cyanide gas, and within minutes of ingestion of cyanide salt.

Once Burksdale was brought into the police HQ, he was quickly processed. Around 6:00 a.m., the activity level is minimal and there is less congestion at the station. The movement of prisoners from *intake* to *processing* and then to the various holding areas actually moves with a modicum of efficiency. Detective Rose waited in an officer's lounge as the new prisoner went through the various steps of incarceration. Rose would be granted an opportunity to speak with Burksdale soon, but knew the prisoner would probably await the presence of an attorney before saying anything. That, of course, is his right, and some prisoners choose to speak freely beforehand—not a wise move. Before Burksdale was moved into an interrogation room, he was placed in a general holding cell with one other recent police *acquisition* from the morning. With his zip-tie hand cuffs removed, Burksdale slowly paced the 20-foot by 20-foot cell. He looked around the dreary, mustard-colored room that smelled like a bad mixture of old urine and cigarettes. Given the foul odor of alcohol and dried vomit emanating from his sleeping cellmate on the far side of the holding area, Burksdale sat down on a dirty metallic bench as far away from the man as possible. He looked at the jail bars and noted they were nearly chrome-shiny at chest-level, probably where the paint had worn off from years of earlier prisoners grabbing the bars. The only sound, other than his snoring mate, was that of large ventilation blowers trying to move the stale air. It was obvious to Burksdale the ventilation system was malfunctioning.

Burksdale had no illusion as to why he was there and what would happen to him. A SWAT team does not enter your home in the early morning hours if they don't have serious intelligence on what you are guilty of. Oddly, Burksdale was mostly disturbed by his failure to understand what mistake he must have made to lead to this point. He relived his victim's encounters, but failed to realize it was actually his own ego that led to his discovery and capture. Burksdale's belief he was smarter and cleverer than everyone else was his downfall.

Burksdale prepared for this day years ago. Perhaps, it was inevitable given his life choices, or possibly because of a secret desire to die, but Burksdale had no desire to go through lengthy inquiries, accusations, and trials. He knew the truth would ultimately come out, and he was in fact, guilty. *So, this is where it ends*, he thought. So be it. Burksdale was miserable with himself and felt he died years ago, anyway.

Burksdale reached into his sweatpants pocket and retrieved the pea sized pellet. He knew exactly what he would experience, and that it would all be over in a minute or so. As Burksdale considered his fate, he thought it was sad, really. He knew so much about the art of poisoning and the physiology of death and dying.

Burksdale placed the pellet into his mouth just over his left, back-bottom molar. Very unceremoniously, he bit down hard and felt the small capsule crack under his mandibular strength. Within seconds he noted a shortness of breath. As dizziness set in, he could no longer maintain his balance to sit on the bench. Burksdale fell to the floor and assumed the fetal position. A sudden wave of nausea caused him to vomit uncontrollably. Soon, he was shaking and gasping for breath. The vomit and saliva were drooling out of his mouth. His tearful, bloodshot eyes revealed the exquisite discomfort he was experiencing. In an odd, distorted way, he welcomed the pain in a location deep inside his body. It was as though he knew he was deserving of this horrible torture. After another nonproductive and painful effort to get needed oxygen into his lungs, Burksdale seized, and then lost consciousness. After another 15 seconds, Burksdale stopped breathing. His inebriated, snoring cellmate never saw a thing.

CHAPTER 54

Glenview, IL

"You've got to be fucking kidding me!" Special Agent Knight shouted into the telephone. "How the hell does this happen? The son of a bitch poisoned himself…are we sure? Didn't anyone search him before placing him into the holding cell? For Christ's sake!" Agent Knight hung up the phone in absolute disgust.

Detective Rose himself could not believe the failure of the lock-up's personnel to follow standard protocol. There was no question Burksdale was clever…but to have a murderer, and a *potential witness* be able to conceal a poison, and then have the ability to use it on himself *while in custody,* was completely unacceptable. Heads would roll on this one, he promised himself.

There was nothing more he could do at this time. Rose placed a call to the Commanding Officer of the unit and would deal with that debacle later. Detective Rose had to get back to the rest of the team preparing to enter the *Yonie* campus. He knew the damn traffic at this hour would create significant delays—using the emergency lane with flashing lights or not.

At 8:30 a.m., Rose was able to meet up with the assembling team at the Glenview Police station. Technically, his presence was not mandated at *Yonie*—this was officially an FBI *raid.* But his investigation into the murder of Bob Margolis was intimately related; he *needed* to be there. Given the absolute disaster with the loss of the apparent murderer,

Burksdale, Rose was as angry as anyone else about the course of events. This entire case, from its conception at *Yonie* to the murder of innocents who worked at *Harris*, made him boil with rage.

He saw Knight going over details with other agents, and Rose caught Knight's attention. Agent Knight interrupted his discussion and came over to Rose.

"I'm sorry for getting so angry this morning. I know none of it was your fault, and I want to apologize," Knight said.

"No apology necessary," Rose responded. "I'm just livid about that screw up. On the one-hand, I can understand how it happened. Burksdale was a smart man, and I'm sure whatever means he used to get a poison through was cleverly concealed. But still…"

Knight interjected, "Look, it's impossible to pat down every inch of everyone. And if he had something very small hidden in his clothes, I'm sure it would have been missed anyway. We have Goodall in our sights now, and that has to be our focus. Obviously, Burksdale was guilty. No one who is innocent and who had his means and resources would have done this to himself. He must have been one troubled guy." Knight put his hand on the shoulder of Rose and said, "Let's keep our eye on the ball and get this other asshole." Detective Rose nodded in agreement. The two men walked over to join the others to continue the discussion.

One of the junior agents asked, "Why don't we just go into the administration building and get him in his office?"

Knight replied, "Actually, it's simple. This is Goodall's home turf. He probably knows everyone in and around his building, or they at least know of him. Don't think for a second that as soon as an FBI vehicle approaches the security gate, the guards won't immediately notify the higher-ups of our presence. Goodall probably knows every inch of this building, and my bet is he has a route of evacuation already planned out…if not for this job, then for others he probably did in the past. This is not his first rodeo, and it certainly isn't mine. No. We need to get him off-guard…in a building or situation that he doesn't know his way out of and isn't in control. This guy will run if given the chance, and if that happens, finding him will be difficult."

"Understood," the younger agent replied.

Knight raised his hands and spoke to the group, "Okay, everyone is onboard…any last questions? Doctor O'Donnell, you good?"

"I'm good, sir," Shamus replied.

"Okay folks, let's go get our perpetrator," Knight stated with authority.

Shamus was the first to leave the station, and he made his way to the *Yonie* entrance gate. The guards at the campus perimeter obviously knew his car and tag numbers. Shamus would typically wave hello to the day-shift guard, Richard. This time he rolled down his window to speak to the guard. "Good morning, Richard…how are you today?"

"I'm fine, Doctor O'Donnell." Although Shamus would only occasionally speak with the guards, Richard sensed Shamus wanted to say more. "What can I do for you?"

"Oh…yes…well, I'm going to be having a few visitors today…just direct them to the visitor center so they can register, and then escort them to my lab," Shamus stated.

"Of course, Doctor. How many are there?" Richard replied as he grabbed a clipboard to begin writing down some details.

"There will be four scientists…I suspect they will be here within the hour. Would you like their names now?" Richard replied.

"No, that won't be necessary, Doctor. We'll get their information when they check in. Do you know if they'll be coming in one car or more?" Richard asked.

"Hmm…that I don't know. I'm sorry," Shamus said with a frown.

"Oh…no worries, doc…just thought I'd ask. Thanks for the heads-up though. I'll get them to you just as soon as they show up." Richard smiled and waved as the entrance gate raised.

Shamus drove on and parked in his usual spot. He knew the security protocols at *Yonie*–everything was watched. By informing the guard at the entrance gate of his expected guests, the FBI entrance would go all that much smoother.

Thirty minutes later, two cars pulled up to the entrance gate. The suited occupants explained the reason for their presence, and as anticipated, the guard requested their ID's. As the guard was copying down their falsified information, a camera in the grass behind the gatehouse photographed the license plates. The government plates had previously been replaced with clean, civilian-issue, vehicle tags. The gate entrance guard radioed for assistance to come to the entrance gate in a golf cart to escort the visiting scientists to the visitor center for photographs and ID's. Once they were processed, the new visitors were brought to the research building where Shamus was located. Shamus welcomed them in as long-lost friends and thanked the escort who then retreated.

Agent Knight and Doctor Cortes went into Shamus's office, which was adjoined to the lab. The other two *scientists* donned white coats and sat quietly by themselves in the laboratory. The lab associates knew better than to ask them anything and went about their business, as usual. They were accustomed to Shamus having visitors periodically visit their lab. The only thing different about these two individuals was that they were as big as horses, and they didn't smile or engage with anyone. The two visitors simply sat quietly without even speaking among themselves. Amy thought she could make out a bulge under the lab coat in the back of one of the men, but she wasn't going to say anything.

About an hour later, Knight gave Shamus the *okay* to make his call.

Shamus went to his desk and lifted the phone. "Operator, can you kindly connect me to Mr. Neil Goodall's office? Thank you."

"Mr. Goodall's office. How may I help you?" The cheerful voice on the other end of the line answered.

Shamus put on his best Irish brogue, "Yes, good morning, dear. This is Doctor Shamus O'Donnell. Is Mr. Goodall in, by chance?"

"Why yes...yes, he is. Mr. Goodall is in a meeting right now...I suspect he will be done in about 30 minutes. Can I have him call you back?" the receptionist responded.

"That would be terrific. Please make sure Mr. Goodall understands this is quite important." Shamus then gave the woman his extension number, repeated it back, and then disconnected the call.

For the next 45 minutes, the three men waited patiently. They discussed most any topic that came to mind, as Knight felt it important to keep the scientists' thoughts occupied. The phone rang, jolting Shamus.

Shamus picked up the phone on the third ring. "Doctor O'Donnell speaking."

"O'Donnell, this is Goodall. You called?"

Shamus replied, "Oh...yes, Mr. Goodall, I'm glad you called back. I have something interesting to tell you...actually, can you spare a few minutes and come here to the lab. I think it would be better to just show you in person."

"What is so important that I need to get my ass down there? I'm knee deep in meetings right now." Goodall replied with annoyance.

"Well sir...we did it...I mean, we have the molecule after just three weeks of work! But I need you to see something...something unexpected occurred. I want to show you something...not only will this work for the prostate cancer vaccine, but...well, this is bigger than we anticipated...please...I need to run back into the lab...just come and I'll show you," Shamus stated excitedly, and then hanging up abruptly.

Knight nodded his head in approval. "I have never met this man in my life, but if what I understand of him is true, he'll come running over." Shamus nodded. He, too, felt he did an award-winning performance. The men all started pacing the crowded room, and then they returned to their seats and waited in silence.

Ten minutes later, a knock was heard on the outside lab door. Amy opened it and was surprised to see the obnoxious administrator.

"Oh…hello. May I help you?" she asked. Goodall almost pushed her aside.

"Why is this door locked? I'm looking for your boss…is he in his office?" As Goodall started walking towards the adjoining office, he noted what he thought were new associates sitting in the lab. Looking at the oversized men, Goodall thought, *What are they feeding those boys?* Without asking for further assistance, Goodall made a beeline for Shamus's closed office door. Goodall knocked loudly once and then entered.

"Okay, Shamus…what's so damn important? Oh…I didn't know you have visitors."

Goodall looked at the two men disparagingly, and then he looked back with glaring eyes at Shamus while awaiting an explanation.

Shamus stood, and stated, "Yes. Yes…I'm glad you came. Oh… yes, how rude of me…let me introduce my visitors in a second. I know you're in a hurry. Let me explain…I opened up the file you gave to me from *Harris Therapeutics*, and look what I see." Shamus waved his hands to indicate he wanted Goodall to come behind his desk and look at something on the monitor. Goodall did so.

"Okay… what am I looking at, Shamus?" Goodall said while losing his patience.

Shamus said, "Here, look closer…let me enlarge the image." Shamus zoomed in on the watermark that Cortes previously unveiled. The watermark clearly displayed the *Harris* logo. It also contained a short disclaimer indicating the contents herein were the legal property of *Harris Therapeutics*.

Outside of the closed office door, the FBI agents removed their white coats, locked the outside door to the lab, and took positions on either side of Shamus's closed office door.

Goodall looked at the watermark. Incredulously, he shrugged his shoulders and looked at Shamus and asked, "So what the hell is this?"

Shamus stated, "Well, Mr. Goodall, that is a watermark utilized to state this is proprietary property of *Harris Therapeutics*. This file was obviously stolen from them."

Goodall looked at Shamus and stated, "What's wrong with you? Of course, this is stolen… how do you think I got it!"

Shamus stated, "I honestly don't know what you did to get it…but I will have nothing more to do with this."

Goodall couldn't believe what he was hearing. He turned around and looked at the two unknown visitors in the office. He then said angrily, "So who the hell are you two?"

"Oh…I'm the guy who put the digital watermark on that document you just acknowledged you stole from me," Cortes said defiantly.

The color in Goodall's face went from pink to white. "Say that again…you are who?"

"I'm Doctor Gene Cortes. I am the developer of the synthesis protocol and…well, actually, *Harris Therapeutics* is the proper owner of that document that is currently being displayed on the *Yonie* monitor sitting on Doctor O'Donnell's desk."

"What the hell is going on here?" Goodall exclaimed. "I'm getting out of here…this is…"

"No, you're not going anywhere," Knight stated as he moved in front of the door. He opened up his jacket and displayed his badge. "I'm FBI Special Agent Knight. You, sir, are under arrest for knowingly stealing proprietary documents from *Harris Therapeutics*, and for acting as an accessory in the murder of Rebecca Sunnis and Robert Margolis, who were employees at *Harris.*"

"Goodall stated defiantly, "I did not murder anyone. And I resent…"

Knight cut him off, "You hired, employed, paid…pick a word, I don't really care. It was under your request that individuals were murdered. You will come with me. Turn around, Mr. Goodall." Just as Knight was reaching into his coat pocket to retrieve a zip tie, Goodall made a quick turn towards the door. He quickly pulled open the door and then suddenly stopped moving. The two bulky *scientists* were now pointing Glock 9mm handguns at Goodall's face.

"This ends now, Goodall. Do not move an inch." Knight stated, as he now pulled Goodall's hands behind his back and tightened the zip tie. Goodall realized that any struggle would be futile. Knight read Goodall his Miranda rights and led him out of the office.

The FBI agents escorted Goodall to their car. At this time, additional agents were called onto the campus. They entered Shamus's office and retrieved his computer with the flash drive still connected. Any additional evidence—printed material, notes, and phone records—were similarly logged into a file and removed. Another team, search warrant in hand, entered the now buzzing administrative building and removed nearly every non-attached item from Goodall's office. His cell phone was still on his desk, and it was carefully labeled and secured.

Knight pulled his own cellphone out and made a call to his boss, FBI Deputy Director Jacoby. "We got him."

EPILOGUE

Chicago, IL

As predicted, Goodall was at first a defiant jerk. He demanded his attorney be present before he would say a word. But his stonewalling didn't last long. Once he was informed of the voluminous information compiled against him, as well as the testimony of Shamus O'Donnell regarding their discussions, Goodall *sang like a bird.* He admitted to his role in financing the acquisition of the mRNA synthesis protocol owned by *Harris Therapeutics.* And, given his culpability regarding the murders, he agreed as a plea bargain to help in the capture of his intermediary, Lucifer Ashwood. The value of changing a prison sentence from *very long* to just *long* is probably debatable, but it was enough incentive to encourage his assistance with this.

As with their previous endeavors, Goodall contacted Ashwood with a supposed new job. Predictably, Ashwood set up a meeting at the same bench on the northern bicycle trail along Lake Michigan. Compulsions had their risks, and Ashwood's consistent behavior made for an easy set up and capture. The agents had him nabbed before Goodall even left the FBI van to meet him—Goodall's ankle monitor and additional recording and tracking devices in place, but not needed.

Ashwood would ultimately inform the agents of his association and eventual payoff to Burksdale. Ashwood had no idea Burksdale committed suicide upon capture. The money trail was then unraveled: The 1.25-million-dollar payment from Goodall to Ashwood, and his subsequent wiring of 1 million dollars to Burksdale was identified.

Yonie's financial records were confiscated, and through forensic accounting, millions of dollars that Goodall manipulated in the past were uncovered for illegal use, bribery, and blackmail. Neither Ashwood nor Goodall would ever see the light of day as free men again.

It was determined that *Yonie Pharmaceuticals* was at the epicenter of another major pharmaceutical scandal. Whether it was bad luck, or the consistent practice of hiring corrupt administrators, *Yonie* was held accountable—again. Their stock value plummeted, and *Yonie,* as an independent company, was effectively destroyed. Its products and various divisions were acquired by competitors.

Interestingly, Shamus O'Donnell was offered the opportunity to work in Gene Cortes's lab as there were obvious vacancies to fill. He came willingly to *Harris* with his associate Amy. Shamus worked alongside Cortes as they were able to now produce the mRNA molecule and utilize it to manufacture the actual prostate cancer vaccine Shamus set out to do for so many years. *Harris Therapeutics* would eventually become a juggernaut in the field of cancer vaccine development, and it eventually made the *billions* that Goodall had sought. William Waters and his company made a transformative impact in the history of medical achievements: their drugs saved millions of lives.

The efforts of the investigators, and the analysis and critical input from the doctors, were all vital to facilitate the capture of the perpetrators and end this most unusual case. Most importantly, everyone's work and effort were performed for the right reasons. When Jay Yamp received the news of all that had transpired, he picked up the phone and called his friend Robert Jacoby and left a simple message.

"Thank you," Yamp stated, "We can get back now to the *real* business of medicine."

Acknowledgements

We are living in a time of challenging medical advances. With the advent of the recent pandemic, there is increased awareness of our need for medical science to carefully and quickly develop the tools, treatments, and methods to maintain our health and well-being. To do so requires our nation's support—both economically and socio-politically. At the same time, some companies in the pharmaceutical industry—those entrusted to produce our needed drugs—have been identified to create a dependency, and in some instances, an addiction to their products. Similarly, the consumer costs for drugs in the United States are exploited and manipulated. We generally pay the highest price in the world for most medicines.

With soaring profits, it appears that some within the pharmaceutical industry have taken advantage of our needs and tolerance for their profiteering. These costs are not sustainable, and along with other problematic situations within our healthcare delivery system, medical-related issues are the most significant cause of personal bankruptcy in the U.S. Although greed has been tempting in many forms in all businesses, in the health care industry, it cannot be tolerated.

This novel is an effort to present a fictionalized version of what greed in the pharmaceutical industry could look like. The question each reader must ask is, *how fictionalized is the story*?

Observing recent pharmaceutical company efforts to maximize profits, the possibility for such industry-driven espionage is not difficult to imagine.

I wish to thank the many individuals who have given me ideas for consideration, shared personal experiences, and helped me understand the impact of their health-related situations and problems. Those ideas and experiences have been blended in this novel to create a story that is reflective of, potentially, real events. I want to extend my appreciation to my pre-publication readers and reviewers who lent me their insight and helped me to write a better story. To Barbara, who gave me superb advice along the way. I want to thank Bill Dorich, my publisher at GMBooks, for supporting my ideas, and my editor, Doug May, for giving clarity to my thoughts and words.

At some point in everyone's life, we are all patients. We depend upon our health care professionals, the many bio-scientists and investigators, as well as the health-industry related companies to provide us with safe and reliable methods, equipment, and medications. My intent with this novel was to provide a fictionalized version of what can go wrong in this industry. I am hopeful such activity remains only in a fictionalized story. But what if…

About the Author

Dr. Michael J. Young is a faculty member at The University of Illinois Chicago (UIC) College of Medicine, in the Departments of Urology and Biomedical Engineering. At UIC, he is the Director of the Division of Urology Innovation and Technology, and functions as a Medical Advisor at The UIC Innovation Center. Currently, he is pursuing the development of new surgical instruments and medical devices, as well as teaching medical and biomedical engineering students at the Chicago campus. Dr. Young holds patents to various medical devices.

Dr. Young's non-fiction book, *The Illness of Medicine,* was a review and commentary on the current status of our healthcare delivery system. It was a compilation of his experiences over more than 25 years of clinical practice. In his previous novels, *Consequence of Murder,* and *Net of Deception,* Dr. Young applied his medical expertise as a predicate for vulnerabilities in the medical environment.

Dr. Young continues to work in the field of medical device innovation. In his free time, he enjoys traveling, photography, and is an avid golfer.

www.michaeljyoungmd.com